MERLIN'S STRONGHOLD

FAERIE CROSSED
BOOK 2

ANGELICA R. JACKSON

Crow & Pitcher Press
SHINGLE SPRINGS, CA

For permission requests, write to the publisher at: Crow & Pitcher Press, P.O. Box 1294, Shingle Springs, CA 95682
www.CrowAndPitcherPress.com

Publisher's Note: This is a work of fiction. Names, characters, places, and incidents are a product of the author's imagination. Locales and public names are sometimes used for atmospheric purposes. Any resemblance to actual people, living or dead, or to businesses, companies, events, institutions, or locales is completely coincidental. Any trademarks, service marks, product names, or named features are the property of their respective owners and are used only for reference.

Book Layout ©2017 BookDesignTemplates.com
Interior dragon illustration via Shutterstock
Interior design by Angelica R. Jackson
Cover design & photo manipulation by Kelley York of X-Potion Designs, using artwork by Angelica R. Jackson

Merlin's Stronghold/ Angelica R. Jackson -- 1st ed.
ISBN 978-0-9987214-4-6
Library of Congress Control Number: 2018959358

Books by Angelica R. Jackson:

Faerie Crossed Series

Crow's Rest
Merlin's Stronghold

Non-Fiction
Capturing the Castle:
Images of Preston Castle (2006-2016)

1

If I'd known this was going to be an intervention, I would have dressed better. Not that a Polo shirt and khakis would have lessened the sting of my mom sticking a "Hello, I'm **Promiscuous**" label on me or anything, but my micro-miniskirt wasn't helping my defense.

My mom and a few of her colleagues were waiting for me to respond to their "concerns about the parade of boyfriends—and even a few girls—over the last few months."

But I know better than to tell a team of medical professionals, "Oh no, you have it all wrong! What looks like a parade is actually a party of one, in different bodies. My boyfriend is a kind of Fae called a corbin who can only come into our world by borrowing a human's body. So every one of those people made a deal where they get a vacation in Faerie, while Lonan gets to spend time with me in their body. Or if Lonan can't manage to switch, I go into Faerie—where I'm pretty much all-powerful, BTW. Or will be, once I get the hang of my magic. If you don't believe me, ask Uncle Tam, who is really Tam Lin and older than he looks by about three hundred years."

And that wouldn't even begin to cover the rest of the weirdness from last summer: like how my crush-next-door, Daniel, ended up in a magical coma and was lost in Faerie for a while. Or how I narrowly stopped a Fae invasion, only to figure out that fixing the Border was just putting a generic adhesive bandage on the whole mess, leaving me to sort out a more permanent fix. While simultaneously learning to control my magic.

Yeah, nobody gave me credit for how hard I'd been working to control my powers, in spite of impulsiveness being hardwired into my DNA: not only handed down from my biological human Dad, but also the scaly, batwinged, dragonish Fae who passed his magic on to me during a ritual Uncle Tam arranged for my conception. So lucky me, the wyvern magic and my dad's Sight had warped into this crazy, chaotic talent called wild magic taking over my life.

But that list of revelations would have landed me in a lot more trouble with my mom than I was already in, so what was the point? I couldn't be the only teen who wasn't telling her mom what was really going on in her life, so why should I fess up now?

But if I was being honest, I didn't like keeping my mom in the dark. Too many people had lied to me, and it had felt pretty shitty when I found out. She deserved more, since she had no idea all the ways the Fae and magic had already affected her.

However, it wasn't the right time or place to spill the magic beans in front of all those other people. For now, I'd continue my policy of not telling her any outright lies.

That meant it was time to go on the offensive.

"Mom, I can't believe you would do this to me," I said. "You know how hard I've been working in school and everything, so doesn't that show I'm responsible? Maybe you could have had a conversation with me, instead of going straight to the hospital's big guns?"

"Avery, you've been different since the summer, and everything seemed to get out of control so quickly. I just want you to be safe."

"What exactly does safe mean to you, Mom? Locked in my room, so you'll always know where I am and who I'm with? You haven't exactly tried to even like my...friends."

Dr. Zapatas (the child psychologist) raised her hands. "Now, now, Avery, you're entitled to your feelings but so is your mom. Let's try to use less accusatory language, like 'I feel' statements."

I rolled my eyes. "Okay, I *feel* like none of you should be a part of this conversation without my consent. I feel like this is more about my mom feeling guilty about how much time she spends at work and worrying her neglect has turned me into a slut. Is that better, Doc?"

Mom threw out her hands and said, "You see? We used to talk about things, but now whenever I try, all I get are smart-ass comments. She seems so *angry* all the time—more than a teenager who only has to worry about school has a right to be."

That made me so indignant, all I could force out was, "*Only* school—you have no idea—but—uuugggghhh! Mom, you have no freakin' clue about the pressure I'm under!"

Not only did she keep on a constant vise squeeze of "keep up your grades for college," but I had Uncle Tam always nagging me to close the Border between Faerie and the human world permanently. And Queen Maeve wanted me to step up my involvement at her Fae Court, but I suspected that

4

was just a way to keep me (and my wild magic) in her sight.

Even my time with Lonan was colored by his aunt's—Queen Maeve's—agenda. When I'd found out Auntie Queen had been urging Lonan to get me pregnant so I'd be further tied to her family, I'd zapped her with morning-sickness symptoms.

Fae don't normally get morning sickness, so her guards thought there'd been an assassination attempt instead—which of course was traced back to me, because the signature of my wild magic was all over the spell. The apology I'd had to deliver for that fiasco had completely rankled my pride.

To top it off, my magic had been leaking out more and more lately, even in this world, whether I wanted it to or not. Like now, when my frustration was bringing the simmering pressure-cooker of wild magic within me to a boil. I clenched my eyes shut and tried to get a grip on myself.

"Avery?"

My name, spoken like it had already been said several times, snapped me back to reality. When Dr. Hume (the OB/GYN) saw she had my attention, she gestured to a door off her office.

"If you'll step into the examining room, I'll give you a checkup and make sure everything is as it should be."

My jaw dropped, and I turned to my mom in disbelief. Any sympathy I'd been feeling for her seized up along with my lady parts, at the realization that she'd signed me up for an invasive procedure. Was it meant to be a punishment?

"Don't look at me like that!" she cried. "I just want to make sure you're...safe."

This time, when she said "safe," it was obvious she meant "not riddled with disease" or "not carrying some grandbastard."

And quick as a transmission with stripped gears, my magic slipped into overdrive. Power hummed through my bones, shooting to my fingers and gathering for a burst. My hands clenched as I desperately tried to hold it back.

Dr. Zapatas must have noticed my trembling fists; she sat forward in her seat, frowning. "Avery, I do hope I'm not going to have to call security. Would you please sit down and calm yourself?"

"I—I can't," I said through gritted teeth. "I—" My voice broke off as the smell of singed fabric rose from my shirtsleeves. *Shit, it hasn't been this bad in a while!* I couldn't even ask these doctors for help, not without maybe putting them in danger too. If I really didn't want to have to explain everything, I'd better try harder to hold a rational conversation.

Then a sharp pain hit between my shoulder blades, progressing to an itching, skin-crawling sensation, like something trying to get out. My eyes went wide as the realization hit me: my wings were attempting to manifest in this world, when they'd only ever shown up in Faerie before.

And they'd chosen to do it for the first time in front of my mom and an assortment of doctors—who already seemed on the verge of locking me up "for my own good." Where would they lock up the wyvern girl, and throw away the key, if it was for *their* own good?

I lunged in the direction of the door, but Mom called, "Avery, we're not through here! Come back and talk to us."

My hand was already on the doorknob. "I've got to go—we'll talk later." The effort of keeping my wings in check made my words clipped and impatient. But that wasn't how I felt—I was scared. For myself and for them.

"No, we'll talk now, young lady—"

A deep-throated growl interrupted her. And it had come from me.

Uh oh—outta time. I wrenched open the door—nearly pulling it off its hinges—and made a dash for the stairwell. While I raced downstairs, my emerging leathery batwings strained the seams of my shirt. The door to the parking garage banged as I burst through it and ran for the dark muscle car idling a few feet away. At the last moment, I remembered the security cameras and threw myself into the backseat.

We sped away, the sound of screeching tires ringing in the concrete box, and I laughed breathily. How would it have looked to the security guards, for the car drive up on camera, only to have me slide into the empty driver's seat? I'd been so careful until now, but one rookie move would have raised all kinds of questions.

I sighed in relief as I let my wings unfurl behind the safety of the tinted windows. Their dark shapes filled my peripheral vision, wafting my sweaty brow with a gentle breeze. At least Nykur had the ability to expand his backseat, giving me plenty of room; having a Fae shapeshifter/car bound to me had some perks. Too bad I'd Hulked my favorite shirt into shreds, though.

With my magic under better control, I tucked my wings back inside my self and crawled into the driver's seat.

Static burst from the radio as the stations rapidly changed—Nykur's way of talking to me when he was stuck in this form. "Where...go from here?"

"Hmm, good question," I answered. "Going home to wait for the gavel to fall is not real appealing right now."

The logical side of me knew it would be better if I turned back and faced my mom, instead of letting her really build up steam, but I just didn't have it in me. At least if I talked to her later, it would just be her and not half the medical crisis team too.

I pulled a fresh T-shirt out of the glovebox and said, "I need to talk to Lonan. I need a nap; you know how bad the crash hits me after I've burned through some magic. We can go to Uncle Tam's maybe?"

The car dipped as he nodded, and then music blared from the speakers. By the time the song finished, we were taking the U.C. Davis exit off highway 50, and turning into the arboretum.

A few months before, I'd created a secret way into Faerie through this strip of living biology lab. I mean, why should I drive all the way to Crow's Rest and Warren Castle to get where I was going, when there were all kinds of places where Faerie nestled up to our world? All I needed was a spot where the Border twined around my ankles like a friendly cat.

I'd found the perfect place in the darkness of an underpass in the arboretum; now if you knew the way—and had a magic car to take you—you could drive through it to Faerie's version of Warren Castle. There, I had the choice of hitting up some Faerie hotspots (like Flynnland, the amusement park/loveshack I'd magicked into existence as my personal playground) or taking shortcuts to destinations in the human world.

In theory, I could hit up Paris, London, Marrakesh, whatever—but today I was only using the passage as a shortcut to not-so-exciting Crow's Rest. In our world, the old mining town was in the foothills, more than an hour from Davis. Traveling this way, it was like twenty minutes, since the time spent crossing Faerie passed in an instant.

Before I knew it, Nykur's tires were kicking up dust on the cemetery's gravel roads and we pulled up at Uncle Tam's cheery yellow cottage.

It was obvious Uncle Tam knew I'd be coming, because fresh sheets lay on my bed in the screened porch when I passed through to the kitchen. As my footsteps sounded on the tile, he didn't even bother to look up from his book—just pointed to the pastie waiting for me on low in the toaster oven.

"Heather—your mom—called to say if you showed up here, I should send you home," he said. "She blistered my ear right well for taking your side. You're staying the night, then?"

I nodded. "I'll call her after I eat." I'd need to at least let her know I was okay, and she never heard her cell phone ring so I could probably get by with a voicemail.

"You know there's an easy fix for all this drama, don't you?" Uncle Tam asked.

I sighed at the start of his familiar rant and sat down to eat my pastie. "We're not talking about that again. If you'd rather I go spend the night in Flynnland, I can."

He harrumphed at my stubbornness, but dropped his argument for now. The power struggle had been going on for weeks: him trying to convince me it would be easier to spellicize my mom into submission so I could concentrate on more important things (namely, closing off our world from Faerie forever), and me arguing that I was not going to mess with my own mother like that.

Not to mention that Uncle Tam didn't seem to see the contradiction of arguing for separating the human world from Faerie permanently so humans could live without magical influence, but using that very influence to make it happen. All that his rants had accomplished was tempting me into messing with *his* memory so I could get some peace.

I knew I'd have to work out a long-term solution someday, once and for all. Not tonight, though, if I could help it.

Before going to bed, I folded some shadows into the shape of an origami crow and invited Lonan to join me. I knew the crow would find him no matter where he was, but there was no guarantee he would be able to get away from his Court duties.

Queen Maeve had promoted him to the Faerie Host, which has nothing to do with a Fae reality show like it sounds. The Faerie Host is an elite guard, and it was supposedly an honor to be included, but near as I could tell it mostly involved standing around the queen and looking buff in overly elaborate armor. Which Lonan admittedly did very well.

But he must not have been able to get away, because I fell asleep by myself, feeling my aloneness like an ache.

2

The next morning I didn't have first period, so I slept in. Good thing Nykur was waiting to take me through the portals and deliver me back to the arboretum, which was only minutes from the high school. I got to second period just in time to avoid getting a tardy text sent to my mom.

At lunch, I remembered they'd finally gotten the pizza station functional in the cafeteria and I raced to get in line. The melty-cheese-and-grease scent was torture, since I was stuck so far at the back of the line that I couldn't even read the menu. I lasted four whole minutes before my impatience overcame my good sense, and I surreptitiously waved a hand in the lunch lady's direction. Just enough to get her attention, magically.

"Avery?" I heard my name called, and I elbowed my way to the front of the line.

A dazed, hair-netted lunch lady asked, "You're Avery?" At my nod, she continued, "These are yours."

She held out two pans of pizza, fresh out of the oven and still bubbling. Only, her skin was sizzling too—she hadn't grabbed oven mitts or anything, just rushed to do my bidding. My magic tended to go overboard without a chant or spell to focus it, and I'd been in such a hurry I'd gotten careless. The flesh of her searing palms smelled eerily like pepperoni, and suddenly I wasn't so eager for pizza.

"Why don't you set those down?" I suggested shakily. "I appreciate you getting them for me."

Still with that blank-eyed stare, she put the pizzas on the counter. I took her hands in my own shaking ones, reciting Uncle Tam's healing spell under my breath. She seemed better then, but who knew if she'd have brain damage from me messing with her mind? Or if she would be vulnerable to magic in some way she wasn't before, because of me? I should have had "poor impulse control" tattooed on my forehead, to warn everyone.

Somebody bumped me from behind as the other students grumbled about my special treatment. One person snickered about me getting handsy with the lunch lady. I tuned them out and concentrated on...Doris, according to her nametag. I spoke to her soothingly, to try to make up for hurting her.

"Why don't you give me a couple slices—use a spatula, Doris!—and I'll let you get back to work?" My personal thrall moved to comply, and I stamped down my guilt in favor of hunger. "Not the pepperoni!" I blurted, far too loud, as my gorge rose at the remembered smell of cooking hand meat.

"Um, cheese, please." I managed a more normal tone of voice.

I took my eco-paper plate, which immediately started weeping grease into my palm, and I slunk off to an unoccupied corner of the room. I had only gotten a few bites in before my bench swayed with the weight of another occupant, and a hand with purple glitter nails snagged my other slice.

"Hey!" I squawked, spewing pizza all over a shirtsleeve.

"Wow, that's sexy," Missa said around a mouthful of my lunch. "Now make soda come out your nose, and I'll ravish you right here."

Not Missa, then.

"Hi, Lonan." At his wink, I continued. "Missa let you take over her body again? I thought she got really mad at you last time, when you dyed her hair blonde."

"I did her a favor—her traffic-cone shade of orange made her look like a Chucky doll. On the other hand, my blonde spiky cut put her firmly into sexy-Gwen-Stefani territory."

I had to admit the Cheeto hair hadn't done it for me either, but then she wasn't my, um, partner all the time. "Still, I'm surprised. Not everybody comes back for another spin on the Lonan-go-round. You don't exactly keep a low profile when you're in their body."

"And yet, Missa keeps coming back for more, so I must be doing something right."

I snorted. "Or she's a total gamer-girl adrenaline junkie, and going to Faerie is more fun to her than any video game could ever be. And it doesn't hurt that she doesn't really care what people think about the naked dance you did on the pool table while she was gone."

He grinned wickedly, not at all embarrassed. "Don't complain. With her, you get to skip the walk of shame all the others feel when they get teased for being your flavor of the week."

It was true, she was a good friend and I knew I shouldn't complain. I'd already lost other friendships over the awkwardness of post-Lonan possession, before we set up a policy that he mostly switched with strangers. But Missa had been my friend for a few years before I'd met Lonan, and she seemed willing to stick around through my Fae growing pains. Even going so far as to switch with him when Lonan and I needed time together, as long as nothing he did got her an actual rap sheet.

Or an incurable STD.

"You know she's a vegan, right?" I asked. "So you can give me back the slice you stole."

I made a grab for the pizza he'd hijacked, but Lonan just started eating faster.

"Urff fusssh a hifforid." He choked, and coughed furiously before he repeated, "You're such a hypocrite—did you even pay for this?"

"Um, no—but I will when I go check on the lunch lady to make sure she's okay."

"Be careful how you ask, or she'll carve out her kidney and give it to you or something."

That stung, since it hit a little too close to my own guilt. I had bespelled Doris on an impulse; maybe I *was* a hypocrite, refusing to use magic on my mom and then abusing it to skip the pizza line. Given the choice to be a well-fed hypocrite or a hangry danger to my classmates, which was worse?

I sighed, before changing the subject. "What are you doing here, anyway? I expected you'd show up at Uncle Tam's last night."

He shook his head and grabbed my unattended pizza crust. "I couldn't get away from the Host, but your origami bird seemed a little melancholy. Thought I'd better spend some time with you, so I agreed to take a history test for Missa today if she'd lend me her body again."

I was silent as I processed this, and then I asked, "How long do you have it for?"

He stopped mid-chew and raised penciled-on eyebrows. "What did you have in mind? You wanna ditch for the rest of the day and spend it in Nykur's backseat?"

"No...but can you come home with me after school? I think it's time I tell my mom what's really going on in my life. What she's imagining is so much worse."

"Whoa, are you sure? Once you tell her something like that, you can't undo it without magical help. How do you know she won't lock you up and pump you full of more drugs?"

"I don't, not really. The other pills stopped working on me weeks ago—I think that big push of magic when I restored the Border flushed them out of my system for good. I guess my magic won, leaving me immune or something. I'm not sure a human institution or lockup could hold me at this point, since I'm not completely human. Not if I went wyvern while I was in there."

He nodded thoughtfully. "You may be right about the last bit; you're a special case for sure. So you want me there when you tell your mom, for moral support?"

I snorted a laugh. "More like amoral or immoral support, but yeah."

I took a deep breath before continuing. "It's... I've been thinking that maybe lying to my mom is nearly as bad as using a spell on her. I'm sure she would think so, if she found out about either scenario. If it *is* just as bad, does it make me any better than the Fae who use people? Or any different from Uncle Tam, who kept Mom in the dark about how I was conceived?"

He shook his head. "Lying so you have time to learn about your magic, and to keep her safe, is nothing like how most Fae take advantage of humans. They don't even 'get' that anything they do is taking advantage. It would be like a Fae discovering free will in a lump of iron ore, and letting it decide if it wants to be used in a ship's anchor, or a car, or a bridge."

"Or whether it wants to be used at all," I said. "But that's my point; how can I expect any other Fae to control their impulses, if I can't control mine? I can't keep letting my magic get away from me and then hold everyone else to a different standard. I can't keep making excuses. If it means I have to spend some serious time in Faerie for some training, I can't just disappear and make my mom worry. So I need to tell her."

He nodded reluctantly. Brow knitted, he leaned over for a kiss, but I reached to stop him with a hand to his chest. It looked like I was grabbing Missa's left boob instead.

"Slut!" Some guy cough-spoke as a group passed. The rest laughed, and one added, "I bet she went down on Doris to get that pizza."

Lonan's expression darkened, and I knew he wasn't above magicking those guys in the middle of the cafeteria, so I yanked him out to the hallway.

"Avery! You're going to let them get away with those insults?" he demanded.

I sighed. "Well, yeah—what am I going to do, un-douchify three-quarters of the school with a spell? It's not the first time I've heard it. Even my mom ambushed me with her concerns about the parade of boys and girls through my bedroom."

I caught him up with what had made me run to Uncle Tam's last night and said, "So you see? I may as well be wearing a scarlet S for Slut. Even though I'm completely, boringly monogamous."

"Not boring," he said, and attempted to pull me into a comforting hug. I dodged him, but he added, "You're not getting away that easily. You need a distraction."

Lonan dragged me into the girls' bathroom and into the handicapped stall. Behind closed doors, I let him wrap his arms around me and heaved a sigh.

"Humans are so weird about sex and love and judgments," he said into my hair. "Don't let them get to you."

"I don't." At his skeptical sound, I added, "Well, not in the way you mean. They can think anything they want, it's a free country—but it does bug me that they think it's okay to say mean shit. To anybody.

"Slut-shaming is so...biblical, and doesn't belong in the twenty-first century."

"Totally." He sounded very grave, but his lips nibbled my neck and made me squirm with ticklishness.

"I'm being serious, Lonan!"

"And I'm agreeing with you. Why shouldn't a wildly magical girl, who's one-third wyvern, be able to love a crow boy who's in a borrowed, tattooed vegan girl's pansexual body without people making it a big deal?"

"When you put it like that..." I kissed him back until the sound of the bell made us come up for air and rush to our classes.

After school, Lonan was ready to pick up where we left off and leave the driving to Nykur while we made out in the backseat. But dread about how to break it to my mom that my wings have nothing to do with a feminine hygiene product—and everything to do with her being tricked during my conception—ruined the mood for me.

I wasn't sure if she'd even believe me—or if she did believe me, would she try to forbid me from having anything to do with magic? I could totally see her trying to do that, and then I'd have to butt heads with her. I'd meant it when I said I didn't want to keep letting my magic get away from me, and I knew from experience that trying to ignore it—or suppress it—made everything worse for everybody.

I didn't even want to think about it anymore. So instead I raided Nykur's magical glovebox full of snacks (Lonan *would* eat pork rinds, ugh) and fortified myself to dump a crapload of preposterous things on my mom. Who confronted us much sooner than I'd expected, when Lonan and I came into the living room and found Mom waiting there.

"Um, hi," I said, and gripped Lonan's hand tighter before he could let go. "Mom, this is my boyfriend."

Mom eyed Missa's obviously boob-bedecked form, her gaze lingering on the tattoos peeking out of neckline and sleeve cuffs, and said, "Uh-huh. Is that the terminology these days? Missa prefers male pronouns now?"

"Missa still prefers 'she', and ten points to you for knowing to ask. But—try to keep an open mind and follow along—this isn't Missa. This is my boyfriend Lonan, and he's only borrowing her body temporarily."

Mom looked back and forth between us, like she was waiting for a punchline. When one didn't come, she said, "Is this your way of getting back at me for yesterday, Avery? Because I'm afraid whatever game you're playing isn't helping your argument that you're...in a healthy frame of mind. Why don't you drop the act and tell me what's going on?"

"Brace yourself, Mom." I started with me figuring out when Daniel wasn't Daniel last summer, and that Lonan had taken over his body, and then about Nykur the magic car taking us to rescue the real Daniel—and that was as far as I got before she cut me off.

"That's enough, Avery!" She got up to get her purse, fishing for her car keys.

I knocked them from her hand and immediately thought, *that's probably one of those impulses you should've controlled, Avery.* I bent to pick them up and then gave her a wobbly smile, trying to defuse her anger.

It didn't work.

"I don't know what—you're coming back to the hospital with me, young lady. Do you have a car, Missa, so you can get home?"

Lonan shook his head. "I'm not going anywhere, and I'm not Missa. Avery's already told you I'm Lonan, her Fae boyfriend."

Actually, I hadn't said the F-word yet, figuring to ease her into the Faerie world-building more gradually. But I hadn't expected her reaction at hearing Lonan say he was Fae—all the blood drained from her face, and she let out a heartbroken wail. Mom dissolved into a sobbing mess, sinking to the floor in the dining room, and I instinctively rushed to comfort her. Shit—what was happening? But my attempt to hug her ended in her curling into a tighter ball, rejecting me as she descended into some dark place.

Crap, leave it to me to screw this up in ways that weren't even on my worry list. I patted her on the shoulder, which seemed to be the least threatening thing I could think of—but also the least effective.

Mom suddenly wailed, "I couldn't save him, I couldn't save him from himself."

When she went back to wordlessly sobbing again, I turned to Lonan in a panic and asked, "What do I do?"

He knelt to examine my wreck of a mother and finally said, "Um...I don't know."

"What do you mean, you don't know? Do people usually freak out this much when you try to tell them about Faerie? How do you get people to listen to your spiel on subletting their bodies without them thinking it's all crazy?"

He shrugged. "There's a spell involved, of course, which lets me influence them to keep an open mind while they listen. I can try it."

"Did you even listen when I said I didn't want to magick her or lie to her?" I took a deep breath, since me panicking probably wouldn't help Mom calm down. "That's not even on the table. What else?"

"You can always say you were joking. Or you were trying to get back at her, like she said."

"And set myself up for an even harder sell the next time I try to have this conversation? I'll have to tell her eventually—if she'd just listen, I'd rather get it over with."

If I could rewind this whole scene, I would. Any fight we would have had about yesterday was better than knowing I'd done this to my mom. Now the only sound in the room was my mom's dwindling sobs, peppered with hiccups, while I thought about how to get out of this mess.

Finally, I reached over and rubbed her back. "Mom? I didn't know you'd be so upset, or I would have...said things in a less-Avery way. Do you trust Uncle Tam? Because he's involved in this too. Would it make a difference to hear his side of the story?"

I didn't know if she was truly calming down or had only run out of steam, but her breathing grew more regular and she seemed to perk up at the mention of Uncle Tam's name.

Trying out a weak smile, she said, "Yeah, maybe Uncle Tam can help."

I took my phone out of my pocket with exaggeratedly slow movements, so as not to spook her. I dialed Uncle Tam's number and relief washed over me when I heard his "Yello" on the other end.

"Uncle Tam, you're on speaker," I said. "I'm here with Mom...and Lonan. I tried to explain about him, and Mom—Mom kind of lost it. Can you tell her I'm not crazy and you know about Faerie too?"

At the word, Mom let out a whimper, and a flurry of curses came from Uncle Tam.

"You broke the geis," he said with a sigh. "Great. I put that on her for her own good, Avery, and you'll have to restore it."

"Wait, what? You put a geis on her so she'd flip out whenever she heard—the F-word?"

"No, of course not. Your father tried to have this conversation with her—if he'd only left it with 'there's somebody else,' it would have been fine. Telling your mom he'd chosen a tree-spirit over her caused all sorts of trouble. She was convinced he'd had a psychotic break and was all set to hospitalize him. I put the geis on her so she'd forget that part of their breakup. Only a Fae mentioning Faerie could break it, in case she was targeted."

Well, nice to have a failsafe, I guess. But stronger than my snark, a rush of anger hit me with the confirmation that he denied my mom the chance to work through her own feelings, on top of everything else. I had to stop and count to ten, to try not to let my magic rise up.

While I was doing that, a garble of Gaelic words came out of the phone and Mom's sobs disappeared. If I was only going by her expression, I would have thought nothing had happened—if it wasn't for the evidence of tears. But I knew something had happened, and I wasn't the only cause.

"What did you do, Uncle Tam? Stop magicking my mom! Isn't it bad enough you messed with her memory before, and tricked her into sleeping with a wyvern?"

"He did what now?" Mom demanded. Suddenly, she was back in Steely-Eyed-Mom mode.

Eep. I'd counted on her still being out of it and not paying attention to what I said. Now I once again faced the decision to backpedal or forge ahead. I went with a combination of the two.

"Oh, um, that isn't the way I wanted to tell you. You see, Tam Lin wanted to create another wild magic child, so he put a spell on Dad's body so a wyvern could add his, um, essence to the...baby. Um, me."

I looked to Lonan for help, but he just cocked one pierced eyebrow at my lame attempt to salvage my confusing recap. I sighed and risked another glance at my mom, whose flaring nostrils showed she'd morphed from Steely-Eyed-Mom into Take-Charge-Mom.

"Here's what's going to happen," she said. "I'm calling Dr. Zapatas and having her do an emergency evaluation of you and your meds, Avery. Then I'm considering taking out a restraining order on you,

Tam, until we get to the bottom of this. I don't know what you've been filling her head with, you and her father both—"

"Mom!" I spoke over her. "Don't drag Dr. Zapatas into this—she can't do anything about it, because it's not a mental health issue. I'm not even on my meds anyway—they don't work with my magic, okay?"

I slammed my jaw shut, but it was too late. *Avery, when will you learn to keep things like that* inside *your head?* Now Mom was going to go ballistic, and I was the one who had handed her the ammunition.

"You took yourself off your pills? *All* of them? That explains a lot. That's it, I'm checking you into a hospital, where they can ensure you take your meds. Where you're not unduly influenced by..." Mom gestured at the phone, where Uncle Tam was hollering about texting me a spell to use before I made things worse.

I leapt to my feet, pacing in agitation. Had we passed the point where I could fix this myself? Should I take Uncle Tam's help just this once? Even if it was just for me to buy some time and work this out...

I was so caught up in wracking my brain that I didn't notice the itching sensation had returned on my back until it was too late. Before I could stop it from happening, my wings swept the ceiling, making a *whump!* like Batman's cape unfurling in the wind.

For a moment, all Mom and I could do was stare at each other. Two figures frozen—one of them inhumanly winged—like a pane in a graphic novel. Until the action fast-forwarded.

Mom tried to scramble over the back of the couch and ended up falling on the ground, where she crab-scuttled away from me as fast as she could. I followed after her, trying to make my "it's all right!" heard over her screams, but the batwings curving behind me only seemed to make things worse. It was all happening in slow-motion and fast-forward at the same time, and I was too much of a wreck myself to figure out what to do right away.

Finally, I backed her up against a wall and tried to speak in a soothing voice while I stowed away my wings. But I think she was too far gone to notice—her eyes were sightless and glazed, breath whistling through her strained throat. The hands she held defensively in front of her face trembled, and it broke my heart to see her like that—and to know I was responsible. Maybe Uncle Tam was right to put a geis on her.

"Mom, please stop." I placed a hand on her shoulder and she stilled, like prey waiting for a deathblow from a predator. "I'm sorry Mom, I'm so sorry—I wish there was a way I could undo all of this."

I waited for her to say something, even if it was only a whimper or to say how much she hated me now. But not a sound came from my mom. It took me a few seconds to realize she wasn't even breathing.

"Lonan, something's wrong!"

I tried to shake her shoulders, but her flesh felt weirdly cold and unyielding under my hands, like half-thawed chicken. Another shake made her rock on her feet, like a statue tipping on its pedestal.

I stepped back in horror, but luckily Lonan lunged forward to catch her. His hands on her waist got no reaction—her face stayed frozen in a grimace of fear. With her hands still raised to protect herself from her own monstrous daughter.

3

While I was lost in my own freakout, Lonan gently set Mom upright again. He walked around her statuesque form, occasionally poking her with one finger to see if she would react. It struck me as a little disrespectful, but I had to admit I was too squeamish to do it myself.

"What's wrong with her?" I whispered, as if afraid I'd wake her after all. A shiver ran down my entire body, just looking at her so...lost...like that.

Lonan answered, "I think she's stuck. Whether it's a time-stopping spell or what, I don't know, but she's definitely frozen."

I whimpered before I took a deep breath and asked, "Have you seen anything remotely like this, so we at least know where to start looking for a counterspell?"

"Uh...no. I'm not sure this has ever been done exactly like this before—but it's got the stamp of wild magic all over it."

Wild magic? As in...*my* magic?

"I did this?" I breathed in horror.

Before Lonan could answer, Uncle Tam's tinny voice came out of my cell phone: "Would somebody tell me what's going on over there?"

Lonan picked it up and explained to Uncle Tam, since I was obviously too much of a mess to do it. "...and then Avery told her mom to stop, and said something about wishing she could undo all this—"

He broke off as I fell to the ground, my legs giving way beneath me. As soon as I heard him say it, I knew—I'd somehow wished this state on my mother. My wild magic and my intentions had worked hand in hand, and once again created a uniquely-Avery disaster. FUed, maybe BAR.

Which meant it was going to be up to me to figure out how to undo it.

But by the next morning, I was punchy and exhausted, and Rictus Mom still lay on the couch. We'd moved her there because at one point I was *sure* I could fix her, and I didn't want her to fall once she suddenly woke up, but nothing Lonan or I tried had worked.

"Now what?" I asked, voice croaky from lack of sleep and too many attempts at spellcasting. "She should be leaving for work soon, and if she doesn't show they'll get worried. Especially since the psychologist knows we had a big fight right before she disappeared."

"Can you call in to her job?" Lonan asked. "Say she's sick—or better yet, that you're going to Uncle Tam's to try to work things out together?"

"Yeah, and it won't be at all suspicious when her 'troubled' daughter calls to tell them Heather's taking an indefinite leave, and no they can't talk to her."

"No, that part's easy; there's a really simple corbin spell to reproduce someone's voice. We use it all the time, to help us blend in while we're in our hosts. If you help me with what to say, I can call in."

So after some coaching, Lonan dialed Mom's work from her cell phone; her boss was completely pissed she was flaking on them. We weren't able to calm him down, so there was a good chance Mom might not even have a job to come back to.

Great. One more thing for me to feel guilty over—even though I bitched about how much time she spent on this job, I knew she also had worked really hard for it. And now she'd be busted back down to nursing again.

There was nothing left to do but wait for it to get dark so we could smuggle Mom into Nykur, and on to Crow's Rest. Uncle Tam had agreed to try a few spells, and if that failed we were going to see if Queen Maeve could help. I'd probably owe her my firstborn child or something if she could thaw my mom, but at that point I'd gladly grovel.

Meanwhile, Lonan and I sprawled on the living room floor, trying to get some sleep. He'd gotten an extension on Missa's body until tonight, and then he'd have to return it to her control.

But I couldn't relax—every time I closed my eyes, I saw Mom's panicked gaze before I froze her. I hated feeling so helpless and out of control. If I had all these powers, enough to freeze her, I should be able to undo it, right? It wasn't fair that she should pay the price for my magic getting away from me again.

After one more stray noise caused me to bolt upright in case it was her coming back to life, Lonan sighed and sat up.

He said, "Okay, there's one more thing we can try. I don't think you're going to like it—and you'll have to help."

"If you think it will work, I'm willing to try anything," I said. "What do we need to do?"

"You're going to have to keep watch over Missa's body, and be ready to call her back if this goes south."

"Where will you be?"

He hesitated before answering. "I'm going to try passing into your mom's body, to see if she's...see if she's okay."

"*What?* Isn't that really dangerous for her?"

"Without the proper spells and preparation—if I'm just free-flying it—she should be able to shove me right out. If she's awake in there."

"That's a lot of ifs. Would you be able to wake her up from in there?"

He shook his head. "I can't say for sure, but it may at least tell us if she's suffering. And if there's anything we can do to help her in the meantime, or if it's a matter of waiting for the spell to run its course. Do you want to try?"

I could still remember what it had been like when Drake took over my body. Could I really wish that on someone who hadn't signed up for a changeling deal? At least I'd kinda known it was possible— she wouldn't even have that clue to let her know what was going on.

"I don't know," I answered. "She's already pretty traumatized as it is. But it's worse to think she could be screaming in there and I didn't know it."

Seriously, every time I'd tried to fall asleep, it was the sounds of her screaming that jerked me awake again. Each time, they'd only been in my head.

After weighing all the pros and cons I could think of, I turned from my pacing and nodded to Lonan. "Walk me through the plan."

So about twenty minutes later, I found myself watching as an amorphous violet cloud flowed around my mom, seeking a way in. It was über-creepy to see Lonan disappear into her still-open mouth, like a reverse exhalation of tinted hookah smoke. My nervousness almost made everything in my stomach come up.

The seconds ticked by, and I watched for any sign of distress or wakefulness in my mom. A full minute passed, and still nothing. I shifted on my feet so I could check the clock again—we only had a maximum of five minutes for Missa's body to stay empty, according to Lonan. Anything longer, and the body could die without medical intervention.

Tick. Tick. *Gaah, this is torture! Do I call Missa back now, and take my chances that Lonan can find his way back to Faerie when he comes out?* I'd nearly decided not to risk my friend's body any longer when a wisp of violet snaked from Mom's mouth.

It didn't so much flow as dribble out as it followed the line of her jaw, to her neck, and down the front of her shirt. By the time it reached her waist, the violet color had weakened, and so had the cohesiveness. The smoky mass gave a few weak pulses and didn't move any further.

Lonan hadn't said anything like this would happen—should I help or not? I extended my fingertips and lightly brushed the margins of Lonan's fading form, and he recoiled sluggishly. Making soothing sounds, I tried again, cupping my palm below one tendril. He lapped at my skin, tasting it, before he curled into my hand like a sleepy kitten.

I carefully moved my hand closer to Missa's face—I had been possessed through my nose and mouth, so I could only assume that was the easiest way in—and finally Lonan seeped into Missa's nostrils. A few stuttering breaths, and then Lonan choked and coughed where he lay on the floor. I patted his back as I stared at my mom, hoping to see some signs of life in her.

Lonan sliding from under my hand returned my attention to him, and he shocked me by scrambling out of my reach. The terror and horror in his eyes was an echo of my mom's. Wait—did that mean...

"Mom?" I asked, my heart flush with hope. "Is it you?"

Missa's head shook in denial. "No—it's Lonan." Another shaky breath, and he was able to add, "Avery, your mom..."

I tried to wait out another coughing fit, but blurted, "My mom *what*? Tell me!"

"She's not in there—there is no *there*. Even if she'd died, there would have been echoes, some residue of her self. But there's nothing there, Avery—only a void. An awful emptiness, apart from anything I've ever come across—even in Faerie."

I hadn't just frozen her—I'd basically created a human black hole where my mom used to be.

Lonan was so tapped out that he thought it would be better to call Missa back to her body so he could go to Faerie to recover. Thinking of handling this without his help sent me into another freakout—or was my life one continuous freakout at this point?

With a few deep breaths to activate my own better nature, I acknowledged that Lonan getting some rest was more important than my worries about how I was going to explain to Missa that she needed to help me carry my mother's body to the car.

We had decided I'd better take Mom straight to Queen Maeve, since this spell was probably beyond Uncle Tam's skills. Until then, I wanted Lonan to hold me in his arms and tell me everything would be all right. But he was uncharacteristically quiet, and even our parting kiss felt dutiful—at least on his side of the lips.

I was about to break away and question him again when suddenly the kiss got a lot more enthusiastic. When the pair of hands squeezed my butt cheeks hard enough to bruise, I didn't need Missa's giggle to let me know she was back.

"You brat!" I smacked her on the shoulder, but she was laughing too hard to notice.

She finally caught her breath and said, "Aw, come on, Avery, I was just screwing around. What's got you so school-marmish?"

Wordlessly, I pointed to the Momsicle still stretched on the couch.

"Damn!" She walked over for a closer look and then stood, shaking her head. "You could make a mint by selling this spell to other—"

I burst into tears and she jumped like I'd burned her. "Whoa! Don't cry—I didn't mean to make you cry!"

So I finally got the hug and "hey, it's going to be okay" comfort I needed—but from Missa instead of

Lonan. She even overcame her vegan principles to heat me up a tray of chicken enchiladas, like a true friend. Although I only took the first bite to humor her, I finished the whole thing and did feel a little better afterwards. But I was still so on edge that the taste of bile in the back of my throat quickly overwhelmed the enchilada goodness.

I guess word was getting around, because Daniel texted me. **hey, nykur said something happed w/ yr mom? hope u can fix it & she's okay**

I replied, **yeah me 2. when she wakes up, don't know if she'll be more mad about the fae stuff or me freezing her. thx for cking in TTYL <3**

It comforted me that, with everything that happened between us over the summer, Daniel still stepped up for me when he heard my mom was in trouble. I would do the same for him, even though we no longer texted on a daily basis. Like those memes on Facebook about "true friends" (never mind that most of them are about being willing to help dispose of bodies).

I guess Missa was one of those friends too, since she was taking my word for Mom's frozen-but-not-dead state. Once it was properly dark out, we carried my mom, disguised with an old Halloween mask as a haunted-house prop, out to Nykur. His back seat flowed to surround her in a cushiony co-coon, padding her in case of any sudden stops.

We set out and Missa slipped her earbuds in; I was left to my own thoughts, which weren't very coherent. I was dreading putting my mom in Queen Maeve's hands—even if she helped thaw her, I didn't want my mom to owe her anything.

Hell, I didn't want to owe the queen anything ei-ther, since her conditions for repayment sometimes involved...well, things I wasn't willing to do. The way I felt right now, I was pretty desperate; had the "things I wasn't willing to do" line moved in this case? If it was for personal gain, for me getting power, no, but the chance to save my mom was dif-ferent.

As much as I joked about how her workaholic ways had taught me to take care of myself, I still felt like a kid sometimes. It turned out that when you're not sure if your mom is ever going to wake up was one of those times. I reached behind the driver's seat and I could just touch her hair where it cascad-ed off the back seat, and I stayed like that the rest of the drive to Missa's house.

After we dropped Missa off, I gave Nykur free rein in the darkened streets. In spite of Davis's col-lege-town feel, it was still possible to travel on rural back roads once you left the strip malls behind. In no time at all, we passed through the arboretum's Gate and came out basking in the bright light of a Fae noon.

I sat up straighter in the driver's seat, readying myself for arriving at Court. Warping the distance, or time and space or whatever it was in Faerie, usually saved a lot of footwork, but with the queen's no-fly and no-magical-transportation zone around her Court, Nykur and I would have to drive or (horse)hoof it. Queen Maeve's palace was one of the few fixed points in Faerie, a trait I was cursing right now since it meant an actual journey instead of willing ourselves there.

I half-suspected the travel restrictions weren't all about safety; the Queen took advantage of the approach to give travelers a hint of what they could expect. The way wound between dark and thorny trees, with sinister limbs crowding the road, until sudden clearings of breathtaking beauty opened before you.

And when you were lulled into a sense of wonder and awe, you'd come around a bend and find a gibbet bearing the corpse of a unicorn—its dazzle rotting away into tufts of felted hide.

I mean, what the hell did a unicorn do to deserve that? Fart a rainbow in the queen's direction?

Not a single view on the way to the Court was straightforward—a flash of unbearable loveliness always lurked among the dark leaves, or a touch of blight borne among the delicate blooms. Where her design sense really held its own was the fanciful wall of briar roses surrounding the Palace proper—a Rococo explosion of carven figures cavorting among the crepe blossoms and thorny vines.

A closer look—which I'd only braved once—revealed those figures weren't so much cavorting as writhing in agony, as the briar rose slowly absorbed them and made the creatures part of its barrier. Why let your enemies' heads shrivel on pikes, when this was so much more lasting? Preserved for every one of the victim's families to pass by on their way to Court as a reminder of what it meant to displease Queen Maeve.

Nykur drove up to the open gates, but stopped to take another form to go inside—his kind may have evolved to include metal in their car form, but the other Fae still had an aversion to a steel chassis. For once, he recognized the gravity of the situation and skipped the snarky T-shirt (or half-naked display), appearing in a dark leather suit as he carried my mom towards the palace. I was touched when four of the Host came out to escort us, but wondered why Lonan wasn't among them.

It wasn't until we entered the palace and its Great Hall that I started to get a weird feeling. I mean, I hadn't exactly been welcomed with open arms by all the Fae before—most of them mistrusted me and my powers, and the ones who said they didn't were often trying to brown-nose me—but the side-eye they were giving me now was more obvious. If there was a Fae equivalent of crossing themselves, they would have done it as we passed.

I tried to ignore them as I scanned the crowd for Lonan. He was up on the dais with his aunt, bending slightly to speak in her ear. In relief, I waved at him like a total dork. He nodded, but turned slightly so he could continue his low conversation with the Queen.

What the...? I hadn't expected him to leap down the stairs and snog me right away, but a little wink or something would have been nice.

I turned to Nykur for guidance, but he was absorbed with carefully setting my mom on her feet. Once he had accomplished that—and removed her Halloween mask—he kneeled and waited for the Queen's attention.

So, I guess we wait. I'm here to ask a favor, so I can totally do that.

And to be fair, I did wait patiently, for a while. But as a series of other counselors took Lonan's place for semi-private conversations with Queen Maeve, my impatience grew. And so did my awareness of the snub she was giving me, in my role as so-called ambassador between the Fae and humans. Yes, asking for her help put more of the power in her Court, but I wasn't exactly pâté.

Mmm, pâté... I was getting hungry, too. While we'd been waiting, the remains of one meal had been cleared away and new courses brought out. But Nykur and I may as well have been furniture, as the servants maneuvered around us and didn't make eye contact.

As the Court went about their business around me, I started to fume—and that wasn't a figure of speech. My tightly reined magic started leaking out my pores, coming off me in blue clouds like my own personal laser-light show. It would be disastrous to lose control here, where the super-paranoid queen took everything personally.

I chewed my lip and tried my best to squash my magic, using some mindfulness exercises which had seemed to help before. But when they'd helped, I'd been in the human world, and here my magic felt so much more raw and powerful. Bigger than me. I could feel it building—along with the euphoria that accompanied a rise in my magic.

I knew if I tried to excuse myself, or if I just left, it would be the height of rudeness to Queen Maeve. I was about to risk a throat-clearing or some other polite bid for attention when my magic decided it had had enough of this restraint bullshit. Even my panic wasn't enough to make it change its mind—in fact, it seemed to fuel my powers.

With a sound like flowing water, wild magic rushed out of my hands, which I hastily pointed down at the floor. A rolling wave of blue energy spread out from me, and when it dissipated I saw the flowered carpet I stood on was now a carpet of flowers. Gloriously fragrant blossoms surrounding me in a saturated-color sea.

That wasn't so bad—it could have gone much worse. I was smiling as I looked up, thinking the queen may actually be pleased with this change, when my jaw dropped open instead.

Every member of the Host had formed a triple-thick wall between me and their queen, each guard armed with wicked-looking pikes or swords pointed in my direction. The rest of the Court scrambled to get out of the crossfire, heading for the doors or for the shelter of a pillar.

They thought I was attacking her. I'd better clear that up in a hurry...

"Your Majesty—wait," I blurted. "It was an accident! You have to believe me!"

I held up my hands in surrender, then realized that pose might be threatening, and lowered them again. What was the universal gesture for "I'm unarmed!" when your actual hands were the arms? I eventually settled them behind my back, and two of the Host warily approached me with magical manacles in their fists.

I took an involuntary step backward at the sight of the manacles—my previous experiences with restraints had not been great—and my wings unfurled in reaction to my fight-or-flight response (emphasis on the flight). I muttered angrily to my wings as I tried to fold them out of sight, until I realized that could be mistaken for a spell too.

Seeing that I might need a bit more time to get control of myself, Nykur stepped in front of me—and got tackled by a group of the Host for his trouble.

"Stop!" I yelled over the commotion. "Just—just slide the manacles over here, and I'll put them on! I promise!"

The guardsman nearest me looked over his shoulder; he must have received some kind of signal from the queen, because he did as I asked. I started to pick them up, but hesitated since I could feel these manacles were not like the ones I'd over-come when Drake attacked me. I was able to even-tually break out of those, once my magic was under my control again.

These were...older. More sinister in an ancient, soul-deadening way. My instincts told me even my wild magic didn't stand a chance with these. A hoarse gasp from Nykur, where he was being held in a chokehold by a guard, reminded me I didn't have much choice but to submit.

I fit the cuffs over my wrists as quickly as I could, and as they snapped shut, my wings folded away—along with my magic. The absence of my powers left me feeling weak and alone, which is probably what Queen Maeve had in mind.

I sank into a drift of flowers, trying to choke back sobs. I had really done it this time: I'd gotten Nykur hurt, and I may have completely alienated the queen—who could be my only hope for thawing out Mom.

I lifted my head and looked again for Lonan—he was there, in the second row of the Host. Looking just as grim and fearful, and ready to lay down his life for his queen, as the rest of them. I didn't even fight when two of the Host came to escort me and Nykur to the dungeons, and put us in separate dank cells.

Without a window in my cell, it was too easy to lose track of time. Of course, time was a funny thing here anyway.

When Lonan had first told me that time and space were different in Faerie, I'd pictured it as having perpetual sunlight or twilight over the land. No sunrises or sunsets, and no seasons, like a forever-summer. Not quite like that, since there was a sun (and two moons), and seasons, and day and night. With Faerie and Earth operating on their own timelines, a week in Faerie could mean an hour at home—or a month.

When I'd spent larger chunks of time here, it felt like the days and nights were longer than twenty-four hours, but my watch didn't work in Faerie so it was hard to tell. Since I'd come here for pleasure more often than business, the only part which had mattered was how much time was passing on Earth; I didn't want to disappear for too long and make my mom worry.

But now she was in Faerie too—or at least her body was—and maybe completely unaware of time passing. So I marked time by worrying about my mom, feeling sorry for myself and wondering if the Queen was taking out her frustration on Nykur. Or even on Lonan, if his loyalty was questioned.

Only the growling of my stomach gave me a hint that I'd likely already missed a handful of meals. And the tray of food the guard eventually brought me wasn't nearly enough—it was good stuff, probably from the kitchens here at court, but once I'd wolfed it down I only wanted more. The warmth of the honey mead on my tongue, the burst of juices as I bit into the berries, became all I could think about. When I dozed, my dreams were of endless feasts and overburdened tables.

My hunger even eclipsed all my worries, and thoughts of anything besides food only surfaced during the haze of contentment following each tray of delights. With no news about my fate, or my mother's, it was a relief to surrender to my anticipation of the next meal delivery, so much so that I didn't even realize something was really wrong until the guard brought me a tray and I was too weak to walk over and get it. I begged him to bring it to me, but with a suspicious frown he slammed my cell door, and left me to crawl across the floor and claim my meal.

As I licked crumbs from the plate, I caught a glimpse of my reflection in the polished surface. My eyes were dark hollows in a skull-tight face, my mouth only a sunken slash. Without the feverish glint in my gaze, I could have been a mummy in a museum case. When I looked down and became aware of more than just food, I saw that my hands and wrists were knobs of bone in a leather casing.

What is happening to me?

But already, the fleeting clarity that came with eating was fading. I dropped into a comforting dream of a magical orchard, where I gorged myself until I thought I would burst.

And when the next tray finally came, I could barely focus through a dark cloud covering my vision. The scent of fruit and mead, out of reach, was torture. I did my best to call out to the guard, to plead with him for help, but I wasn't sure if a whisper even left my cracked lips. My eyelids rustled as I blinked once, twice—and then everything went dark.

4

A familiar smell filled my nostrils, making them twitch like a rat's. *Is that choco-late...and hazelnut?* I cracked my eyes open, and caught the glint of a foil wrapper inches from my face. And, so close I couldn't focus on it proper-ly, a pile of unwrapped chocolate squares. *All I need to do is stick out my tongue...*

So I did, and a velvety smear of chocolate re-warded my withered tastebuds—this wasn't a dream, it was real. The initial rush of sugar gave me enough strength to reach out a hand and cram some of the squares into my mouth, nearly choking as my dusty salivary glands kicked in. I ate as fast as I could—until everything started to come back up.

Would my cause of death technically be "irony," if I choked on vomit from eating too fast after a brush with starvation? I didn't think I could ever live that down in the afterlife. Even my own wheezing laughter sounded dusty in my ears.

Having learned my lesson, I gave each new bite a little time to settle before taking the next. I moved on from chocolate to pasties, and then ate some of the fruit the guard had brought earlier. Strangely, the Fae food didn't taste nearly as good as it had before, but the jug of mead helped me wash down all the rest. When I couldn't eat any more, I lay back to let the food coma set in.

But surprisingly, I didn't really feel the need to rest. Instead, something goaded me to get up and get moving. *Get up, get out, get away,* the voice urged. I obeyed, and made my shaky way over to the door of my cell. At my touch, it swung inward, and I stumbled back, expecting this to all be a trick. But no one jumped out and yelled "Psych!" and only a few sounds carried from the corridor. Supporting myself with the jamb, I swung drunkenly out the door to check for guards.

Nobody but me and a bunch of blue torches to know I puked again, thankfully. I wiped my mouth and looked longingly at the jug of mead still in my cell, but I'd never be able to carry it in this state.

So I carefully put one foot in front of the other and whisper-shouted "Nykur?" as I weaved.

It took a few tries, and some fits of giggling, before I heard an "Avery?" in answer. I headed towards the two meaty fingers waving from a food slot down the row, and shook them in greeting.

"Heeeeey, Nykur, ol' buddy," I said, and then burst into tears. Why wasn't he as happy to see me as I was to find him? He should be hugging me right now.

"Avery? What's going on? How are you out of your cell, and why do you sound so weird?"

"No, you're the weird cell." I tried again. "The weird sound. Wait, what? Come out here and say that to my face."

I pushed his cell door open, and nearly followed it into space, before a pair of hands caught me. I smiled up at Nykur, but he recoiled, nearly dropping me.

"Gods! What did she do to you, Avery? You look like a corpse."

I waggled a finger at him. "Uh uh, you won't turn my head with that pretty talk—'you look like a corpse.' Ha!"

But he didn't laugh along with me; instead, he pulled me into his cell and cradled me carefully on his lap. With a sigh, I laid my head on his shoulder.

"I'm so tired, Nykur," I mumbled. "And I was so alone."

"It's all right now," he soothed. "Can you tell me what spell the queen used on you? Did she torture you?"

Did she? I didn't remember any torture sessions with a harsh lightbulb in my eyes and a henchman with bloody pliers, like in a movie. But the queen, she'd be more subtle than that, wouldn't she?

I shook my head. "I didn't see her at all. Nobody but the guards who brought me my food. It was never enough food, so maybe it *was* torture. As soon as I'd eat what they brought me, I was even hungrier for more. Like I could never get enough. I had dreams where I ate so much that I split right open, and still I wanted to eat."

"What did they bring you to eat?"

I leaned back in a languid stretch. "Oh, it was über-fantastic, Nykur! These berries were like cherry cordial—no, like marzipan—or maybe the best flavor of Jelly Bellies. I can't even describe them, they were...the best. And there was this mead like a beautiful cloud princess peed in my mouth—I know that's not the right way to put it, but it was magical and sweet and warming, like a cloud princess' pee would be."

He studied me, turning my face so he could get a close look into my eyes. "Avery, you sound like... Of course! The manacles!"

I whimpered as he grabbed my wrists. "I don't want the manacles!"

"No, I'm not going to put them on you, but where are they? How did you get them off?"

I stretched my muddled thinking, but shrugged and said, "I don't know. Are they in my cell? We could go look. I have food! Real food. Are you hungry? Let's go eat."

He propped me up from behind as I led the way to my cell, where I fell on the trays and started eating again. Nykur came and knelt by me, showing me that the manacle's cuffs were hanging open, scorched at the seams.

"You really don't remember how you got these off?"

I started to reach for the jug of mead, but he moved it away and waited for me to answer.

"No, I don't," I said, pouting. "Is it important?"

He nodded. "It might be. Remember how these took away all your magic? You shouldn't have been able to break out of them. These are a relic from King Oberon's time, and were used on Merlin to bind him millennia ago."

"Oh." I reached out a tentative finger, but I didn't feel anything from the manacles. No magic, or even the residue of magic. Inert.

"But...it's probably a good thing you did," he continued. "If I'm right, these manacles deadened your magic to the point where you were completely human; all the Fae food they brought you didn't do you a bit of good. It burned you up, like fruit from the goblin market does to young humans."

"So I really was starving? It wasn't my imagination?" I shivered at my close call.

"I think so. But the real question is, did the queen know this would happen? Maybe that was her plan all along."

Nykur made me eat more of the "real" food which I'd apparently magicked into my cell, then I washed it down with plain water since he wouldn't let me have any more mead. As my giddiness cleared, I realized most of my drunken behavior was probably from the aftereffects of my wild magic overcoming the manacles, and not the mead. Once I had magic in my system again, the Fae food didn't affect me the same way.

In fact, I felt so much better that I wanted to go pay the queen a visit. Most of my fear of offending her, of her retaliating with her magic, had evaporated along with the manacles' magic. Instead, my anger and magic seemed set to a low boil, just under my regained ability to talk like a normal person again instead of a manic pixie sprite.

Now that inner voice was saying, *Maybe she needs a little reminder that if I stay at the Court, it's because I choose to—not because she put me in the dungeon.*

But once again, Nykur acted as the voice of reason and convinced me not to leave my cell, and to pretend the manacles still held me—even though they were about as secure as an edible chastity belt at this point.

By the time the Host came for me, I'd discovered that sealing the manacles closed with magic didn't reactivate their powers. These guys never looked too close anyway, thankfully, not even when they motioned for me to get to my feet and follow them.

Out in the hallway, another pair of guards was just leading Nykur from his cell. He hadn't been shackled, but moved like he'd aged several years; a result of him being away from water so long, according to him. I gave him a grimace of sympathy and waited for him to catch up.

As we passed another hallway, a final pair of guards joined us with another prisoner.

"Lonan?" I took a step towards him, but he shook his head as the Fae put their hands to their weapons. I blew him a kiss and found my place next to

ANGELICA R. JACKSON

Nykur again. Lonan and his escort walked in front of us as we took the stairs.

Was it my imagination, or was Lonan moving like he was hurting? A little hitch in his gait as he raised a foot to the next step. How did he go from being the queen's protector to becoming her prisoner in the dungeons?

But I didn't get a chance to ask him, because once we were into the palace proper we were separated. I found myself in a small but rich chamber, where a horde of Fae girls descended on me—which was alarming enough after being in solitary confinement, but these girls were armed with sparkly dresses and lots of floral-scented makeup pots.

"Whoa," I said, "keep those to yourself. My clothes are fine."

But they giggled their bell-like laughs and one said, "We'll burn those, after you've had a bath to wash the human-world stink off you."

"Shows what you know! This is dungeon stink," I retorted. "I've been there for...how long *was* I in the dungeon? And why am I even out? Did the queen send for me?"

But the mention of the queen seemed to remind them of their duty, and they didn't speak again, just wrestled me out of my clothes and into a bath scented with gardenia-like blossoms. They scrubbed my protesting skin until it was red, a few of them slyly copping a feel whenever they thought they could pass it off as part of the bathing.

I would never in a million years have let them get away with it under normal circumstances, but I was afraid if I got too worked up then my magic would make itself known. Not a good thing, when I was supposedly magically shackled and neutralized. So I spent most of that private-hell time gritting my teeth and thinking of pink elephants getting slapped.

In the end, they had their way, and I stood perfumed and polished and primped, whether I liked it or not. The dress was actually kind of nice—a drapey botanical print which would look at home in the pages of an Anthropologie catalog, if not in my own closet. And it made my boobs look amazing.

Ugh, if Nykur or Lonan make one crack about Barbie Avery, I will zap them—shackles or no.

Then I paused to wonder if I would even see them again—the queen wouldn't have bothered to put me in this getup if she was going to publicly execute me or something, would she? Or if she was going to make me watch Lonan or Nykur on the execution block? I tried to question my "handlers," but they just giggled and ignored me.

Except for the one who leaned forward to whisper-breathe in my ear, "Are you the daughter of the Tam Lin?"

"Kinda," I whispered back, bracing myself for bad news. "Why? Did the queen do something to him too?"

That started an even more hysterical fit of giggling, but she didn't answer my question. She whispered to some of the other girls, and among their *squee*ing I caught "that beauty is worth any punishment" before another girl shushed them as my guards arrived.

They may as well have not bothered prettying me up, because the elaborate up-do they'd created was a mess by the time we got to the Great Hall. Between my nervous tugging on the tightly braided sections and my untwisting the new curls as an outlet for all my pent-up anxiety, one entire section flopped into my face.

Even not counting that, if I had wanted to appear calm and collected as we entered, I failed miserably. My emotions were just too heightened for me to monitor all of them at once, and to also walk without tripping on my long skirt. I couldn't get an answer from the guards on what sort of reception awaited me—a trapdoor dropping me back into the dungeon? A public flogging?

Whatever it would be, there were plenty of Fae here to witness it. Definitely standing room only with all the Court and their entourages. But once those nearby recognized me and my shackles, a circle cleared around me and my escorts.

"Where's Nykur?" I whispered to Lonan, who waited for me in front of the dais, flanked by another pair of guards.

He shook his head, but he didn't look too worried, so I turned my focus back to the Great Hall. Rich tapestries covered the wall behind the throne, and wispy banners—or was it bunting?—draped between the pillars. These were all new since the last time I'd been here; they gave the Hall a somber look.

Gulp. Were these the types of decorations you put up for a sentencing at the Faerie Court, or for an execution? They sure didn't look like anyone would be spelling out "Welcome Back, Avery!" in fireworks.

The crowd in front of the dais cleared enough that I could see the queen now, but her face was hidden by a curtain of hair as she leaned to speak to the guy seated to her right. I'd never seen him before but he was definitely human, and he stood out among the Fae and their false beauty. Those cheekbones could have cut glass, but it was the way his full lips curved into a sensuous smile which seemed to have captured the queen's avid gaze.

She giggled at something he said, and you could almost see cartoon birds and hearts circling her head, she looked so smitten. It would be kind of sweet, if I didn't know some of the humans at Court were here unwillingly—or unwittingly—under a spell.

Was this guy under a glamour? I narrowed my eyes, trying to focus my Sight, and his outline wavered. Yep—definitely glamoured. This magic was stronger than most, and it took some intense concentration for me to strip away the layers until an older man sat in his place. With those sensuous lips and cutting cheekbones back under his white beard, where they belonged—and where they couldn't creep me out for thinking they were attractive.

I started to call out "Unc—" before Lonan stomped hard on my foot.

Shit, that hurt! Did he transform his foot into an anvil? But through the tears springing to my eyes, I caught his glare of warning. Ohh...I probably wouldn't be able to see Uncle Tam through the glamour if the manacles were still sapping my magic.

I nodded, but kicked Lonan in the shin to pay him back (not that my measly human foot made much of an impact). Lonan hissed at me to knock it off—the first words he'd actually spoken to me since we'd come from the dungeon—and we went back to waiting for some acknowledgement from the queen. Instead, she rose from the throne without speaking to us.

Uncle Tam resisted the coy pull of her hand, and her pout turned stormy until he stood and whispered in her ear again. I don't know what he said, but she actually *blushed*. And she simpered—I've never actually seen somebody do that outside the pages of an historical romance novel. His words must have been persuasive enough for him to get permission to come talk to me, because she let him step down from the dais.

Torn between relief that I wouldn't have to face the queen just yet and annoyance that this would drag out longer, relief won when Uncle Tam gave me a tight smile. He wouldn't be smiling if it was that bad, would he? Unless he was just baring his teeth...

I lifted my hands as he approached, planning to give him a hug, but the manacles reminded me I wasn't supposed to be able to see the real him. So I awkwardly turned my reach into a head scratch, and promptly got some of my hair tangled in the manacle chains.

"A little help here?" I squawked.

As Lonan disentangled me, he breathed in my ear, "Would you stop drawing attention to those manacles? Do you want everyone to notice the queen doesn't have any real power over you?"

I shrank under the heat of his anger, but he was right—I needed to keep a low profile, if I didn't want to get thrown back into the dungeon. Or worse.

Uncle Tam stopped in front of me, and I nodded politely as if I was greeting a stranger, before his gaze dropped to my now-purely-decorative manacles.

"Go find yourselves some refreshment," he said to the two guards behind me.

One turned to obey, but the other sneered and said, "I take orders from my queen only—not her playtoy. Why don't *you* bring us some drinks, if you're not needed in the queen's bed for now, old man?"

Uncle Tam stiffened into his full height, and his glamour crackled with magic. He seemed on the verge of really letting the guard have it when Lonan cleared his throat. There weren't any allergens in Faerie, so it could only be an attempt to break Tam out of his impending rageyness, and it worked. With a sigh, Uncle Tam left off with the laser eyes and leaned in so we could talk in somewhat-privacy.

"The queen knows those manacles have become useless," he murmured, "but she's looking the other way to save face. Don't give her an excuse to call you out—she believes if it comes down to a battle, her magic is greater than yours. Not testing that belief may save all our lives yet."

I gulped, before I whispered back, "She really considered killing me? It was only some flowers, and my unfortunate timing! I didn't mean any harm.

"And where's Nykur?"

Uncle Tam pursed his lips. "At his lake, as he still needs to soak a bit and he wants to keep out of the queen's attention. But you should know Lonan tried to defend you, and it got him a sound beating. Nephew or not, she was furious he could appear to side with you over her. None of us may be safe from her wrath."

I looked questioningly at Lonan, and his nonchalant shrug made it clear he didn't want me to make a big deal about it. But knowing he took a beating for me *was* a big deal, and we'd be coming back to it later. And maybe I'd be bringing it up with the queen.

Uncle Tam waited out the silent communion between me and Lonan before he continued. "Fortunately, Lonan had already gotten a message out to me you'd been imprisoned. I was able to persuade her to release you all—for now—in exchange for certain concessions. But tell me: are you well, Avery?"

My mouth twisted at the memory of that all-consuming hunger. "Let's just say, your bloodline could have ended in the queen's dungeons. How long was I in there, anyway?"

"A fortnight or so, in Fae-time. I've been here about four days."

"Why *are* you here?" I asked. "I mean, not that I'm not glad to see you—but didn't you vow never to set foot in Faerie again? Let alone set other parts of you in the queen's bed, as seems to be the talk of the Court?"

He winced and said, "Those concessions I mentioned—some of those are mine alone to take on, and not for you to worry about. Much of how the queen handled your, er, *lapse* can be lain at my feet. On my advice, you delivered her the perfect leverage to use against you."

He sounded so upset that I instinctively patted his arm in comfort. But then my hand stilled. "Wait—what leverage? You mean Mom? Where is— the queen hasn't fixed her yet?"

Uncle Tam shook his head. "Queen Maeve has said she will revisit trying to reverse the spell on your mother, once you have shown you will abide by her conditions for your presence in her Court."

My intake of breath had a dangerously reptilian sound to it. Unfortunately, my magic didn't see much of a line between fear and anger, and this news had dragged me across that line. I'd been trying to respect the queen's role in her own Court, but if she couldn't even respect that my mom should be off-limits in negotiations, then we weren't starting on an equal footing.

Lonan quickly stepped to my side, surreptitiously placing himself between me and one of the guards. His presence calmed me down enough that I was able to grit out, "What conditions are we talking about?"

Uncle Tam ticked them off on his fingers as he said, "Firstly, to encourage your obedience, Lonan will wear a crown of thorns at all times. If you rebel, the queen can cause him great agony, even from afar."

I glanced at Lonan, who nodded, barely hiding a grimace. I did not like where this was going, but I motioned for Uncle Tam to continue.

"Magic lessons have been arranged to teach you control over the wild magic. Your attendance is mandatory, and you'll basically be under house arrest until you can show your impulses are no longer ruling your magic."

I'd already been thinking along those lines myself—well, not the house arrest—so that was a condition I could agree to.

"I'll want to see the fine print, but what else?" I asked. Somehow, I got the feeling Uncle Tam was stalling before he laid the really bad news on me.

"You are not to be alone with Lonan, Nykur, or myself; we will always have one of the queen's trusted Host or courtiers watching over any meetings and assignations"

I barely stopped myself from snorting. Yeah, as if the queen actually trusted anyone—those watchers would likely each have three watchers watching over them. It got another nod.

He paused. "This last one...you're really not going to like it, but I hope you'll keep an open mind...and you should know there are ways we can delay fulfilling this part."

"Just tell me."

"The queen wants you to bear a Fae child."

"That again! I've already told her Lonan and I won't be doing any babymaking—"

"Not with Lonan," Uncle Tam interrupted softly, and his words shocked me speechless. "The queen will choose your—she will choose the father of the child."

5

The laughter of a couple nearby suddenly sounded sinister, and my own silence carried a new weight. Lonan looked about as sick as I felt, but he wouldn't meet my gaze. Was this another case of him giving me space to make my own decisions, or did he really not care? I cared—and so did my magic, judging how it prowled under my skin, ready for me to call on it.

I absolutely want credit for taking a deep breath before saying, "She knows I'll never agree to that, right? Is that what she's after, a reason to keep me locked up forever?"

"No..." But Uncle Tam didn't sound very sure.

"Right—I'm so out of here. Whether I go back to the dungeons or to the apartment in Davis, I don't even care at this point. Let me know when the queen is ready to be reasonable. A baby, my ass—"

Uncle Tam blurted, "You can't leave, Avery! It's either meet her conditions and have some freedom in the Court, or live out your days in the dungeons. If you try to escape, the Wild Hunt will be on you before you are two strides from the gates. The Wild Hunt is even older than the queen; older still than wild magic, and none can evade or survive them. You may last longer than most, but I can guarantee they will make you regret even trying. Promise me you won't do anything impulsive?"

When I didn't answer right away, Lonan sighed and said, "Look, will you at least let Tam take word back to the queen that you agree to the first two conditions? It will make it a lot easier for us to talk if we can go somewhere quieter."

"But I haven't agreed to them," I said sharply. Oh crap—there was the blood-simmering sensation which meant my magic was getting impatient with my holding it back.

Uncle Tam and Lonan started to speak simultaneously, with variations on "You need to take this seriously" before I held up my hands.

"Look, you may not have noticed, but I'm barely holding it together over these new demands from the queen. If you guys want me to seriously consider them—the first two, at least—you're going to have to give me a chance to think. If it needs to happen in my cell, fine, take me away."

The last part was spoken loudly to my guards, but Uncle Tam hastily said, "That won't be necessary, quite yet. Why don't you and Lonan get some food and talk?"

I knew Uncle Tam thought if anyone could persuade me to see reason, Lonan could. But there were limits to my reason, as I'd demonstrated on more than one occasion. Still, why not spend some time with my boyfriend before we went back to our separate cells?

I rolled my tense shoulders into something like a shrug and walked towards the banquet table, letting whoever wanted to follow me come along. Lucky me, it turned out to be Lonan and the especially rude Fae guard. I filled a golden plate with some choice morsels, and Lonan and I found a relatively quiet corner.

"Tell me you're not okay with this baby thing," I demanded as soon as we sat down. "What does she expect to get out of me having some Fae spawn, anyway?"

He grimaced. "I'm not okay with it; that's why I ended up in a cell. I argued with her about it so much she was forced to do something, or she'd look weak. She started with the beating, and when that didn't work I was sent to the dungeons—the next step would have been me working in the mines, or exile."

I swallowed a half-chewed bite before I said, "Whoa, she's really serious about this. But...it's a dealbreaker, Lonan, I've got to be honest. Even if I decide to have a kid down the line—for my own reasons, and not as part of a bargain—there's no way in hell I'd let her have anything to do with it. Or let her have any say in the baby daddy."

"Yeah. Tam said something about trying to delay it, but I don't know if he has an actual plan or if there even is a solution."

I gave him the side eye—it seemed like Lonan was going to say something else, there at the end. Whose side was he really on, anyway? Well, nothing like the direct method of asking—softened with some humor, as always.

"If it comes down to a battle between me and Queenie, whose side would you be on, Lonan? Is blood thicker than other bodily fluids?"

He laughed, but sounded very serious as he said, "You know you have my heart, and whatever you decide, I'm with you. Always."

I leaned over and kissed his cheek, but mostly so he couldn't see my frown at a completely new set of worries rising up. How long was "always" when he was virtually immortal? The queen could lock me up and wait for my life—or my will to live—to run out. Sooner or later, Lonan would have to make up with his aunt after my death and make a life for himself in Faerie again.

It was always the case, that I might turn out to be longer-lived than the average human, but odds were I was not headed for centuries of partnership with a corbin. Should I even hold him to it? I shouldn't even have to worry about this on top of everything else, but it wasn't like it hadn't occurred to me before—it just fell lower on the priority list when I had bigger things to worry about.

Like surviving the queen and my own magic.

I sighed, and he put his arm around my shoulders. Why did everything have to get so complicated when Fae were involved?

Well, that wasn't entirely fair; I'm sure I would have found an Avery way to complicate things with my mom, even if magic wasn't involved. But most mother-daughter relationships survive the teen years, right? Eventually?

I asked, "Lonan, where is my mom? Can I see her? It might help me make up my mind."

"Before I got sent to the dungeons, I moved her. If she's still here, I put her closer to the windows so she could feel the sun on her."

His consideration made me tear up, and he gave my shoulder a squeeze as he said, "I know she may not be able to tell, but I thought if she could..."

I wiped my eyes. "Yeah, thanks for thinking of it. So will you take me to her?"

He stood and took my hand, even though the manacles made it awkward.

As we made our way through the crowd, Lonan said, "The queen will be back later, and we'll be expected to eat at her table. I don't know if you'll need to give her an answer by then, but you should at least try to convince her you're thinking about it. Oh, and about the magic lessons, you might want to know—"

He broke off mid-sentence and suddenly pulled me in a different direction.

"Wait, where are we going, Lonan? I thought we were going to see my mom."

"We'll do that later; for now, let's go back and wait for the queen. We don't want to miss the chance to talk to her."

I dug my heels in. "I don't want to wait nicely for the queen—I want to see my mom. What's going on?"

"Nothing. Will you just come with me, please?" There was a desperate note to his plea, and I very nearly gave him a pass and did as he asked for once. But something didn't feel right.

I shook his hand off me and looked around the Hall. We'd been pretty close to the large bank of windows before Lonan had changed direction, and that was where he said he'd left my mom. I stifled an urge to yell "Mom!" into the crowd, like when I was a kid and had lost her at the farmer's market.

Most of the courtiers were talking in small groups, no doubt passing the time until the queen came back. From the looks of the smolder she had sent Uncle Tam's way, though, it could be a while. Court involved a lot of waiting, and these Fae looked resigned to it.

One crowd over by the windows was especially boisterous, however, and my eyes kept returning to them. A tattered-looking creature, probably a brownie, was perched on a stool in front of an easel, with a paintbrush in his hand. Some of the Fae looked over his shoulder, laughing uproariously at whatever he was putting to canvas.

Another group kept changing poses, and doubling over with laughter. In spite of myself, I smiled; it had been a while since I'd heard genuine

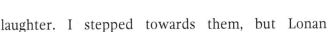

laughter. I stepped towards them, but Lonan blocked my path.

"Avery, don't."

"I want to see what's so funny..." I trailed off as I realized how anguished he looked. "What's wrong?"

He didn't answer me, and my eyes narrowed as I looked beyond him. "Is it—are they tormenting a person over there? A human, I mean?"

I didn't wait for him to answer, and barged over to the brownie artist. He was putting the finishing touches on a grouping of Fae, all captured in poses of simulated terror. These same Fae now stood at the painter's shoulder, hooting at their caricatures. But there were only three here, and four figures in the painting—*oh, shit, I recognize the person in the center of the composition.*

I raised my eyes to where another group was posing with the statue of my mom—one guy was standing behind her, honking her boobs and leering. Another one had climbed halfway up her body, trying to position himself just right to—

"If you put that in her mouth, I can guarantee you it's coming off." My voice was so bass and growly, it cut through their mirth, and all the nearby Fae turned to me.

The guy mounting my mom her didn't seem to notice my tone, however, and said, "No, it's funny!

See, there's these things called selfies that humans do—"

"Yeah—no," I said. "This is your last warning to back the shit away from her." My magic pulled at its fragile leash, surging to my fingers and ready to go on the attack. I was nearly at a place where I would let it.

Finally, it must have registered how serious I was, because the two Fae stepped away from my mom. "No harm meant! It was only a bit of fun—"

But it was too late for apologies—my voice deepened even further, and my wings burst out, knocking over a few indignant courtiers.

The queen was supposed to help my mom, not let her subjects mock her. It was hard to believe that she'd ever intended to help her—or to help me. Only to use us, as leverage and as her pet wild magician.

Well, I wasn't her pet and she couldn't tame me or my magic—and I was done trying. As my anger rose, so did my magic, like magma rushing to the earth's surface. I'd never felt it this strongly before: true to its name of wild, my magic crested like a tide. Lapped against the edges of my body.

Cries of alarm spread out from where I stood as blue lightning crackled across my skin, and the guards struggled to reach me through the crowd.

"Avery—" Lonan's voice sounded as if it came from a great distance.

"My mother is not a photobooth prop," I roared.

The manacles fell away to ash, and my beating wings carried me aloft. Through a blue haze, I saw the queen and Uncle Tam across the Hall, caught mid-step as they were returning. Just in time to make her realize that everything that happened from here on out was her fault, that she'd driven me to defend my own.

"Queen Maeve!" I screamed. "You wanted my answer: well, you can keep your Court and your kingdom. I want no part of any of you—and in the meantime, you can all burn!"

As I spat out those last words, a gout of blue flame followed it, and some nearby fabric hangings caught on fire. Screams sounded as it spread, ignoring all natural laws by jumping across the crowd to spark new fires on tablecloths, rugs—even the hair and clothing of the crowd. Magic, running wild, turned the scene into a fire storm.

I should have been worried, should have been trying to get the fire to obey me, but I honestly couldn't give a shit anymore. Not even the sight of Lonan doing his best to shove people out the shattered windows moved me—he was trying to save the same Fae who had been groping my mom just moments ago. They didn't deserve to be saved.

The only one who didn't deserve this was my mom—she'd never done anything wrong, other than bringing me into the world. I grabbed her up in one clawed hand and flew off, and let the chaos and burning Hall recede as I winged towards home.

But I never made it to Davis, or even Uncle Tam's. As I flew over the twilit landscape of Faerie, the worst post-magic hangover ever began to sap my strength. I didn't even have the energy to be properly angry anymore—or did my magic fade because my anger did? Still, I had hatred, and that kept me going a while longer.

But soon, I could barely lift my wings, let alone my mom. Instead of trying to make it all the way across the Border, I ducked into Flynnland—getting through the door in time to drop my mom's leaden weight.

I screamed as I crash-landed on the midway, my scales falling away and every muscle aching as I returned to normal size. No wonder Bruce Banner went out of his way to not turn all Hulkish. The aftermath of anger and transformation hit me like sudden-onset mono, and it was all I could do to crawl into the seat of a bumper car before I fell asleep.

When I woke up, the inside of my mouth tasted like someone had been using it to age blue cheese. That grossed even me out and a need to get to a bathroom and brush my teeth got me up and moving. I stumbled through the amusement park, put off by its oblivious, happy pseudo-families.

You see, when I'd created a pocket of wild magic in Faerie, I'd been pretty new at this spell thing. So even though it looked like crowds of people mobbed the midway, they were only scenery. A closer look revealed their individual faces were out of focus, or repeated throughout the group.

Numb, I walked right through some of the figures, as if they were holograms, on my way to the Honeymoon Mansion I'd built for trysts with Lonan. Then I ran a bath while munching on some Pop-Tarts I'd been hoarding—the best I could do for real, human food for now.

But as I soaked in the hot water, listlessly splashing at strawberry pastry crumbs, I started to sob. All the other emotions I'd had to set aside to be the Avenging Wyvern seeped back into my awareness.

Did I really light the Great Hall on fire and not even care? Yeah, those Fae molesting my mom were totally deviant, but was that deathworthy? I had just let the flames spread—and I left Lonan there. Uncle Tam and Nykur too, and any number of Fae who were possibly innocent.

If this is what I turned into when I really let loose with my magic, I didn't want any part of it. Maybe both worlds were better off with me magically manacled and fading away in a dungeon. Or, maybe I should just stay here in Flynnland.

Only Lonan, Nykur, and Daniel had entry privileges anyway, so I could be happy in exile with some visitors, right? And their deliveries of food from home, of course. I could already picture it: my new routine of no school but plenty of carnival rides, conjugal visits from Lonan, maybe letters from Uncle Tam and Missa...

The only flaw was, that wouldn't get me any closer to unfreezing my mom, and there was no way I was going to let her suffer for this most epic of my epic failures. Not just for my failing to fix her, but also for my utter loss of control, like a toddler upset because no one would play by my rules. So much for the promises I'd made to myself when I magicked the pizza-lady.

But I could only soak all-angsty in the bath for so long before I had to admit one serious truth to myself: I'd have to go back to the Court and make nice with the queen. More than that, I might have to agree with everything she had demanded. Plus whatever else she came up with, since there was a good chance her "conditions" would never end.

I shuddered at the thought of submitting to one of those creepy Fae princes for enough sessions to get pregnant. Would it be cowardly to find a spell to let me dream the whole ordeal away? I could go to sleep and wake up with a post-pregnancy body, but no other lasting effects on my psyche.

How sad was it, if that was the best-case scenario?

I took my time drying off and getting dressed, dreading the moment when I'd have to face the queen and plead my case, and maybe tally up the deaths I was responsible for. Because as much as I tried to blame my magic getting out of control for what had happened, it was ultimately my fault if anybody had died in the fire.

And the worst part was that even though cutting short a very long Fae life should be tragic, a little part of me thought *it depends on the Fae.* I've never hated someone—or something—enough to actually want them dead, but even that was changing.

Nothing had been easy since I'd discovered my wyvern side—but finding my morality could be as flexible as other Fae's was the worst. I'd always been so sure of what was right and what was wrong, back when I only had human worries. But Fae politics and blood-ties polluted everything, and my own growing wyvern nature wouldn't let me go back to being just a girl—even if that was an option outside of daydreams.

But eventually, I realized my over-analyzing things was only a way to put off returning to Court. I had to admit I was as ready as I was going to be.

I planted a kiss on my mom's cold cheek before I opened the door. And the fact that I was looking back at her, over my shoulder, was the only reason I didn't notice anything wrong right away. But when I tripped over something and burned my palms by trying to stop my fall, that got my attention.

I hastily scrambled to my feet, sneezing at the ash I'd stirred up. Red light from the burning husks of nearby trees surrounded me. *What the—*

Don't say Hell, Avery, because that sure as heck is what this feels like.

6

Once it really sank in that this wasn't the basement of Warren Castle, I turned to look back at the door I'd come through. Set in a blasted stone wall—all which remained of the castle's foundation, apparently—the sounds of Flynnland poured out of the doorway. But instead of the cheerful calliope-and-carnival soundtrack, it sounded garbled and muted.

I felt a pull towards it—a literal sucking sensation—and stepped back through. Inside, Flynnland swirled like shower water after a color run, with all the hues draining into a single, dark hole. A magical black hole? Only, I'd never thought up anything like that before—so where had it come from?

I didn't have much time to wonder, as the strength of the black hole or whatever it was made it more difficult to even stay in place. Beside me, Mom's body teetered, and I made a grab for her. I probably looked like the world's most convincing mime as I struggled to drag us through the exit. As I fought it, an entire Tilt-a-Whirl lifted up and tumbled into the darkness.

Oh, shit—I didn't want to find out if that was going to happen to us.

I managed to grow some claws and anchor us to the dirt with my toes. But the absence of sound behind me loomed larger somehow, and it seemed only a matter of time before I'd get Dysoned if I stuck around.

Thinking my wings might work against me here, I wound my tail around my mom's ankle and used my clawed hands and feet to free-solo the horizontal rock face of the ground. I slipped a few times, and I was terrified we weren't going to make it, but I finally felt ash and seared grass under my palms and dragged us the rest of the way through.

As I lay gasping, I looked over my shoulder and saw the remains of Flynnland were sort of collapsing in on themselves. From the outside, it didn't look like a black hole so much as a canvas mural being crumpled by a giant fist. I thought the force of it would stop once it folded so small it disappeared with a slight *pop!,* but if anything it felt worse.

Now it wasn't completely a physical sensation of pulling—it was more like bits of my essence draining away. My life force, or my soul—or something equally drastic. My magic? Flynnland was a part of me, a part of my learning to use my powers, and the wrench of it disappearing hurt like nothing before. Resisting it only made the weird feeling stronger—like my panic was feeding it somehow.

I tried to calm down, tried ignoring it, but I could feel myself getting weaker every moment. I rallied for one more effort, and as the connection to Flynnland snapped the recoil of power threw me back into my body, gasping and choking.

An odd tanginess lay on my tongue, like the taste of an unfamiliar fruit or something—but not something completely unfamiliar. Sort of like the first time I'd had a plantain and could recognize its banana kinship from the flavor. *What is that—*

But I didn't get a chance to think on it too long; a scream from right next to me made my eyelids fly open, and my hands raise in defense. I rolled over as my mom continued to scream. Wait, she was screaming! If I had to give up Flynnland to unfreeze her, it was totally worth it.

It took me a few calls of, "Mom. Mom! MOM!!" to get her attention, and her screams finally died.

We both sat up at the same time, and she looked around in panic.

"Avery, where are we? What happened?" Her eyes widened even more. "You—you were—you had wings!"

Between the smoke in the air and the tears in my eyes from hearing her voice again, I had to clear my throat before I could talk. "I'll tell you where we are—and what happened, but you have to promise not to freak."

Her bark of hysterical laughter made me jump. "Promise not to freak! I think we're so far beyond that now, Avery."

I stood and dusted the ash from my pants. "Oh. Yeah, probably true. So, okay, what's the last thing you remember?"

"You said something to upset me, back in the apartment, and then...then...I must have had a breakdown or something, because I swear you had devil-wings!"

"Well...technically the Devil and I both have wyvern-wings, since those illustrations of the Devil are based on some long-lost relative of my wyvern dad." She gaped at me as if I was speaking a foreign language. "But we don't really need to get into it right now."

At least she didn't seem to remember all the things the Fae did to her while I was in the dungeon. Hopefully, without those other things in her psyche too, I could salvage our relationship.

"Maybe we can start with where we are," she said faintly.

We both looked around, trying to spot something familiar. The shattered building definitely looked like a castle, but whether it was Warren Castle or the shadow Fae version, I couldn't tell. Both of them had trees fairly close, and a road leading to them, so it was a tossup.

I opened my mouth to answer, when the sound of galloping hooves approached.

"Nykur?" I called.

But instead of a huge black stallion, a unicorn came running out of the blackened trees. Ashes flecked its star-bright hide, and its eyes barely rolled in our direction as it sped past.

"Run!" It gasped. I obeyed and grabbed my mom's arm, trying to get her to run with me.

But she dug in her heels and asked, "Was that a... Tell me it wasn't a *unicorn*!"

"I'll tell you whatever you want, really—but we've got to get someplace safe first, Mom!" I tugged on her again, until her feet finally started moving.

We followed the unicorn's dust trail, onto the road and down the hill. It wasn't until I saw the first car that I knew we weren't in Faerie; the red SUV was crushed into a misshapen lump, as if Godzilla had stepped on it. Another car was in flames, on top of the half-collapsed roof of the old residence for the Warren School of Industry's superintendent.

But at least that building let me know we were in Crow's Rest, and that Uncle Tam's house should be less than a mile away. I was about to ask my mom if she'd let me fly us there, when a dark-winged shadow swept across the sky and dropped a fire truck into the middle of the street. The ground shuddered so hard Mom and I both fell to the asphalt, which may be what saved us as the dragon made another pass and torched the fire truck.

Oh my God, I hoped there weren't any firefighters in there—there was no way anybody could survive that, even with their turnouts on. I dragged Mom over to a low wall along the street, and the rocks dug into my back as I tried to hide us in its shadow. A spell would be more effective than just old-fashioned hiding, but I was too afraid of drawing attention to try anything.

But I also hadn't just gotten my mom back, only to have a crazed dragon get us. Judging by her glassy-eyed stare, Mom wasn't going to be much help. And I didn't have the convenience of using another way out, since the door which led from the Castle to the botanical gardens was no longer in existence.

I dug my cellphone out of my pants pocket and tried calling Uncle Tam's number.

Dammit, a busy signal—which likely meant his phone was out, since the voicemail should have picked up even if he was on another call. I tried Daniel's, and my dad's—the same thing. Missa's number was the only one where I got a real live person.

"Missa! Shit, I'm so glad to hear your voice—"

"Avery? Where are you? Things are totally crazy in Crow's Rest!"

"Yeah, tell me about it! A dragon almost squashed us with a fire truck. Have you heard from Uncle Tam? Lonan? Anybody?"

"No! But it's all over the web and the news stations—at first they thought it was some kind of natural disaster, or even a terrorist bomb. When a pack of these weird furry creatures knocked down a reporter and started *eating* him, I knew this was some kind of Fae invasion. Didn't you say you *stopped* this kind of thing when you restored the Border?"

"Yeah, I did...well, I thought I did. Something happened at Court, and my magic got out of hand. I don't know what's going on."

"Shit, Avery, do you think you started this? Because that is majorly screwed up; it's spreading, and it's not only Crow's Rest anymore. If you caused this, you have to fix it!"

I dropped my head between my knees and tried to take some calming breaths before I answered her. "Missa, I don't *know* if I did this, or if I can stop it. Something weird attacked me when I left Flynnland, and I don't know if it was part of this shitstorm, or what caused it. I think I need to get to Uncle Tam's and see if I can get answers from him, or from his books."

"If his place is still there. The whole town was ground zero of whatever happened, and the shots from the helicopter made it look like a battle zone. Then something attacked the news helicopter, and now there are only satellite images on rogue websites. I'm sorry, Avery, but you'd better have a backup plan. If you get out of the blast zone, I can try to meet you—"

My phone went dead. Like, not even dropped the call. I was left holding a useless bunch of plastic and electronics.

Okay—if technology was failing, I'd need to try the magical channels. I molded some shadows into an origami crow, whispering a message to Lonan into its spiraled ear.

When I released it, though, it came at my face instead of taking flight. I batted it away, getting a stinging slash like a paper cut in return. A derisive *Caw!* sounded from its beak as the crow flew off—was it even going to look for Lonan? Stupid runaway magic!

"Urrggh!" My mom cringed at my frustrated outburst, and I hastily tried to calm down for her sake. "We've got to get to Uncle Tam's, Mom. Will you do what I say and follow my lead?"

She reached out to grab my hand, but didn't say anything. That would have to do. *Now what? Do I try to fly, and risk the dragon coming after us?* Probably not a good idea.

I took a moment to close my eyes and silently called out to Nykur with his true Name; if he was anywhere nearby to "hear" it, he should come to me. I strained my ears to hear hoofbeats, or even the revving of a souped-up muscle car. But I heard only the crackling flames, the distant screams, and some far-off sounds like gunshots—pretty much what we'd been hearing since we emerged from Flynnland.

Well, Nykur might catch up to us, but we had better get moving. I applied all the stealth moves I'd learned from watching cop shows and military movies as Mom and I skulked down Palmyra Avenue and towards the center of town.

We didn't see many humans, only a few hold-outs armed with guns and wearing camouflage. The Doomsday preppers may as well have been shouting "I told you so!" as they fired at unnatural creatures from their barricaded buildings. One guy—was he the math teacher from the junior high?—helpfully spread some cover fire so Mom and I could run across an intersection. I saluted him and moved on.

By the time we reached the edge of the cemetery, where Uncle Tam's caretaker's cottage would hopefully offer some refuge, I'd hoped we'd made it through the worst of it. I was now physically propping up my mother, since the pack of jackal-headed creatures who tailed us for a while seemed to have pushed her over the edge of tolerance. She'd progressed from glassy-eyed stumbling to a walking catatonia.

I pulled her into the shade of a crypt and tried to get her to talk to me, to at least tell me this wasn't some leftover damage from being frozen. In desperation, I finally started crooning a lullaby she sung to calm me when I was a child.

> *Sleep my child and peace attend thee,*
> *All through the night.*
> *Guardian angels God will send thee,*
> *All through the night.*

By the third repetition, it seemed to be helping. Her breathing was more regular and I started to relax a little myself. A quiet *shuff* of wings nearby put me back on my guard, though, and I looked up to see an actual angel land on the roof of the crypt above us.

I gaped at the angel as it gazed down at us, and realized something about it seemed familiar. Its features were so perfect they looked almost carved, and that's what clued me in. I'd seen it before, right in this cemetery—I'd even played at its feet.

"You—you're one of the Ladystones. The angel with the anchor and chain, right?" It nodded, and I laughed a little. "You have no idea how glad I am to see a friendly face! Everything else seems to want to kill us or eat us—and not necessarily in that order."

The angel shuddered and gave a melodious cry of dismay. "Oh dear me, no, you won't catch me running down prey. Far too uncivilized."

My smile faded as I realized it hadn't exactly denied eating "prey"—only the methods. Those episodes of *Dr. Who*, the ones with razor-toothed stone angels, ran through my mind.

"So...you don't want to eat us? You're friendly, right?"

"Well, I might not eat *you*—but that one with you doesn't look too long for this world. If you're done with it, it should be nice and ripe after a few weeks in a crypt."

"No, you can't have my mom! I'm definitely not finished with her." Aghast, I pulled Mom closer to me, in case the angel got any ideas. "To be clear, you're not eating either of us."

It smiled indulgently and said, "I would much rather have a pulpy, aged corpse."

Well, wasn't that comforting? And what happened when it and its kin cleaned out the local cemeteries and ran out of aged corpses? Did they all do like it had just suggested, and wall up a living person against the shortage of bodies?

"You're—you're not really the same Ladystone who's been here for a hundred years, are you? You've come here from Faerie."

It laughed its musical laugh again and winged away, settling on an obelisk at the top of the hill. A few other figures came to join it, looking like a squabbling murder of stone crows against the late afternoon sky.

I really needed to get to Uncle Tam's and sort this out—it was only a few hundred feet to the cottage now. But I couldn't leave Mom here—she was too vulnerable in this state. So I poked and prodded her into movement again, and we toiled up the hill.

I was relieved to see Uncle Tam's cottage intact, though Daniel's house hadn't fared so well. The entire back side of his house had been sheared off, leaving some of the furnishings hanging into empty space. The sycamore tree between the houses loomed larger and more wild-looking. A familiar figure standing beneath it waved to me.

"Uncle Tam!" I called. I dropped Mom's hand and ran towards him; before I got there, a weight struck me and pinned me to the ground.

I struggled against some kind of net, but my flailing only caused the strands to turn white-hot and shrink against my body. I screamed, until Uncle Tam's voice overrode mine.

"Stop fighting it, Avery! You'll only make it worse. Just hold still."

I did as he said, and the net retreated enough to let the cool air on my skin. I breathed a sigh of relief, but then asked, "Wait, how do you know how this net works? Why am I trapped in it?"

"Because I set it up. It's to hold you here long enough for me to make sure you'll listen to me."

I shifted inside the netting, trying to get so I could see him better without triggering its defenses. "*What?* I thought you were on my side."

"I was," Uncle Tam answered, "until you dragged both worlds into your tantrum. You can't let your wyvern side rule you any longer, not when you have the power to cause this much destruction."

I had a moment of utter shock that he could actually believe I'd wanted something like this to happen, before I turned defensive. "Hey, I may be an impulsive pain in the ass sometimes—and sure, I was furious when I left the Court—but to take it out on the entire world? Two worlds? Even my wyvern side can't see the sense in that. Maybe somebody else has been screwing around with magic they don't understand, but it wasn't me this time! Let me out."

But Uncle Tam's jaw hardened and he shook his head. "I'm going to take you straight to Merlin so you both can fix this."

"But I didn't have anything to do with it! Why won't you listen to my side of the story?"

Uncle Tam paced. "I want to trust you, Avery, but this disaster has the taint of wild magic all over it. You may not have done it on purpose, but your magic has got to be the source—and the only way to fix it. If you truly didn't want this, prove it by making it right with Merlin's help."

When Uncle Tam got this determined about something, it was nearly impossible to divert him from his own agenda. What hope was there of clearing my name when Uncle Tam didn't even believe me? If I was going to prove I hadn't done this, I needed to be free—of this net, and of Uncle Tam's agenda. Especially if his agenda was biased against me.

I tested the strands again and got a blazing pain for my trouble. I could probably eventually short it out with a major surge of my magic, but who knew how long that would take—or how much it would hurt in the meantime? I didn't know if I could get free on my own, but maybe I didn't have to.

I squeezed my eyes shut and Called Lonan's true Name. "Krrkennen. Please come."

Lonan flew in, taking his humanoid shape as he landed. He started to take a step towards me, but Uncle Tam laid a heavy hand on his shoulder to stop him. I struggled before curling into a ball, away from the burning net strands, as I pleaded again to be let out.

But the sound of distant horns cut across my voice.

"That'll be the Hunt," Lonan said, shrugging off Uncle Tam so he could kneel beside me.

The Wild Hunt? Everything I'd ever heard about them ran through my head: the unearthly horses who tear into your flesh (if the Hounds don't get you first), and how death is no escape since they'll pursue you into the afterlife. So that they could run you down and rip you apart over and over.

That sounded worse than this net, or even the dungeon.

I panicked inside the trap holding me. The strands flared up in response and I screamed, my body gripped in its own response and no longer listening to my brain. A protective layer of scales sprouted all over me, and my wings stretched the net to its furthest reaches—only to have their delicate membrane start to scorch.

I let out a roar, the pain in my wings turning to a burning anger throughout my entire body. I gripped the strands of my snare, pouring all my anger into the magic acting against me. The net glowed so brightly I could barely stand to look at it, before it started to melt and fall away from me. Soon there were only a few lines of ash which I easily shook off.

I turned to Uncle Tam and his pale expression made me pause. Great, I'd basically confirmed Uncle Tam's worries that I didn't know my own power. Even Lonan was in fight-and-flight mode, with a ruff of feathers standing up around his shoulders, and his eyes completely violet.

Forcing my breathing to slow, I tried to calm down enough to regain control over my shape. I returned to merely a kick-ass girl, only to feel the cool air on my naked skin. Oops, my clothes were in tatters on the ground—thank goodness Uncle Tam magicked an outfit onto me. I was about to thank him, when the hunting horns sounded again—closer. And the baying of Hounds joined them, louder as they neared their prey.

Over the cemetery, the stone angels took flight, circling as they screeched in delight. My own wings itched to take me away from there, to let my self-preservation kick in and save me from the approaching threat.

But I couldn't do that—not if I wanted any hope of mending this rift between the worlds, and between my own loved ones. I bowed my head and flushed the last of the anger and fear out of my system, leaving an aching sadness and a resignation.

"I'll go to Merlin and try to mend the Border," I said. "But on my own terms, not as a prisoner of the Hunt or anyone else. Call them off, Lonan."

Lonan shook his head. "Unfortunately, it's not in my power. They'll pursue you until they have you in hand, and then deliver you to Queen Maeve."

Alarm flashed across Uncle Tam's face and he argued, "To the queen and her Court? No, she needs to go to Merlin. That's the only way to solve this."

"Perhaps the queen will still send her to Merlin," Lonan said, "but the Hunt is already on the scent and the queen wants her. That's all there is to it at this point."

As punctuation to his words, the horns and Hounds blared.

Right then, the front door of Daniel's house banged open and he made a run for the driveway. Since the houses weren't far apart, he saw the three of us and froze.

"Oh my God, you're all right," he said. "You guys—don't just stand there! It's not safe here!" At another blast of the horn, he did a cartoon-character running in place that would have been comical in other circumstances. "They're coming! Everybody in the car," he called as he threw a duffel bag through the window of his dad's SUV. When we all just stood there, he tried to drag me and Uncle Tam.

But Uncle Tam stood his ground, and pulled me with him. "She's not going anywhere with you. She needs to come with me to Merlin's and fix this mess she's made."

But Daniel looked in confusion from Uncle Tam to me, and then to Lonan. "What mess? What are you talking about?"

"This mess," Uncle Tam said, gesturing to the ruined town below. "The mess you're trying to escape."

"You think Avery caused that?" At Uncle Tam's grim nod, Daniel shook his head violently. "She didn't—she couldn't have. She wasn't even around when it happened."

"What do you mean?" Uncle Tam and I said together.

Daniel looked up at the "angels" circling the cemetery and said, "Look, I'll explain on the road. We can't stay here, it's not safe."

"She's not going anywhere until I hear what you know, Daniel," Uncle Tam insisted. I shrugged off his hold and nodded.

"But you'd better convince us quick," Lonan said, "or the Hunt will be upon us."

Daniel took a deep breath. "Okay, look, I went to Flynnland because I hadn't heard from Avery in a while and was worried about her. I saw the statue of her mom—or, I guess it *was* her mom—inside the door, and so I went to find Avery to tell her I was sorry her mom was still frozen."

I made a "wrap it up" motion with my hand, and he blurted, "But you were in the bath, Avery. You were crying, and I chickened out. You know how tears make me nervous now—"

"Daniel, get to the point!" Lonan cried, as the sound of hoofbeats grew.

"I-went-back-through-the-door-into-our-world-and-everything-was-fine-for-about-ten-minutes-and-then-all-hell-broke-loose," he said in a rush. "I could see the Border tear open, and then the ground shook so hard beneath my feet—and it wasn't long before Fae started spilling out into Crow's Rest. There was nothing I could do—nothing anybody around could do. It definitely wasn't Avery—she was still back in Flynnland, safe behind the door. But I couldn't get back in, and I had to hide from the dragon—"

"None of it matters, if Merlin is the only one who can make everything right," Uncle Tam interrupted. "We need to go to him now, Avery.

Lonan argued, "It's too late. Hopefully the queen will listen to Daniel."

Daniel nearly fell over. "I'm not going to the Court! I'm sorry, Avery—not even for you. I know the things that go on there."

He was already running to the waiting SUV, and I took a few steps after him. "Daniel!" I turned back to Uncle Tam. "You know without Daniel's story the queen may not listen. I need to convince him to come back with me, but it will take time. Time we don't have if the Hunt takes me now. I'm going to have to make a run for it."

I dashed to join Daniel. Uncle Tam sputtered, "Don't—wait!", but Lonan's footsteps followed mine.

I jumped in the front passenger seat, and as the door swung shut I could see horsemen reflected in the side mirror. A pack of Hounds boiled under-hoof, and the Hunt's horned masks swayed above them.

Lonan dove into the backseat, hollering, "Go, Daniel!"

7

Daniel didn't need any more urging, and the tires smoked as he peeled out of the driveway and turned down the hill. I looked back and saw Uncle Tam flagging down the Huntsmen, but the Hounds were already after us. Their blood-red ears flapped like sails as they put on more speed. Before I could blink, a huge white head pulled even with my window, and gobs of slobber slapped me in the face.

Ewww! I tried to roll up the window, but the Hound turned its head and shattered the glass with one dire fang. I screamed, and at the same time the back of the car fishtailed. The tires squealed in place, before the back bumper ripped off with a screech of metal. The car lurched forward and a few of the Hounds fought over their prize behind us—

but the one at my window had been joined by another, who loped at its shoulder.

Lonan was cringing away from his own open window, when a sudden frenzy of barking by my ear made me scream again. For a minute, I thought one of them was in the car with us, but then I recognized the furious brown form of Bobbin. His barrel-shaped body swung half out the window before Lonan could grab him.

Daniel's cries of, "Bobbin, knock it off! Get back in here!" went unheard by his dog, who was too worked up to listen to anybody. One of the Hounds turned its head, its mouth gaping and ready to swallow Bobbin whole, until Daniel swerved suddenly and knocked it into a tumbling roll.

"Don't hurt them!" I yelled. "That won't get the Hunt on our side."

"You do something, then!" Daniel yelled back.

Shit, using magic on them could just as easily hurt them, especially with my recent luck. What should I do? In answer, something rolled against my foot and I bent to pick it up.

"Lonan, do you have a good grip on Bobbin?" I called over my shoulder.

At his grunt of "yeah," I stuck my arm out my window and gave the squeaky ball a good squeeze. *Vweee!* At the sound, those blood-red ears shot forward, and the Hound left off snapping at Bobbin to stare fixedly at my hand. With another squeeze for good measure, I threw the ball as hard as I could into the roadside blackberry bushes.

With a yelp, the Hound broke off and dove in after it, and the others joined it. I had enough time before we took a curve to see heads prairie-dogging above the brambles as the joyous Hounds searched for their prize.

"Whoohoo!" I called, and reached back for a high five from Lonan. I tried to get one from Bobbin, too, but instead he nipped my fingers.

"It was his favorite ball," Lonan said for him.

"I'm sorry, buddy. I'll get you a new one. Come on, gimme a kiss," I crooned at him, making kissy noises until Lonan leaned over and licked my cheek. "Gaah!"

Bobbin must have decided that was punishment enough, because he enthusiastically licked me too. Ugh, how many times was I going to accidentally French-kiss this dog?

"Get a room!" Lonan said, egging Bobbin on.

I flipped him off and turned back around, asking, "So, where are we going, Daniel?"

"Over to Grantland—there's, like, a refugee camp there, and my parents are waiting—"

At my sudden scream, Daniel wrenched the steering wheel and reflexively stomped the brakes. "What???"

"My mom!" I wailed. "I totally left her back there! What kind of shitty daughter leaves her mom with the corpse-eating statues and the Wild Hunt? We have to go back!"

"No way!" Daniel said, the same time as Lonan said, "You are *not* going back there!"

"You guys, it's my mom! I didn't get her out of Faerie, only to hand her to the Hunt! She needs to get to this refugee camp, too."

Daniel looked into the rearview mirror, meeting Lonan's gaze. I could tell neither of them was going to go along with my plan.

"Look, I can fly back there, get her, and still be at the camp before you guys—"

Lonan growled in frustration, making Bobbin yelp in surprise, and said, "So, you want to know she's all right? Avery, call Tam on Daniel's phone."

"Oh," I said in a small voice, "good idea. But if he doesn't know what happened to her, or if he doesn't answer, I'm so jumping out the window."

Lonan leaned back and scowled at me, but I was already dialing Uncle Tam's number. My heartbeats sounded loud in my ear in between each ring.

"Yello," Tam answered.

"Uncle Tam! Is my mom with you? Is she okay?"

"John!" he said. "It's so good to hear from you!"

"What? No, it's A—"

"Listen, I can't talk right now, I've got company—but you'll be glad to know the heather's in bloom. Right here in my yard."

Did he have a stroke or something? "What are you talking about? Are you being deliberately—Oooh, Heather. Like my mom? She's there with you and she's okay?"

"Yeah, I hear you! But I'll have to catch up with you later. I'll see you at the next railroad meeting?"

I put my hand over the phone and whispered to the boys, "He's being really cagey, but he's saying something about catching up at a railroad meeting? Do you guys know what that means?"

"The refugee camp is set up by the old locomotive at the fairgrounds. Maybe he knows about it?" Daniel asked.

"That must be it," I said to him, before going back to Uncle Tam. "Yeah, I'll see you there. Hope that heather is still blooming when you get there."

"Sounds good!" A gravelly voice intruded, sending chills through me—I couldn't understand what it said, but it sounded unhappy. Shit, the "company" he'd mentioned must have meant the Huntsmen were still there!

"Gotta go." The phone beeped—Uncle Tam had hung up.

I'd only ever been to the fairgrounds in Grantland for the Italian Picnic, and a few county fairs when I was little, so I wasn't expecting much luxury at the camp. I was pleasantly surprised to see neat rows of tents in the distance as we joined a long line of cars waiting to get in. Bigger, camouflage tents loomed over the rest, too—like some kind of Army Circus had come to town.

A few of the smaller midway rides which had been stored in a back lot seemed to be up and running, and I was starting to think this might not be so bad. At least I could pretend like we had a bit of the lost Flynnland back. Too bad the line to get through the gates was more like Disneyland at the holidays.

I craned my head out the window and tried to see through the haze. *Oh, shit.* I twisted to face the backseat. "Lonan, we have a problem. They seem to be checking everyone in the car, and they just put some winged creature down on the ground—at gunpoint. I think they're checking for Fae."

I gestured to the lush mane of feathers adorning his natural, humanoid self. "Can you do anything about that? Like, shave it or something?"

In a very birdlike gesture, he rubbed his cheek on the feathers before grinning at me. "You know you'd miss 'em, baby."

I rolled my eyes at him. "I'd miss *you* more, if the Army sends you to a Fae Guantanamo—"

"No, I think it's the National Guard up there with the guns," he interrupted. At my glare, he said, "You're worrying for nothing. I'm not in somebody else's body anymore, with all the limitations that come with that."

His head morphed into a crow's head, sized for his human body. The wicked-sharp beak snapped in my direction, making me flinch in spite of myself, before he shrank down into a normal-looking crow on the backseat.

"If you can manage to keep your own wings—and scales—tucked out of sight, Avery, you guys should be fine," Lonan said as he flapped to the edge of the open car window. "Smell you later!"

I blew a kiss after him; Bobbin scrambled to jump after the crow as it flew away, but I snagged him by the collar and brought him into the front seat. His warm weight on my lap was comforting—until he let rip a truly rank fart.

I gagged and sputtered as I hung my head out the window, and Daniel laughed his head off. "You *know* he gets farty when he gets excited, and the last few hours have been pretty exciting. Plus, Mom gives him his pills wrapped in cheese, so it kind of cancels out the anti-gas meds."

I held my breath and waited until Daniel started the engine again to move forward one car length, before asking, "How are your parents? They got out okay?"

"Yeah, they were both at work, but we had arranged a meeting place in case of an emergency. Who knew we'd ever use it for the Faeriepocylpse? My parents took some Disaster Preparedness class, and it's actually pretty impressive how prepared the county is. The last wildfire was really a shot in the— actually, I should call them and let them know I made it this far."

While Daniel caught his Mom up—"yeah, I got Grandma's soup tureen, though I don't know what good it's going to do you"—I inwardly cringed again at the thought of how easily I'd left my own mother behind.

I mean, being captured in an enchanted net was a pretty valid distraction—but once I'd decided to make a run for it, how could I have not remembered to bring her? Especially since I'd basically blown off the queen over my mom's treatment at the Court—and then *I* turned around and treated her like she was still an unresponsive statue.

It felt like my priorities had all gotten so screwed up lately—some of them out of my control, but some which should still be under my control. I didn't even know whether to count my magic in the "under my control" or "not bloody likely it's under my control" column.

That fire I'd caused was bad enough, but Uncle Tam had seemed pretty sure about the mark of wild magic being all over this unnatural disaster. I didn't think he would have tried to capture me without some sort of evidence. Where had Lonan been when I called him, and what had he been doing? He hadn't exactly rushed into my arms like he was glad I was safe—Daniel had seemed more relieved than my own boyfriend.

I broke off that train of thought as we finally pulled up to the guards. They kept their weapons at the ready; a pair of them walked all around the SUV, using an oversized dentist mirror to check the underside. Daniel and I each got our own personal inspection, from an unsmiling guy in fatigues and reflective sunglasses. His nametag said "Smith," but it may as well have said "Archetypal Badass Stand-in."

This was hardcore. I started to squirm—*holy shit, they're not going to do cavity searches or anything, are they?*—when my guard said, "I'm going to need you to keep both hands in sight, and stretch your arms out the window, ma'am."

I didn't even bristle at this use of "ma'am" on a girl my age, because I was freaking out and wondering whether he was going to try to put manacles on me. Did they know I was a fugitive from Fae justice? Maybe they'd been told to watch for me—or were under a geis, and didn't even know they were doing it.

"Ma'am?" the soldier barked, shifting into a more aggressive stance since I'd failed to comply with his orders.

I snuck a peek at Daniel, and saw he hadn't been cuffed or anything. Holding my breath—to help keep my magic from deciding it needed to defend me—I pushed my arms through the window. I wasn't completely brave: I shut my eyes while I waited to see what he would do.

A tickling sensation on the inside of my forearms was the last thing I expected. My eyelids flew open, and I saw the guard was running a bouquet of St. John's wort up and down my skin. I burst out laughing, I was so relieved, and that got an involuntary smile from the guard before he restored his Serious Mask.

Daniel was getting the same treatment, and we shook our heads at the bizarreness. I thought they'd wave us through, but the guard on my side said, "We'll need to do the dog, too."

"Wait!" I said, and grabbed the soldier's arm without thinking.

Three guns instantly pointed at us.

"Sorry!" I let go and slowly raised my hands. Fear sweat started on my palms, faster than it could dry in the dusty air. "It's just that—he'll eat it. Bobbin eats everything—even poo. Um, you probably don't need to know that. The gist is that St. John's wort will make him sick. Do you have any salted bread? It would totally work, too, if you're trying to see if he's Fae."

My babbling was met with silence, while the mirrored sunglasses exchanged a few glances. Maybe I should start talking again—at least it seemed to keep them from shooting. But Smith put the St. John's wort through his belt, and reached into a pocket for some hunks of bread, glittery with salt grains.

Good, at least my hunch that they were prepared for Fae was right. Bobbin nearly took off the guy's fingertips as he snapped up the bread, but Smith didn't seem to notice as he watched the dog closely. Bobbin gulped a few times, and the guns started to lower. Until, with a "hraaaacckkk" sound, the dog's body started to convulse.

I didn't know whether to pound on his back, or fling him away, in case he was some Fae spy in disguise. Before I'd made up my mind, a hunk of soggy bread launched onto the dashboard—where Bobbin promptly licked it up again. Then looked around for more.

"Sometimes he eats too fast," I said weakly. "That's all it was—he ate too fast."

Smith looked a little disgusted, but he called "Clear!" to his fellows and waved us through. I put my face in Bobbin's humid fur, trying to muffle my hysterical giggles, as Daniel followed the directions toward parking.

We finally found a spot, way in a corner of the fairgrounds, and I was dreading having to schlep all these bags back to the populated areas. Luckily, Mrs. Dawes had been ready for everything—Daniel pulled two folding wagons out of the SUV's cargo well. They were the really sturdy kind from gardening catalogs, and we had no trouble loading up the wagon beds with all the gear. With Bobbin perched happily on top of one load, we started the long trek towards the tents and smell of cooking.

I was pouring sweat in no time, and secretly used a little magic to help my overloaded wagon along. I grinned as I passed up Daniel and his huffing-puffing effort, and he said my name in a warning tone.

I turned to stick out my tongue at him, and then screamed as a shower of sparks cascaded from a nearby lamppost. Daniel and I both stared as the arcing electricity faded, leaving a smoking lump where the streetlight bulb had been.

"What the—it wasn't even turned on, right?" I asked Daniel.

He shook his head as a couple of guys came running up.

The one in fatigues barked, "What happened?"

We explained the light had gone haywire when we were walking by, and the other guy left to find somebody with electrical experience to come take a look at it. Fatigues Guy started to put caution tape around the post—his Army Surplus pants gave me the impression this guy was a volunteer/civil serv-ant—when a radio clipped to his belt crackled to life.

Daniel and I exchanged a shrug and kept walking.

But he called after us, "Hold up a minute! Are you the ones who came through the gate a few minutes ago? Who knew about St. John's wort and salted bread?"

I didn't feel like I owed this guy an answer, so it was Daniel who said, "Yeah, but I'm on my way to find my parents. Can this wait?"

"I wanted to ask how you know about those...charms. We can talk while you walk."

He fell into step with us, giving us no chance to brush him off. "Who are your parents, by the way?" he asked Daniel.

"The Dawes—Jack and Jill. Yeah, I know, their names are hilarious." Daniel usually tried to cut off any jokes about his parents' names before they happened, but Fatigues Guy didn't even try.

"I know them," he said instead. "They're helping out in the Mess Hall. I can show you where their tent is—you're both going there?"

"I don't know," I said, when he looked expectantly to me. "I might need a separate one for my family, if there are still empty tents—I'm expecting my mom and my uncle too."

"And you are?" he prompted.

Something about this guy rubbed me the wrong way and I debated giving him a fake name. But they had my real name at the gate, and him checking it was only a radio call away. "Avery Flynn. And you are?"

"I'm Block Captain Lane." He nodded like I'd confirmed his suspicions on my identity, and pulled his radio off his belt to say, "Where do I take Avery Flynn? I've got her."

I stopped in my tracks. "You what?"

He stowed his radio and answered, "You're on a list, to go directly to HQ when you arrive. The guys at the gate should have caught it, since you match the description too. Come on."

He started walking briskly away, and then noticed I wasn't following him. "Come on, they'll be ready for you."

That's what I was afraid of; too many people wanted to cage or kill me lately for me to wander off casually with some guy who thinks he's G.I. Joe. "Not until you tell me who's waiting for me, and why."

He blustered, "Just do as I say, Flynn." Yep, this guy was definitely civil service material. Or maybe school front office.

I waited him out. "You don't know why they want me, do you? Until they send someone who does, I'm sticking with the Daweses."

He scowled and looked to Daniel. "Tell her to stop acting like a child and to do as she's told."

Daniel shook his head and said, "Ain't no power in the 'verse..." and we both burst out laughing. I mean, he kind of mangled the quote, but still funny.

We left Block Captain Lane behind us, complaining into his radio, and we followed our noses towards the Mess Hall. Bobbin helped by leaning out like a figurehead, guiding his ship to a bounty of corn dogs. Or at least, that was the dominant food smell on the breeze.

But I'd barely got in a couple of hugs from Daniel's parents before a more-official-looking guy in fatigues came up and asked, "Avery Flynn?"

I sighed and said, "Yes. That's me."

"I'll take you to HQ."

Daniel and I started to protest at the same time, but Mrs. Dawes patted me on the shoulder. "It's okay, your dad's had the guards on the lookout for you. He just wants to know you're okay."

That pulled me up short. "My dad? He's here?" We hadn't spoken in a while—a month, maybe—and that was in Faerie, where he spent most of his time with his boyfriend.

"He's not here," the Guardsman said. "He's at the—he's on the phone for you."

So after promising Daniel I'd catch him up on what my dad said, I went with my escort. He turned back a few times, impatient with my dragging pace, though his military training kept his face stony. Only his fingers tapping on his thigh gave away how much he'd like to hurry me along so he could get back to more important things.

But my mind was on important things too, like what to expect from my dad. We'd made up somewhat since last summer, but maybe that was because on the phone it was easier to stick to small talk and jokes, and not get into the big stuff. Plus, Corriell often acted as a buffer, and he was honestly a great guy—maybe actually a better guy than my dad.

I mean, I still loved Dad, but after he'd sold me out to a rogue wyvern, my trust was gone. He swore up and down that he regretted it, and would never have done anything like that in his right mind. But could anyone affected that much by Faerie ever be in his right mind again? Even if he wanted to? Like how some former drug addicts never seemed to reclaim those fried brain cells.

My escort cleared his throat and broke me out of my reverie as we approached the biggest Army circus bigtop. But we didn't go into it like I expected—instead, we passed it and continued down a few rows until we came to a slightly smaller, khaki tent. A couple of guys in front of it, chopping wood, nodded as we went in.

It may have blended in with the other house-tents on the outside, but as soon as we stepped inside it was obvious this place was much more serious. A bank of fans blew cooling air across boards of blinking lights, and computer casings lay open so uniformed techs could fiddle with their innards.

They barely looked up at me as I made my way over to an open laptop, where my dad's smiling face flickered on the monitor.

"Avery!" he said, "You made it! I was so worried."

The poor quality of the video distracted me—what was he even talking on, an Inspector Gadget watch?—before I answered, "Yeah, I'm fine." I caught myself smiling, in spite of my dread from a moment ago. He was still my dad. "And you? Where are you guys?"

"We're someplace safe, further from the front lines."

From off-camera, another voice piped up, "Hi, Avery! Is that rotten corbin still treating you right?"

I waved into the camera and blew Corriell a kiss. "Of course he is! He—"

"Let's try to focus here, Avery," Dad interrupted. Then he said something sharp over his shoulder, and Corriell didn't speak up again.

"The Army is willing to provide whatever support and protection you need to do your job," my dad continued. "They've established a secure perimeter around Corriell's tree, in exchange for me helping them to understand the Fae threat from behind the front lines."

There was that word again. "The front lines? Have you picked up military-speak, or is this really a war?"

"It's the latest battle in the ongoing war between human and Fae, like Tam has told us about. If we do it right, this could be the last battle, and they'll never bother us again."

His gaze through the monitor had a familiar intensity as he continued to rant, and I tuned him out. I should have known that he hadn't been worried about me for my own sake, but more about how I could benefit him. But it still hurt; he was still my dad.

When he paused in his rant to take a breath, I tried to get him back on track by asking, "Let me guess, you want me to use my wild magic to win the war? How exactly am I supposed to do that?"

"Finish what you've started. You've already torn the Border to pieces, so close it off completely. Then we'll be safe."

I was already shaking my head. "First of all, I didn't do anything to the Border this time; I'm as mystified as everybody else by what's going on. Secondly, even if I separated our world and Faerie, it's not like we'd all fall into world peace. There would still be humans of questionable morals and motives around here. And what about Corriell? He may not survive if the worlds are separated. Aren't you worried about him?"

"Of course I am. That's why I'm doing this, trying to get on the right side."

And really, that was probably how he saw it—not as trading someone else's safety for his own and Corriell's. Last time it was me on the auction block, and this time it was both worlds. Well, it was kind of me and my powers on offer again—at least he was consistently turncoatish.

But would he even have come looking for me, if he didn't think I was the key to winning this war?

8

Suddenly, exhaustion hit me. All I really wanted to do was get some food and some sleep, and to know my mom and Uncle Tam were okay, but here was Dad expecting me to jump in and do what he'd promised. But they were his promises, not mine.

I put on my agreeable-daughter mask (honed through years of practice with my dad and mom), and said brightly, "Listen, Dad, I'm glad you and Corriell are safe. I've had a really long...well, couple of weeks, really. I need to get some rest, and then we can talk about what to do next."

I pushed up from the chair, but he said, "Wait! Even if you're too tired to shut down the Border right now, we should at least come up with a plan so we can start on it as soon as possible. We need to minimize the losses as much as possible."

Finally, something we agreed on. "Fewer dead people—human and Fae—is a good thing. I'm happy to talk to whoever is in charge of things, and to help where I can. But let me be clear that until I know the whole story of the Border's destruction, I won't even know if I *can* do anything to help. So, unlike your situation, I'm not making any promises, to save my own ass or otherwise." Okay, so my agreeable-daughter mask slipped a little.

Dad started to sputter some protest, or defense maybe, but I didn't even care anymore. I reached out to close the laptop, but before my fingers made contact, a blue bolt zapped from my hand. An arc of electricity flashed along the wires from the laptop, frying everything in the network with a sound like party poppers going off.

Techs dove for wires, trying to unplug stuff before it was a total loss. Only a few blinking lights showed once the smoke cleared. It was a lot quieter in the tent without all those fans running.

"Ohhhhh," I said. "That explains my phone and the lightpost."

Everyone stared at me, or glared at me. "Um, sorry, this is a new thing. I'm not even sure if it was magic, or electricity, or some hybrid of the two."

Nobody said anything or made eye contact now; they just went back to fiddling with the equipment. Was that because they were socially awkward nerds, or because they'd been ordered not to?

"Well, I'd better leave you guys to it..." I trailed off, as it became obvious no one was speaking to me. Turning on my heel, I exited the tent and almost ran smack into one of the guys outside. He smelled like wood chips from splitting firewood, but seemed friendlier than the guys inside.

"I can show you where your tent is," he said. I nodded wearily, and he fell into step beside me.

"My tent isn't near any generators or power lines, is it?" I asked, only half-jokingly. "Maybe I should go stay in the old miner's cabin in the museum section—nothing for me to fry in there."

"Actually, it's wired for an alarm, and the sound system that plays the canned tour recording."

"Oh," I said, brilliantly. I glanced at him sidelong—he was older than I had thought at first, like maybe late forties. The muscles bulging under his shirt had kind of thrown me off. An aura of easy power came off him. "You're not just a grunt, are you?"

He smiled and said, "Your dad said you were perceptive, and the uniform wouldn't fool you for long. I'm a federal agent, working with the Fae and magical creatures."

"Like an auror? Or X-Files?" I gasped and turned to him. "Are you Mulder? I mean, like a real Mulder, and they based the character on you?"

He flinched, before he composed himself. "Do I hunt down aliens and other weird stuff like that? No, that's on TV. But the Fae, we've known about them for a long time."

Hmm, his flinch said maybe I'd hit too close to home with my Mulder question. Maybe the other agents teased him about it? I guess I wasn't too tired to think that image was really funny—or maybe it was because I was so tired that it was so funny to me?

Letting it go for now, I asked, "So are you who I'll be talking to about what happened with the Border?"

"Yeah, once you've had a chance to rest. Can I ask you a few questions while we walk?"

"Sure, I guess." We paused to let a golf cart towing a small water tank cross the "road" in front of us.

Then he asked, "About your dad—is there something going on between you I should know about? Some conflict over the Fae?"

I eyed him before answering. I didn't know him, so should I trust him? But then I thought about how a lot of the mess lately started with me keeping things from Mom, and maybe with other people and Fae not being straight with me. I didn't want to be part of the web of lies anymore.

So I said, "Well, this past summer was my crash course into Faerie and the Fae. Before then, I didn't know anything about them. Then I found out I'm... He told you about my parentage?" At his nod, I continued, "A wyvern dryad-napped Corriell and held him as a hostage to get my dad to turn me over. Which I wouldn't have thought would work, but it did—that wyvern psycho, Drake, got his hands on my wild magic, and *I* nearly disappeared. All because my dad chose to protect Corriell over his own daughter."

"That's brutal," he said. "But what's your take on your dad now—should we trust his information? Is he on the side of humans or Fae?"

I stopped to think. "My dad knows a buttload about the Fae, for sure, and his Sight is at least as strong as mine. But I don't know that I completely trust him to be loyal to humans. I like Corriell, but hearing stories from my mom of what my dad was like before, I think Dad's relationship with the Fae has changed him. Whether it's because of a truly obsessive love for Corriell, or if there's magic in play, it's always going to affect his decisions. I'd keep that in mind, if I were you."

He grunted in acknowledgement, and then said, "Should I have the same kind of worries about you and your boyfriend?"

"Huh?"

He nodded at a crow perched on a telephone post, watching us through violet eyes. Way to keep a low profile, Lonan. I sighed. "No—Lonan and I— we're good."

"Your files say you are—mostly. That should be good enough for now," he said.

He had files on us? How long had we been on his radar? He hooked a left and led me down another row of tents. These didn't look occupied, not like the ones we'd passed with laundry hanging off the ropes and shoes outside the flap.

"Where are you taking me now?" My voice shook a little, but I was too tired to muster too much paranoia at this point.

"I agree you might be better off with some distance from our power supply, and if you're getting Fae visitors then I definitely don't want them mingling with the civilians. This ought to be far enough out."

He stopped in front of a tent and I asked, "About the Fae...you know they're not necessarily the enemy, right?"

"Well, historically we haven't exactly peacefully coexisted, but all the signs seem to point to them being as hard-hit by this disaster as we've been. So I'm willing to give them the benefit of the doubt until we know otherwise. My old sergeant used to say 'Act in good faith, plan for bad dealings,' so that's how I'm treating this situation."

"Fair enough." I stuck my head in the tent, and saw it was empty. "Um, where do I sleep?"

"I'll send somebody out with the basics—cot, blankets, a lantern. Did you bring any stuff with you? They can pick that up too."

"No, these are all I have." Some of my favorite outfits had been in Flynnland, dang. "I—I'd just gotten out of Queen Maeve's dungeon before this all happened, actually."

"Really?" His eyebrows rose, making him look younger again. "Sounds like a story I'll want to hear later. Insider information on the queen is always helpful. The bathroom's two rows that way if you want to wash up, and they should be here with your kit by the time you've finished. I can see if Mrs. Dawes can grab you some clothes out of the Red Cross bin, too."

He turned to leave and I called after him, "Thanks for your help."

He walked backwards and answered, "No problem. At least you won't starve." He pointed as Lonan landed on a tentpole, a half-eaten hamburger in his bill.

I made a face, but then I said, "Hey, I don't know your name! What if I need to ask for you?"

"It's Boulder—Special Agent Brock Boulder." With that, he turned and hurried off.

I burst out laughing, and Lonan dropped his hamburger as he said, "What's so funny?"

"I'll explain when I get back," I said. "I'm going to the bathroom, so do you want to meet me here after they bring the cot and blankets? And if you don't mind, can you find me something to eat? Something that's not already chewed on."

"Picky, picky," he scoffed, but flew off towards the mess hall.

They had hot showers and everything in the bathroom, but I figured I'd save a proper shower for when I had clean clothes. So after a token sponge bath with some paper towels at the sink, I wandered back to my tent, half-dead on my feet. A crew of guys exited the flap, and waited for me.

"You're all set, Miss. We left some things for the family members you're expecting, too."

At least I got "Miss" this time, instead of "Ma'am." I thanked them, and then blessed them when I saw they'd actually made up a cot with pillow, sheets, and blankets—waiting for me to fall into it. I did, and a few moments later a sweep of wings let me know Lonan had joined me.

I cracked open an eyelid, and saw he was handing me a jelly donut, only slightly battered from its flight. "Thanks—I hope I can stay awake long enough to chew it. If I choke, promise me you'll remove the evidence from my dead windpipe so nobody knows it was death by donut."

"Will do," he said, trying to crawl under the blankets with me.

"Lonan," I whined, "this cot isn't made for two of us, go get one of the other ones."

"Just—shift over a little and I'll be the big spoon."

I grumbled some more, but we managed to make it work. And considering I hadn't really spooned with him in weeks, it was worth the crowding. We both had powdered sugar around our mouths by the time we fell asleep, two warm bodies curled against the chill of the autumn air.

I woke up to Lonan gently shaking me as he whispered, "Somebody's coming." I moaned and burrowed further under the covers, but the scratchiness of the blanket reminded me I wasn't at home. My eyes flew open as I remembered Lonan was wearing his own shape, and not everybody was supposed to know about him.

"Do your bird thing!" I hissed. I could hear the approaching footsteps now, crunching in the dirt, so they must be close.

He grumbled, but shrank down to a blackbird, scrambling under the pillow as a voice called, "Hello? I never know how to knock on a tent."

"Daniel," I said in relief. "Come in."

Bobbin burst through the flap before it had completely lifted, and was in my lap washing the powdered sugar off my face before Daniel stepped inside. When I finally fended the dog off, he barked and rooted under the pillow until he flushed Lonan out. The two of them rolled around the tent floor, happily squawking and growling, while Daniel and I rolled our eyes.

"Oh my God, is that breakfast I smell?" I blurted, and then remembered my manners. "I mean, good morning."

He laughed and showed me the paper bag in one hand. "Yeah, I thought you'd be starving since they hauled you out of the mess hall before you had a chance to eat. I brought enough for two, since I figured Lonan would be here."

"Don't worry about him," I said. "He stuffed himself with all kinds of stolen food when we got here."

Lonan-the-blackbird shifted back into Lonan-the-nearly-human-looking and said, "Stolen food tastes the best, but that was hours ago and I'm hungry again, so fork it over, Avery."

I growled at him as he made a grab at my breakfast burrito, but I let him take the one still in the bag. Bobbin came to sit on my feet, his eyes on my every bite.

"Mwhaf's in fee uffer bag?" I asked around a mouthful.

"There's the delicate flower I love so much," Lonan said in a come-on voice.

"I fwuz—" I stopped to swallow, "—talking to Daniel, smart ass."

Daniel handed me the grocery bag and said, "My mom put together some clothes and stuff you might need."

I shoved the last one-fourth of burrito in my mouth—ignoring Lonan's passionate moans at the sight of my cheeks distended like a greedy hamster's—and dug through the bag. A jacket, a pack of white cotton underpants still in the package, some socks, a bundle of maxi pads, a pair of cargo pants that look like they'd fit, a T-shirt—

I nearly choked on the last of my breakfast as I held the T-shirt up for the boys to see the words "Public Enemy" scrawled across the front. "Passive-aggressive much, Mrs. Dawes?"

They both laughed, and Daniel said, "That's a perfectly legitimate vintage T that my mom probably didn't have to dig through an entire pile of less specific ones to find."

As I washed down my burrito with apple juice, Daniel added, "Oh, and the showers have a really long wait right now, so I wouldn't rush to get in line."

Damn, that was next on my list. Okay, plan B. "Well, then can you guys tell me your version of what happened with the Border? I still haven't really heard the complete story, and I'd like to before I talk to Special Agent Boulder."

Daniel said, "I'll start; I don't really know what happened along the entire Border, though. Like I said, I'd come out of Flynnland and was on my bike heading home—oh, yeah, my car was broken down again, so I got there by bike. I hadn't even gotten past those boarded-up houses when there were a bunch of weird booms and concussions, and the sky over town looked like it was moving. Remember how you said the Border had gone all 'unravelly' last summer, like the Northern Lights on steroids?

It was kind of like that, but with smoke too, and big shapes flying around. I thought at first they were planes, and maybe terrorists were planning to crash them or drop some bombs, but then I saw one of the shapes breathe fire and I knew something else was going on. I was closer to home than the meeting spot, so I swung by to get Bobbin and then pedaled all the way to the fairgrounds with him in my backpack."

Bobbin whacked my shins with his tail when he heard his name, so I petted him until he rolled over for belly rubs, and Daniel continued.

"Mom and Dad were already here, so we met up and that's about it. Tam called and checked on us regularly, and after about ten days it sounded like things had cooled down enough in our immediate neighborhood that it was worth trying to come back and get some more stuff."

"Wait, what?" I interrupted. "Ten days—but I was only in Flynnland for, like, one night. I don't think it would have even been a full twenty-four hours. And it took me maybe three or four hours to get from the Castle ruins to Uncle Tam's. Are you sure of that timeline?"

Daniel frowned and looked to Lonan, who said, "I've overheard other humans, and they're all saying it's been about a week and a half since everything went crazy. In Faerie, it was more like a week."

"How can that be?" I asked. "There isn't usually a huge time difference between Flynnland's little pocket of magic and the human world—I made it that way on purpose. If anything, it always worked so more time in Flynnland was just a blip at home—not the other way around. Wait...you said it was a week in Faerie, Lonan? Tell me what it was like. What happened to make you believe I'd done it?"

He looked uncomfortable. "It wasn't something I jumped to conclusions about—there were definite signs of wild magic—"

"We'll come back to that," I said, "tell me what *happened*."

Lonan nodded and said, "Okay. So, the fire you started in the Great Hall burned for days and made the whole place unlivable. The queen and her inner circle—including Tam Lin—went to stay at Castle Crag with the Massif family. They're an old Oread clan—old even for mountain Fae, I mean. I guess the queen felt they'd been out of Court politics long enough that she could trust them, if this was the start of some kind of takeover by you."

I raised my eyebrows at that, but didn't comment.

"I stayed behind, and worked on containing the fire since we couldn't put it out. It burned itself out a few days later, but not before some truly odd things started happening around the Palace: live butterflies bursting out of murals, food turning to moldy leaves on the platters, the lake icing over. But those things, they were almost...prankish. I half-expected to find you hadn't left the Palace after all, and were causing trouble to thumb your nose at the queen. Then things turned kind of sinister. The worst one was when all the creatures trapped in the rose hedge suddenly found themselves released— but in the middle of celebrating their freedom, they all dropped dead."

My slight smile at the "prankish" things disap-peared. "All of them? There were at least a hundred in the section I walked along one afternoon."

Lonan nodded soberly. "We collected the corps-es, and they were so light it was like they were made of paper. Even the ogres' bodies weighed no more than a hornet's nest. The families asked for their loved ones' remains, but at that point the bod-ies were part of an investigation. It almost caused a riot—they'd gone from thinking the queen had somehow shown mercy, and then seeing the life torn from their kin permanently."

I shuddered—this was somehow worse than the slow absorption into the rose hedge they'd escaped.

"And while we were trying to figure out what happened, we heard from those in the Great Hall that at the time of the deaths, the flames had also flared hot enough to burn the royal throne. The throne is sacred, made from the ancient wood of Yggdrasil's heart, and nothing natural or magical should have been able to touch it. We hadn't even bothered to move it out of the Hall, and it went up like sawdust.

"Then, like it had used up the last of a spell, all the flames went out and the unexplained magic stopped. Once the smoke cleared, we didn't have to look too hard to find that wild magic tainted everything."

I stood and paced a few laps in the tent, before I asked, "What does it mean, when you talk about the mark of wild magic? I've heard it before, but don't really associate my magic with...a stain, or whatever. I mean, I can see my magic as blue energy while it's active, and I see other Fae's magic as different colors while they're spellcasting, but it doesn't really linger."

Lonan thought for a moment and then did his best to answer. "Okay, so most Fae magic doesn't really change the essence of something. Say I turned Daniel into a frog—"

"Leave Daniel and frogs out of this scenario, please," Daniel interrupted.

Lonan rolled his eyes. "Okay, say I turned your pillow into a bowl of strawberries and Cool Whip— I can make it have the taste, texture, smell, and weight of the real thing. But eating it would give you about as much nutrition as eating the foam or feathers inside a pillow, since its essence would still primarily be that of non-food stuff. Although, since Fae are *made* of magic, they can get magical sustenance from it. Humans, not so much."

"*That* dynamic I'm familiar with," I said ruefully, thinking of my meals in the dungeon. "So what makes wild magic different?"

"Wild magic doesn't only change the appearance of things, while the essence stays unchanged: it combines with magic to create something entirely new. Like how mutations in a child's genes can distort what they would have normally gotten from their parents. The act of changing it leaves behind... I don't know how to describe the residue. A scent, like fumes—or maybe a taste—or it could be visual, like a mark. It's not really anything I could consciously put my finger on. We just *know* and recognize when wild magic has been operating."

I paced again and mused, "Would you describe it as tangy, maybe? Like a taste that's kind of familiar, close to one you've had before, like how banana and plantain are cousins?"

Lonan shook his head. "For a sentence which makes no sense, it does a pretty good job of capturing the elusiveness of describing it. But to me, the sign of wild magic isn't really even close to anything else, it's very much unique. Honestly, it feels wrong."

I told them what had happened when I'd exited Flynnland: the feeling something was draining my magic, and the smell/taste I'd noticed when the connection snapped.

"What if," I said, "what if that was somebody else's magic—wild magic, I mean? Could it be like when somebody borrows your sweater: to you, your sweater doesn't smell like anything, but your friend says it smells like patchouli?"

"Your magic smells like patchouli to you?" Daniel asked, obviously out of his depth.

"No, that's my point. Other than the blue color when I'm actively using—or leaking—magic, my own wild magic doesn't have any signs at all to my senses. I'm wondering if it's like how you don't really smell your own natural odor, but you're sensitive to others'?"

"But I'm smelly a lot," Daniel argued, "and I know when I'm smelly."

"Well, yeah—you're a stinky teenaged boy. I'm trying to use an analogy, or metaphor, or whatever, to try to figure out what's happening. Lonan, do you get what I'm trying to say?"

"Sort of—but there's a huge flaw in your theory, Avery. There isn't anyone else with wild magic, so how could that be what you encountered?"

That stopped the gears in my head momentarily. But then I said, "There's Merlin, too—I mean, wild magic has come about twice, so why not a third time? Maybe Uncle Tam wasn't the only one exper-imenting by putting unsuspecting human couples in a Fae threesome?"

One side of Lonan's mouth drew down as he considered. "It would be a really difficult thing to hide."

"Uncle Tam managed it for sixteen years—"

"He wasn't precisely hiding it in you, as much as suppressing it—"

"The point is, Lonan, nobody knew about my wild magic for years, even though Uncle Tam was really hoping to see it in the early years, before he gave up on me."

Lonan and Daniel exchanged a look which I easily interpreted as "she's not going to let go of this, just humor her."

"You may be right. It's worth considering," Lonan said.

I rolled my eyes at his attempt to pacify me. "Yeah, if you have any other theories, feel free to share them."

"Well..." Lonan hesitated so long that it became a full stop. At my raised eyebrow, he said, "What if you *did* do something to the Border, Avery? I mean, when you fixed the unraveling. It wouldn't be your fault exactly, if you messed it up worse because you didn't know what you were doing."

My stomach dropped as I thought this theory through. Could it be what happened? How would I even know if it was true, either way? Even though I'd learned some things about my magic since last summer, it still didn't feel like I was anywhere near expert level.

"I don't think that's what happened; even if I didn't know what I needed to do, the Border did. It had a sense of what it was supposed to be, how it was aligned, and I guided it back in place."

I remembered something else and said, "Hey, I've been wondering how and why my mom unfroze right when Flynnland was destroyed? Was that actually something to do with my magic, or maybe the other wild magic I think was there?"

"You mean, like you think some other magic was involved in freezing her in the first place?" Lonan asked. "I know you might want to believe that, but I was there and..." He trailed off.

"And what?" I challenged.

"And that was you. It was your magic, no doubt in my mind."

"I guess I'm not back in the running for Daughter of the Year after all." My sarcasm was weakened by my own sadness, though.

We were all silent for a moment as we processed. I shook my head, saying, "We should probably at least mention all this to Uncle Tam when he gets here. Have either of you heard anything from them?"

Both boys shook their heads, and Daniel said, "Do you want to use my phone to try to call him?"

He held it out before I could stop him, and blue sparks shot out of it as soon as it got within my reach.

"Oh...I guess I should have warned you, technology and I aren't friends lately," I said.

He stared at the melted hunk of metal and plastic in his palm before sighing. "Yeah, a little warning would have been nice. It's not exactly easy to get a replacement phone these days. I suppose that means we shouldn't let you too close to the vital operations, like the mess tent, then? Which means Lonan and I will continue to be your meal delivery service. Yay."

"Yes, please," I said, giving Daniel a hug. "And I like your food better—Lonan eats like a toddler trying to get diabetes."

Lonan sputtered a denial, while Daniel stood up to leave, saying, "I'll keep that in mind. And Avery, I think you should go try to shower now. I think you must even stink to yourself at this point."

I didn't even need to sniff my pits to know he was right. "Yeah, yeah, I know. Sorry about your phone."

"I'll try to call Tam from HQ, and see if he's still going to try to join us."

"Thanks!" I waved as he left, and I packed the stuff Mrs. Dawes had sent back into the bag so I could take it to the showers with me. Lonan flew out the flap ahead of me, just one more camp-follower bird off to scavenge from the trash.

Yuck, I think I'll try to score some mouthwash for him while I'm out, for later.

9

For all her passive-aggressiveness in her choice of T-shirts, Mrs. Dawes was at least a good judge of my size. Everything fit, and although I'd thought about wearing the shirt inside out, I decided to flaunt my Public Enemy stripes on a walk—away from the vital areas and their vulnerable electrical fields, of course.

I wandered around the parking lot at first, trying to avoid people and give myself time to think over all that Daniel and Lonan had said about how the Border disaster had played out. Once I accepted the timeline, I could see that there were some common themes: a strong release of magic when the Border fell (like the one after Flynnland disappeared entirely, maybe?), plus a lot of chaos and, um, magic running wild until it just wound down.

But if that's all it was, why hadn't things gone back to normal? According to reports coming in from Crow's Rest, people were still disappearing or reappearing, and so were parts of town. Fae came and went at will—maybe contributing to those people and places disappearing and reappearing? And it sounded like the Fae had never experienced something like this in their very long recordkeeping either.

I couldn't shake the feeling that in spite of me being very sure I hadn't caused this, I was still linked to it somehow. Maybe because I'd been the last wild magician to work with the Border? And maybe I was tied to it, like Lonan had suggested? I just didn't know, and I didn't even know how to find out, or who to ask. Besides the queen, of course, and I wasn't ready to be on speaking terms with her yet. Short of going back to the Court and reading through their archives myself, it... Oh yeah. Did the archives survive my fire?

My guilty conscience shied away from that question, and urged me to find some way to make myself useful, here and now. I followed the earthy smell of manure towards the old race track.

The infield, and track itself, was now a maze of pipe corrals and makeshift fencing, thronged with everything from alpacas to Zebu cattle (the miniature ones). At first, I wandered around, petting the critters who seemed friendly, but when I noticed several empty water buckets, I pitched in and started filling them. I even helped a little girl bathe her hog, a huge red beast outweighing her by at least fifty pounds.

It felt good to be helpful, so when Lonan flew up beside me and said, "Avery, you need to come check this out!" I ignored him at first. But he kept pestering me, and I was afraid somebody would notice the crow with the suspiciously human vocabulary, so I sighed and followed him deeper into the maze of corrals.

This was the section with horses, and most of the pens held up to half a dozen companionable equines—including some donkeys and mules. One round pen held only a huge black stallion, his restless hooves churning up the turf. He had on a bridle, but the reins dragged in the dust, somehow not tangling in his legs.

"Nykur!" I called. Other than swinging his enormous head in my direction, with his ears pinned back, the stallion didn't react. Maybe we were wrong, and this was a different nykur or something? It sure looked like him, minus the intelligent glint in his eyes. There was a wickedness in his gaze, yes, but more like he was thinking about eating a person than how to romance one, like he usually was.

I looked around for Lonan and spotted him in a nearby black locust tree. "Is that our Nykur?"

He bobbed his head yes, but didn't answer me. I was about to question him, when he said, "Tweet! Tweet tweet chirp!"

I laughed and said, "What the hell was—" I sighted a woman walking towards me and stopped mid-sentence. I turned my gaze back to Nykur and tried to look nonchalant, but she stopped a few paces away from me.

"Hey, kid! You don't want to mess with that horse. Get away from there."

Oh, so she was one of those "hey, stupid kid, you'd be dead of stupidity if some non-stupid adult didn't tell you what to do" kind of women. Well, I hated to disappoint.

"Who, me?" I said, letting a little spittle track down my chin as I finished speaking.

"Yes, you," she said, impatiently. "That horse is dangerous."

"You mean Asshat? He won't hurt me."

She made a face. "You know this horse? And his name is..."

"Asshat, yeah." And before she could stop me, I ducked between the rails and into the pen.

"Stop!" she hollered, and Nykur sidestepped in alarm.

"Don't yell," I called. "That'll make him worse. You have to know how to speak to him." But good thing my back was turned to her, so she couldn't see how white my face got when Nykur snaked his head in my direction.

Now that I had his attention, I was rethinking this impulse. His hooves were soundless on the dirt, as he stalked me like he was the world's biggest border collie staring down a sheep.

"Nice horsie," I said weakly. His lips peeled back from his gums, and his teeth were like picket-fence boards. His ears stayed folded back, and his gaze held me like I was a mouse to his cobra. Okay, so "nice horsie" didn't work—I'd have to try something more tailored for Nykur.

"Boobies," I said. "Panties. Brassiere." Nykur's ears tilted forward.

"What did you just say?" The woman asked from behind me.

But I ignored her and continued with my naughty list. "Bum. Nipple clamps. Rumpy pumpy." Each word allowed me to get a little closer.

"Negligee. Fanny. A little slap and tickle." I could almost reach the reins, which was good since I'd nearly run out of the euphemisms I knew and would have to move on to the more graphic words. Finally, my fingers closed on leather, and I had hold of him. I sighed in relief as his massive skull nudged me—in the boob, of course—and he exhaled with a flapping of equine lips.

"Good boy," I said for the woman's benefit—and whispered "bad boy" for his.

"I'll go enter his name in the logs," the woman finally said, still frowning. "You're sure that's how you want it written down?"

"Nah, his real name is Master Roger Funnybottom the Third. Asshat is his stable name."

She walked away, shaking her head and still frowning. Lonan swooped down and landed on Nykur's hindquarters, digging his talons into the horse's hide to keep his balance.

"What was the 'tweet, chirp' nonsense?" I asked him.

"I was trying to do a bird call to warn you someone was coming."

"Well, next time, maybe you should try 'caw caw' if you're trying to be subtle."

He cocked his head, all slyness. "But then you wouldn't have known something was up, would you? My way worked."

"Fine, it worked. So what's up with Nykur? Why doesn't he seem to know me?"

Lonan pecked Nykur on the backside, and waited for a reaction. All he got was a shiver of skin and a stomp of hoof. "Hmm...maybe take off his bridle?" he suggested.

I undid the buckle on the side, and slipped the headpiece off as the entire bridle fell into my hand—slimy bit and all. "Yecch." I turned away and tried to shake some of the drool off of it.

"Hey, let me put a ball gag in *your* mouth and see how much you salivate," a voice said.

I whipped around to face Nykur in his manly form, with Lonan perched on his shoulder. "It's you!" I threw my arms around him and he patted my ass comfortingly. Lonan pecked him hard in the ear, and Nykur hastily moved his hands north.

"What was up with the horse form? Why were you stuck like that?" I asked, stepping out of his embrace.

He rubbed the back of his neck sheepishly. "Well, I wasn't feeling quite myself earlier, after I was hit by some kind of blast. I was staggering around—looking for you—and this woman with a truck and horse trailer came by. Apparently, she was evacuating some horses and decided I needed help too."

"And she sweet-talked you into putting a bridle on?"

He turned red. "Well, I wouldn't say she *sweet-talked* me—you know I have a weakness for bossy women."

"You mean she was even bossier than Avery?" Lonan stage-whispered.

I glared at him and said, "But didn't I read something about how kelpies can be captured? Doesn't it mean you're her—thrall or something?"

"Not now that you've taken off the bridle," he said. "I'm not answerable to her now—although, I may do some sniffing around tonight to see which tent is hers..."

"The crow says caw, caw!" Lonan said as he took flight. "Someone's coming, so you'd better decide if you're a horse or a man here."

I felt horsey breath on the back of my neck before a fatigue-clad guy jogged up.

"Miss Flynn, Special Agent Boulder would like to see you back at your tent."

"Yeah, okay, thanks." I called. "Just let me give my horse some water and I'll meet him there."

I told Nykur I'd come back later tonight, and left him eyeing some skittish mares in the next paddock. *Man, I hope none of them are in heat and willing to let their hormones overcome their natural horse sense.* Lonan flew off, planning to meet up with us both after dark.

When I got to my tent, Special Agent Boulder had made my bed and set up the other cots, too. I started to say thanks, but he waved away the small talk.

"There's been a change in plans," he said. "Your uncle and your mom are on their way and will be here later tonight or in the morning. Then you'll be leaving tomorrow."

"Leaving for where? And what's changed?"

He ran his fingers through his flattop, a nervous gesture which immediately had me taking this more seriously. He'd seemed pretty unflappable yesterday.

"Things went south shortly after you left the communications tent. It took them a while to get things back online, and when they finally did, they found a ton of messages. HQ had been trying to raise us and were about to send in troops since they couldn't get a reply. At about the same time as your blowup of our equipment, the front line took a big jump. Areas which were still 'normal' are now experiencing magical phenomena, and the people who stayed are nowhere to be found. The really weird part is, the area affected is not a random section— it's like a tentacle reaching out for something. Like it's got a purpose."

I shivered, in spite of the warm fall afternoon, as my sense of safety fell away. "That sounds...creepy. So which direction did it go?"

"It's heading straight at this camp."

"And because of it," I said, "you want me to leave? You think it's connected to me in some way?"

"We do. The fact that your magic fried our equipment at the same time is too much of a coincidence, and after years of dealing with Fae magic I no longer believe in coincidence anyway. Having you here may put all these refugees at risk."

"Not to mention if the Hunt comes after me, that's a risk, too," I added with a sigh. Sure, that had already been in the mix, but up to now I'd been successful at putting it out of my mind.

Agent Boulder shook his head. "Queen Maeve has called them back for now—you can thank Tam for his influence. He's managed to buy us all some time."

I snorted. "What did he have to promise in exchange? Seven youths and seven maidens?"

But the special agent didn't play along with my joking this time. "I don't think tributes were on the table; Tam claims he was able to convince her that whether the disaster originated with you or not, your wild magic may still be the best hope for fixing it. To try to fix anything, you need to get control of your magic, and there's only one person who is genuinely qualified to help you."

"Let me guess—Queen Maeve? Because I really don't trust her—"

"No, not Queen Maeve," Boulder said with a tight smile. "You're going to Merlin's."

I nodded, not really surprised. Uncle Tam had been pushing for that already, and Merlin's letters to me over the last few months had started the teachings a bit. But in writing we'd only covered some basics, like how much my emotions and magic were tied together, and it was obviously time for some in-person lessons. Really, *past* time for that.

When I went to rub my face, I smelled horse— and worse—on my hand, so I said, "I think I need another shower."

"Okay." Boulder didn't seem thrown by my change of gears. "I need to get back, anyway, and check in with HQ before dinner. Should I have Daniel or one of my guys bring you some food later?"

"Probably a good idea," I said. "And, um, if I know of a Fae who accidentally got brought into the camp, is that going to be a problem? He can mostly pass for a human, but I know he wouldn't show up on any of your roll sheets or anything."

Boulder paused in the act of lifting the tent flap. "Do I need to worry about him causing any trouble?"

"No-oo-oo," I said, and hastily added, "Well, there might be a few bruised hearts when he leaves, but that's about it. I think. And maybe you should have some antibiotics on hand for an outbreak of STDs."

He peered at me under skeptical brows. "If you give me a name, I can add him to a list. Do I need to put him on the 'watch' list, or is he genuinely mostly harmless?"

"Oh, he's like...a puppy." A dirty, filthy puppy. "He goes by Nykur."

Boulder nodded and left me to make my way to the showers. When I wandered through the gathering twilight back to the tent later, I found Lonan already in there, eating the last of a pastie.

"Hey—was that mine?" I grabbed the crust from his hand. "Somebody was supposed to drop off dinner for *me*."

"Calm down, Miss Grabbyhands. There are two more in the bag—this one was beef, so I was saving you from it."

"My hero." We sat back-to-back, and I polished off the other two pasties. The soft light of the lantern and my full belly made me sleepy, so I pulled

Lonan onto the cot with me. We'd only snuggled for a few minutes before I tried to sit up; Lonan pulled me tighter into his body.

"You're not going anywhere," he said. "This is comfortable, and we'll have company in here soon enough."

"I told Nykur we'd come back for him—"

"Special Agent Man asked me to deliver a message to Nykur about some rules of behavior, and I got there just as Nykur ducked into the bossy woman's travel trailer. Judging from the rockin' that started, I didn't think a knockin' would be welcome."

"Eww. He doesn't waste time, does he?"

"No, and I'm busy making the most of our time while we have our tent to ourselves. So snuggle up."

I smiled and did as he said. Our breath synchronized, but I wasn't really sleepy anymore. *Hmm, maybe I should turn around and see if we can get this cot rocking. Naah, if my mom walked in, that would be hella embarrassing.* "Lonan, are you still awake?"

"No," he said, his voice muffled in my hair. I rolled over, poking and prodding him to give me room so I could face him instead.

With a sigh, he propped himself up on an elbow and said, "Is this going to be one of those nights where Avery's brain won't shut up, which means Lonan doesn't get any sleep either?"

"Maybe, but face it—every night has a pretty good chance of that happening." I kissed him on the chin. "Anyway, I'm wondering what you can tell me about Merlin's wild magic. Like, how was he born?"

"You mean, like, his origin story?"

"Yeah, I guess. Have you ever met him?"

"No, I haven't met him. He spent some time in the human world after he set up the Border, and then came back to Faerie—but no one has seen him in years. Hundreds of years in Fae time. He manages to communicate with a select few—like Tam Lin, apparently—but has otherwise kept to himself."

"Why? Did he have a falling out with humans and Fae?"

"I don't know, it was before my time, and all I know is the stories passed among the corbin. He's always had a hard time getting along with Fae and humans: never quite trusted by, or comfortable in, either world. I've always thought it must be a terribly lonely existence."

I was quiet as I thought about isolation and judgement. Was that what I had to look forward to, in a life with wild magic? Because it fit with my experience of the Court so far, and my own mother didn't react well to seeing my true nature.

"Do you think it's why he talked Uncle Tam into trying for another wild magic combo?" I asked. "Because he didn't want to be alone? That makes me feel really bad for him, but also pretty angry he'd doom someone else to a life he couldn't bear."

Lonan rubbed my back and kissed me softly before saying, "I don't think it's quite that simple. Maybe you'll have the chance to ask him, if you're serious about having magic lessons with him."

"I guess so." I sighed and turned back around so I could try again to sleep. But then my eyes flew open and I sat up. "Hey—did you say there are corbin stories about Merlin? What are they?"

Lonan sat up too. "If I tell you a story, then will you let us get some sleep?"

I grinned. "Well, after the story, maybe I'll need a glass of water, and you'll need to check under the bed for monsters—"

"All the monsters but you left hours ago. They wanted some peace and quiet."

I stuck my tongue out at him. "Ha ha. So, what's the story?"

He piled up some pillows and got comfortable before he spoke. "In the human legends, Merlin was fathered by a dark spirit who came to his mother in her tower, and they got it mostly right. In our stories, his Fae father was a corbin—it's a love story.

But let me do this properly, and keep in mind this is translated from the old corbin language."

He put on a serious voice and intoned, "Once upon a time, a long while ago, a king locked his only daughter in a tower, after she had once again refused a suitor of his choosing. Contrary to his royal wishes, she continued to insist she was the best judge of her own heart and mind, and of the man who would suit them.

"And so the years passed in a stalemate, while the princess idled in her prison. She spent her days alone, but for the meals delivered by an old family retainer, and but for the company of her canary in its golden cage. The bird was her only confidant and she treasured it dearly, until one day in a fit of empathy she set it free. Her own spirits soared along with her friend's, before a falcon struck the spot of gold from the sky.

"A passing crow heard the princess's lamentations, and harassed the falcon into dropping its prize. Once he returned the battered body to its mistress, and witnessed her grief over her lost friend, the crow offered to sing to the princess in its place. If she was startled to find the crow could sing, let alone speak like a person, she did not offer offense by showing it. Instead, she graciously accepted the crow's proposal and entertained him as she would a guest, every time he came by. Those visits became more frequent, and he confided to her that he was not an ordinary crow, but an enchanted creature called a corbin.

"He also declared his love for the princess, and if she had come to return his feelings, there was a way for them to be together as man and woman. The corbin revealed he could abide in a human's body, just as he did with a crow's. However, her enthusiasm for such a scheme was dampened by the news that any human he occupied would risk losing their mind."

This was all sounding really familiar. "Hey, wait a minute," I said. "Do you guys all use the same script?"

Lonan laughed and said, "Well, we've had thousands of years to try out various speeches, and we've learned what works on gullible humans."

That got him a sock in the arm, which probably didn't even hurt since we were in such close quarters. He pulled me into his lap, and kissed me soundly in retaliation.

When he finally let me come up for air, he asked, "Do you want me to finish the story, or is your lack of attention span a liability here? Would you rather have the song version?"

"There's a song? Why didn't you say that in the first place? Yes, sing to me, o sweet corbin." I fake-swooned in his arms.

"Okay, so you probably already know this tune, since there's a bastardized human version with lyrics about a blacksmith which I know Tam has performed. As if blacksmiths were as cool as blackbirds! Maybe you've heard the version by Steeleye Span? That's the closest to the Fae tune—"

"Less talking, more singing," I interrupted. Lonan really did have a gorgeous singing voice, so I shivered in delight when he launched into the song.

Oh, a blackbird courted me, through wind and weather
He fairly won my heart, softly as a feather.
He told me of rare lands, with his tongue so clever
And if I go with my love, I could live forever.

Our love it is so strong, we'll not be parted
But is our courtship done 'fore it can be started?
I fear his gentle wings cannot warm me in my tower—
He's sworn to find a way to turn my cell to bower.

I wake to find my man, but ask not why or how;
The sure touch of my dear is his solemn vow.
Tis only for one night that we may lie together
Ere the morning sun sends him back to feather.

I thought he was pausing for effect, but when Lonan didn't continue, I opened my eyes and looked up at him. He was frowning, and staring off into the distance.

10

"What is it?" I asked. "Why did you stop?"

"I said it was a love story, but I never said it was a happy story. I was thinking about how all the love stories between Fae and humans seem to end in tragedy."

Whoa, talk about splashing some cold, dark water on the romance. I sat up. "We're not talking about Merlin's parents anymore, are we? Are you having doubts about me...about us?"

He sighed. "I... Look, I enjoy our lively banter as much as you do. I know humor is your default mode, but lately I feel like you're using it to keep me at arm's length. We were apart for a pretty crappy few weeks, and you're acting like nothing major's happened. You just picked up where we left off."

I sat up and scooted away from him, needing some space for this serious conversation. "Hey, so did you. Maybe I was waiting for you to answer some questions."

"Questions you haven't asked, you mean? Like what?"

Those questions had been bottled up, since I was unsure where or when was the right place to ask them. He obviously had noticed my retreat into "banter and sarcasm" default mode. Well, if he wanted unfiltered honesty, so be it.

"Like, what did you hear at Court—before I'd even gotten there with my mom's statue—that convinced you the queen needed protection from me? I saw you whispering with her, Lonan, and after I accidentally made the carpet flowers bloom, you looked just as willing to put your sword through me as the rest of the Host. And, what's up with Uncle Tam and the queen too? How did he go from harassing me to permanently shut down the Border, to trying to convince me I should 'compromise' by basically giving the queen everything she asks for? I'm having trouble trusting both of you, since I don't really know if Queen Maeve is using you both as puppets."

He pushed past me to stand up, and ran his fingers over his head, making the feathers stick out in all directions as he paced. "It's not that black and white, Avery."

"Then let's talk it out." He hadn't actually denied any of it, had he?

"Brace yourself, Avery Girl, because you're not going to like my answers." He sighed. "I hope you know by now that I truly love you, but I have other obligations too. To my family and ruler. Protecting the queen against a threat, like when you were at Court, is one of them. And that's not one I have complete control over—when she's under immediate attack, she can take over her Host. We all become an extension of her will."

"What do you mean? Like a hive mind?"

He nodded miserably. Whoa, so my puppet comment wasn't totally off-base. How deep did her control go? How did I know—or how did Lonan know—whether he really loved me, and wasn't acting out a script?

And Uncle Tam—were all those times when he didn't act like himself, when he was "two-faced," actually the queen acting through him? That would be some advanced evil-genius shit, to have a counterpart to do your dirty work without anyone being able to tie it back to you.

"What are you thinking?" Lonan asked, when I didn't say anything right away. "I know you well enough to guess your brain is worrying full throttle."

"Oh, I'm just questioning every interaction I've ever had, and whether I can trust anyone again. Or if I can even trust myself or my instincts."

But the anguish in my voice didn't fit my flippant comment, and Lonan came to put his arms around me. I let him, so I must have still had some faith in him.

"Hey, don't ever doubt I'm on your side," he murmured. "I'm Team Avery all the way. It's...complicated, with my family. And my queen."

"Well, I wish it wasn't. Couldn't I—" I paused, horrified that I'd been about to ask whether I could use my magic to override hers. How was that scenario any better for Lonan, to switch whoever was pulling his strings?

And now that I'd thought of the possibility, what was keeping me from doing it anyway during one of my "tantrums?" Was Lonan wrong to trust *me?* When I didn't even know if I could trust myself?

If I ever did anything to compromise Lonan's free will, or endanger his life, it would mean I'd become as bad as—well, as bad as all the Fae and people trying to use me and my magic. Like the queen, who threw geises around as casually as ordering takeout. Maybe it would be better if he wasn't so close to ground zero. Where he would be safer, at least from me.

I turned and started making the bed. Without looking at him, I said, "Maybe you should go back to Court for a while. Until all this is over."

He turned me towards him, searching my face. "Is this because you don't trust me anymore? Are you trying to break up with me?"

I shook my head and went back to making the bed, but I know he saw the tears filling my eyes.

"I don't want to go. Do you want me to leave?" He asked softly.

I shrugged, not wanting to influence his decision. After giving me plenty of time to answer, he stepped towards me and I felt his breath on the back of my neck before he placed a kiss there.

"I can fix this," he whispered, then ducked out the tent flap.

I stood, torn, before I ran outside. Just in time to see a dark shape against the night sky as it winged away.

"Lonan, are you coming back?"

No answer. I shivered in the midnight air for a few minutes, before I went inside and curled up alone in my now-spacious cot.

I couldn't fall asleep right away, I was so fidgety from our conversation. I didn't feel like it had settled anything—in fact, it had left me pretty unsettled. Maybe it would have been better if Lonan hadn't called me on my weird behavior at all, because it sent me into a space in my head that I didn't visit very often. That space was serious and dark, and I knew if I spent too much time in there that I'd have trouble getting back out.

Soft voices woke me sometime before the sun came up, but I merely groaned and burrowed further under the covers until they went away. When the scent of breakfast sausage and maple syrup tickled my nostrils later, I emerged to find my mom and Uncle Tam watching me.

"Yay, you guys made it!" I croaked blearily. "And did you come bearing gifts of food?"

Mom laughed, a warm sound to my ears. "Yes, Avery. I knew you wouldn't be half as excited to see me if I was empty-handed."

"That's so not true, Mom," I said, and leapt out of bed to engulf her in a hug. Any distraction which didn't let me dwell on the fight with Lonan was welcome. "Escaping under dragon-fire doesn't exactly count as a reunion. You can talk while we eat."

Uncle Tam shook his head. "We dropped our bags off earlier, but you were cocooned in your blankets, so we left to eat. We brought you some French toast sticks, and sausage gravy to dip them in—the kind of disgusting combination you love."

I snatched the bag from his hand, and made Homer Simpson-esque moans of ecstasy. As I raised the first gravy-laden piece to my lips, Uncle Tam made a face and said, "I'm going to go shower. You two can catch up, and I'll be back after you've finished that slop."

Mom laughed at his disgust and grabbed one piece for herself, sans gravy. Letting her have some of my food was a reflection of how much I'd missed her—normally, taking food off my plate without permission was as risky as taking a bone from a junkyard dog.

"So, Mom," I said around a mouthful of food, "what do you remember from the last few weeks?"

She hesitated before saying, "I remember us fighting and then Lonan sending me into a meltdown by talking about Faerie...it feels odd to say 'Faerie' aloud, but at least I don't have a meltdown now. Tam fixed it, since he says I need to be able to discuss the Fae, and to recognize them. Now that I know my daughter is one of them."

I choked a little before I could swallow my bite. "Yeah. That must have come as a shock, when my wings unfurled back at the apartment. Are you okay with it?"

Half of her mouth turned up, and she shrank a little. "We've both seen all the same Hallmark Channel movies, where the mom tells her child that nothing they could do would ever make her stop loving them. It's true—the love is still there, but I feel like I never really knew you. Or your dad, or Uncle Tam. You've all been part of this world I never even suspected was real outside of fairy tales. Avery, you've been exposed to dangers I can't even imagine, and you were facing them alone."

She had no idea how much I was worried I had been alone the whole time, even when I thought I had people I could trust in my corner. But it wasn't like I would ease her guilt by telling her that, so why bother?

Instead, I said, "I'm not sure how much you re-member, or what you've been told, but I'm not ex-actly a helpless gerbil. I'm kind of a badass." Or at least I was feeling more like one now that I had a good breakfast in my belly.

"Well, that's good, I suppose. My point is, you should have been able to come to me; what hurt more than anything was when I could feel you pulling away from me."

I looked down at my lap and fiddled with my napkin. "That was worse than me freezing you? Lonan said you were...gone, like your soul had disappeared. I was so scared I'd lost you—I never in a million years wanted that."

"Oh, Honey, I honestly don't remember any part of it. As far as I'm concerned, I went from our apartment to that street with all the smoke and the dragon. Not an easy transition, at all, but I'm not traumatized by you freezing me. Not that I ever want to repeat it."

"Noted," I said, writing an imaginary note on an invisible tablet with a French toast stick. "And I want to say sorry for leaving you behind, with Uncle Tam and the Hunt—you weren't treated badly or anything, were you?"

She frowned. "The Hunt are—strange. When Tam was persuading them not to follow you, it was hard to tell if they were even listening. Or could understand what we were saying. They eventually camped out on his lawn and ignored us—you need to be really careful of them, Avery."

I wiped my mouth hastily on a paper napkin and blurted, "I thought the queen called them off?"

"A messenger came and told them to hold back, but I got the impression they're not entirely under her control. Maybe the Hunt only obeys when they want to? So watch out, in case they decide you're fair game again."

I nodded, and scooped the last of the sausage gravy out of the container with my finger since I'd run out of French toast sticks.

Mom made a face and said, "Well, telling you that supernatural hunters may come after you certainly hasn't affected your appetite."

I smacked my lips, just to annoy her, and said, "Seriously, Mom, I can handle them. Didn't Uncle Tam fill you in on my badassery?"

"Yes...but I suppose it doesn't seem real to me. Like it's an elaborate hoax."

"I can fix that. Wanna see my batwings again?"

I didn't give her time to answer before I unfurled my wings. They spanned from corner to corner inside the tent, and I had to hunch over to fit within the canvas confines. I waited out her shock, and after a few minutes her breathing slowed. She reached a tentative hand out to touch the nearest membrane and its tracery of veins.

"They're warm," she said in awe.

"Well, yeah, I am still a mammal, in spite of the scales."

"Scales?"

I nodded. "Yeah, there's more—are you sure you're ready for this?"

"N-no, but do it anyway."

My magic was waiting under the surface of my skin, so it would be no trouble to unleash it and let myself go full wyvern. But—dammit, these were the only clothes I had. Mom's eyes grew wide as I got naked.

"Um, trust me, this will make sense in a second." My muscle-y scaled form burst out, like biscuit dough from a can.

Mom hadn't even begun to take in my form before the tent flap lifted and Uncle Tam came in. He stopped short and said, "That may not be the smartest thing to do, Avery, when we're surrounded by people who are talking about bombing the monsters who drove them out of their homes."

"Oh," I said, deflated. As in, literally deflated to my girl self and ducked behind my mom to dress. "Are people really saying that?"

"Well, some are also threatening to cut off my balls, but that's just the usual—" Nykur broke off as he entered behind Uncle Tam and saw my mom. "Ah, so nice to see you again, Heather."

She started at his familiar tone, and said, "Have we met? Oh—are you Lonan?"

I blurted, "God, no!" at the same moment Nykur said, "Gods, no!" and I laughed.

"When you met Nykur before, Mom, he was a car. And he has other shapes, too, so if a black hare hops into your shower stall, don't be fooled."

Mom raised a skeptical brow as Nykur stepped forward and kissed her hand. She asked, "A hare, and a car? So are you like a VW Rabbit?"

"No, no—a big black muscle car. A sexy one," Nykur murmured, his lips now on the inside of her wrist.

Mom snatched her hand away and turned bright red. "Now I remember. The seats were very...warm."

"Eww, Nykur, did you use your massage trick on my *mom*?" I glared at him, sending a mental image of me putting his bridle back on him, and leading him to the vet for gelding.

He nearly fell over backwards in his haste to put some distance between himself and my mom. That was better.

"Well, I'd better let you get to your plans," Mom said, flustered now. "I'm due at the infirmary tent, anyway." She turned to leave.

"Wait!" My voice made her pause in raising the tentflap. "You're not coming with us when we leave?"

She glanced towards Uncle Tam, but he avoided her gaze with a frown. It had the flavor of an old argument, and I knew Uncle Tam must have been nagging her once again for choosing work over me.

"Avery," she said, "it's just that—"

"No, I get it, Mom," I said, trying to keep any pang of accusation out of my voice. "You can do more good here, helping people, and you'll be safer. Right?"

"That is what I was thinking, yes—but if you need me, then I can go with you. You don't need to do this alone."

"It's fine, Mom," I said. When she started to speak again, I added, "No, really. I'm not just saying that—I agree you'd be better off here. Nykur and Uncle Tam will be more help than you would for this."

If I let myself step back from the lingering guilt and fear from having almost lost her when she was frozen, even I could see it wasn't worth putting her life at risk. We didn't really know yet where we were going or what we'd meet along the way.

She searched my face and nodded before she exited the tent. Uncle Tam came over and gave me a hug, and Nykur patted my shoulder.

I sighed and said, "It's really not a big deal, guys. I guess the flip side of no longer feeling I have to be 'normal' around my mom is recognizing how little we have in common anymore. We're worried about things on a completely different scale."

Uncle Tam was still watching me carefully, and I changed the subject. "Have either of you talked to my dad recently? He's crazy-obsessed with protecting Corriell, and I don't trust him. Is it a dryad-magic thing, that Dad's so stuck on him? How does it even work?"

Nykur made a raspberry, that still managed to sound like a horse flapping its lips, on his way out of the tent, saying he was going to get something to eat. At least he didn't say some*one* to eat, but he was obviously avoiding the subject.

I turned to Uncle Tam. "Well? Are you going to duck my question too?"

Uncle Tam chewed his moustache as he thought it over. "There's certainly some magic operating to reinforce the bond, but Michael genuinely loves Corriell, I think. Though it took him a while to admit to himself that he could be attracted to males and females, or those with a mixture of traits like Corriell."

It took me a few seconds to process that; I couldn't settle my brain on whether to ask more about Dad, Corriell, or Fae genders. So I just went where my mouth took me.

"You think he was having trouble coming out and that made it more complicated? I get that, but what I don't get is why Dad thought it had to be an either/or situation with Corriell and our family. It might have helped Mom to understand what was really going on, if she had all the backstory. I mean, before Lonan, I would have labeled myself completely hetero—but then he started showing up in girls' bodies occasionally and I discovered it wasn't a dealbreaker. It didn't matter to me what parts he or she had, as long as it was Lonan."

Uncle Tam snorted. "You make it sound simple, but it's not. You didn't even tell your mom about Lonan until recently."

"True. So why did Dad loving Corriell have to end our family?"

Uncle Tam shook his head. "That, I can't tell you. You'll have to ask your Dad."

"Yeah—if I speak to him again."

Uncle Tam said, "I wouldn't be too judgmental about the influence Corriell has on your dad, if I were you..."

"What's that supposed to mean? You think I'm a Faephobe or something?"

"It would have been easier if you were more anti-Fae. You would have already closed the Border and none of this would have happened. No, I mean you may very well have strong magical influence yourself. Merlin's hold over others was one of the reasons both Fae and humans were set to annihilate him."

"Yeah, right." But Uncle Tam didn't join in my laughter. "Wait, you really mean it? Like, my wild magic can enthrall Fae?"

"I don't know how else to explain your effect on Nykur—he's the most commitment-avoiding creature I've ever come across, and yet he's thoroughly devoted to you."

"Is he? He's probably already slept with half the women—and all of the mares—in this camp."

"But I'd wager none of them have claimed his fidelity, as you have. And none ever has before."

I gaped at him. There was no way I had some kind of weird hold over Nykur—unconsciously or not. I didn't remember checking the box for "include control add-on pack" when my powers installed. In fact, I'd rather have no powers at all if thralls were part of the deal.

Before I could process his theory completely, Uncle Tam brought the conversation back to our earlier topic. "So, are you going to speak to your dad if he calls again?"

"He's still waiting for me to call him back and say I'll close the Border permanently, like he wants. Actually, you used to be pretty vocal about that too, Uncle Tam—have you changed your mind?"

He sighed and sat down, pointing me to the rickety camp chair across from him. "It's more that, in light of recent events, I am no longer certain the Border *can* be closed or repaired. We genuinely don't know what went wrong with it, or how your wild magic might have played a part. That's why we need to find Merlin and ask his help."

"Find Merlin? You mean you don't know where he is? I thought you two kept in touch."

"We're not in constant contact; he's not just a text away. I know where he was last, but he seems to have moved on from there. We'll start at the last known sighting, then see if anything there points us in a direction."

"I expected getting to Merlin's to be...a formality, not a quest. Does the queen know where Merlin is? Can't you or Lonan ask her?"

"I've already asked her, and that's how I know Merlin has moved on; the messengers who Maeve sent returned without finding him."

"Oh. So, what's the plan?"

"We'll leave in the morning and head to his tree. Although he's probably retreated to his stronghold, where he can conserve his own wild magic while he waits for us to join him. Which is complicated by the fact that no one knows where his stronghold is, and since it's in Faerie it could move around—"

"Hey, shouldn't we wait until Lonan gets back before making any concrete plans?" I interrupted, as the thought occurred to me.

An awkward silence descended, and then Uncle Tam said, "Lonan won't be coming right away. He's got some business at Court, and if he's free to join us later then he can catch up."

"He said he'd fix whatever it was—I know he'll be back."

"He could be a long while, Avery, and we have no time to lose."

I narrowed my eyes at Uncle Tam. "Queenie didn't stick him in prison again, did she? Cause I've had enough of that—"

"It's not that. Don't get your heart set on Lonan joining us, all right? Let him handle his worriments, and we'll handle ours."

Yeah, we'll see.

11

Uncle Tam had been around me long enough to know I wasn't likely to give up that easily, and he seemed determined to keep me distracted and busy for the rest of the day. It wasn't too hard since we really did need to pack some stuff—in saddlebags, as it turned out.

A dazzling, sun-colored mare had shown up in Nykur's pen, fully tacked and ready. Uncle Tam claimed her, in spite of the fact that he'd never owned a horse as far as I knew. What was really strange was Nykur seemed to have a healthy respect of her—she could herd him across the pen with only a look.

If that wasn't enough to clue me in she was probably magical, when Uncle Tam had me check the supplies in the bags hanging on either side of her shoulders, I found the saddlebags were much larger inside than out.

I came around by her head and said, "Hey, you're a Fae, aren't you? Are you another Nykur?"

She came out of her doze long enough to curl her lip in disgust, and then fell back into her drooping-head, relaxed posture.

"No use pretending," I said sternly. "I'm onto you. I have the Sight, you know, and I'll be able to tell if you're not just a horse."

The derisive swish of her tail was the only sign she'd heard me. Uncle Tam walked up with an armful of turkey jerky packets, and I said, "Hey, what's this horse's deal? Is she Fae, a boghorse, or what?"

"This is Epona—named for a goddess. As a royal mount, she's the best I could ask for, and won't put up with any of Nykur's harassment."

"Nice to meet you, Epona." I pulled my hand back in time to avoid her snapping teeth. "Um, what does Epona eat?"

Uncle Tam laughed and stroked her now-willing cheek. "She doesn't eat girls—not even hybrid ones. She'll come around to you eventually, if you don't act too foolish. She can't abide foolishness."

"Good to know. Does she talk? Oops, by the look she gave me, I already blew the 'don't be stupid' rule."

Uncle Tam laughed and gave Epona a friendly slap on the shoulder before going back to packing.

I wished I had more stuff to bring, to take advantage of those bottomless saddle bags. But I only had a few changes of clothes that Uncle Tam had brought from his place, plus another outfit I'd gotten from the free pile.

I trailed Uncle Tam back to our tent for more supplies, then whined, "Why can't we take the car, anyway? Nykur has climate control and everything."

"We'll be traveling through some really unstable areas, Avery, what with the wild magic areas spreading. His metal chassis may not go over well in some Fae-dominated territories, and Nykur's horse form is more natural—as is Epona's. Less threatening to both human and Fae."

"Fine, but do we at least get some Harry Potter-esque tents? Completely outfitted for magical glamping?"

"Nope, just plain ol' Army surplus tents. Less to go wrong with them."

We finished loading up the packs, and I had time for a shower before Mom came back to join us for dinner. On my way back from the bathroom, I slipped over a few rows into an unoccupied tent. I reached into the shadows and started to fold one into a messenger crow.

"What are you doing?" The voice behind me startled me into jumping a few feet off the ground, where I stayed as my wings kept me aloft.

"Nykur, what the hell?" I landed and tried to untangle my wings from the clothesline strung across the tent's peak. "What are *you* doing?"

"Aah, aah, aah—I asked first."

I narrowed my eyes and asked, "Are you following me? Spying on me?"

"I prefer to think of it as looking out for you."

"Yeah, right—what are you afraid I'm going to do?"

He sat in a camp chair and crossed his arms before drawling, "I don't know, maybe you'll call Lonan's Name, or send him a message, thereby screwing things up for him."

"What do you mean?"

"Did he try to talk to you before he took off? What happened?"

"I don't really know what happened—Lonan said he had something to fix, but...I just want to know he's okay. That we're okay."

Nykur shook his head. "I don't think this is something you can help with; he needs to work out his own family issues."

"But what if he can't? What if whatever hold the queen has on him is stronger than what we feel for each other? He's already raised his sword against me, because of some stupid Host thing—"

Nykur interrupted my whining, saying, "It's part of being in the Host. It's even stronger than a geis, and he's not able to tell you the full details. As in, not physically able to tell you."

"So, like, the first rule of Host Club is—"

"A setup for a joke, yeah. But it's also true."

I sighed and unfolded another camp chair. "Okay, tell me about it, please. If you can."

"Of course I can. I'm not foolish enough to take the Host oath." He settled back in his chair. "I know you're not well-versed in geises and how they work, but their power most often comes from imbalance—when a debt of some kind is created. So if, for example, after he's specifically been told not to, a dashing Nykur seduces the queen's tasty hand-maiden—thereby ruining the girl's chances at a successful, royally-approved marriage, because how could she wed a dusty old duke after sampling the pleasures of a robust stallion of a Fae—"

I cleared my throat and lifted an eyebrow at him.

"Sorry." He was clearly not sorry about either bragging or the seduction, but he continued. "If a Nykur did do something like that, he owes a debt. It could be to her family, or as in this case, to the queen herself."

"And then he finds himself sentenced to life as a car in the human world, until he works off the debt?"

"Exactly. The geis on me had all kinds of strings attached: I couldn't talk, I couldn't show my true nature overtly, I couldn't return to Faerie until the queen decided my debt was settled."

"But...you did talk, sort of. And once Lonan outed you, you were able to show yourself as a magical car."

He leaned forward, scooting his chair closer to mine. "Yeah, after I'd spent some time in the company of your wild magic. Between that, and my shifting loyalties, I was able to find ways to bypass those strings until I was entirely free of her geis."

I shifted uncomfortably in my chair. Was that what Uncle Tam was talking about, when he hinted that wild magic can overcome other magic?

Nykur gave me a quizzical look before continuing. "The queen wasn't too happy about my ties to you overriding her own, of course, but she wouldn't risk punishing me further without a good reason. In case you saw a move against me as a move against yourself, when she didn't know the full extent of your powers."

I cleared my throat and asked, "So her solution was to invite Lonan to join the Host? I'm still not seeing the connection."

"Her *first* solution was to put a royal geis—which doesn't need the debt component, so it's basically magical marching orders—on Lonan. To maintain his loyalty to her, and to force him to spy on you and report back."

"So that's what's been going on? She made him spy on me?"

"Nope, it didn't work. Her geis didn't last five minutes after he got around your wild magic again. Truthfully, it may not have worked better to begin with, because it was meant to *maintain* his loyalty to his aunt, and he'd already fallen for you.

"Anyway, when the geis didn't pan out, she strongly 'invited' him to join her Host. Lonan refused, but then he found out her 'Plan C' was to have him killed and make it look like Tam Lin had done it, leaving you without any real allies. Your dad was already under Corriell's thumb, and could be easily manipulated into convincing you the Court was your best refuge."

"So he decided joining the Host was the lesser of evils?"

"I assume so, and maybe he thought your magic could override that, too. But as we saw when you magicked the flower carpet, he had no choice but to fulfill his Host duties. The queen's magic takes over her guards when she's under attack, so they can act in unison to protect her and follow her orders. It's true of every liege and their Host."

"The magic takes them over? So, she *is* like a puppet master."

"A closer equivalent might be a hive-mind or a queen bee; the puppet strings only kick in under extreme threat."

"Like flowers blooming at her." I made woo-woo finger motions in disgust at her overreaction. "But when he does come back, how will I know if he's working for her, or being sincere about something? I'm going to be second-guessing everything he says and does now."

"Yeah, if you're smart. You should be wary of everyone anyway."

I smacked myself in the forehead; these magi-political convolutions were giving me a headache. Nykur scooted his chair over and rubbed my back; I tensed for a pinch, or a roaming hand, that didn't come. He met my side eye with a smoldering look of his own.

"Nykur?" I asked hesitantly. "Why do you—why are you my sidekick?"

He reeled back, hand to his heart. "Sidekick? Oh come on, I'm at least a partner-in-crime. Or maybe I'm hanging around until you break up with that loser corbin."

"No, seriously. How do you feel about me—and *why* do you feel about me? Uncle Tam said maybe I, like, have a hold over you—the way Corriell does over my dad. But with my wild magic."

He blew his horsey raspberry and shook his head. "The original geis I had on me, from the queen, wasn't even focused on you. She sent me to spy on Tam, to see if there was a way she could get him to come back to her and Faerie. Once Tam figured it out, he pawned me off on you. I mostly stick with you because you're more interesting."

"But what if that's not all it is, and I'm controlling you? I'd really hate to think you don't have free will around me—that you're only with me because you're my thrall."

"You mean thrall with benefits, don't you? Because I'm okay with that."

I scoffed and kicked his camp chair legs out from under him. Laughing, he turtled on his back until I helped him up, and then he tried to lead me out of the tent.

"Wait," I said. "I'm serious about this, Nykur. I want to—we need to see if there is more to this connection between us. Do you think I can break it? Do you want me to try?"

"Meh. Worst-case scenario, if you do have some sort of control over me and we break it, you're down another ally when you need us most. Even in the best-case scenario, where there's no thralldom involved, we'd be wasting time and energy testing the theory. I vote we leave things as they are, and concentrate on fixing this wild magic eruption."

Of course, he would say that if he was under my control and thought he was telling me what I wanted to hear. So if I ordered him not to tell me what I want to hear and it worked, would it mean he was following orders or not under my spell any longer? Ugh, this was total brainhurt.

I sighed and returned to our previous conversation. "Why would it be a bad idea to call Lonan's Name?"

"If your magic is able to overcome the queen's once again, she'll be—"

"—royally pissed," I finished. "Okay. I'll let Lonan do things his way for a while, but I'm not promising to be patient forever."

Nykur winked. "If you last the night, I'll call it a victory. But yeah, you should give it longer. By the way, I think you'll regret it if you don't at least call your dad before you go."

I made a face but this time when he tugged on my hand, I let him lead me out of the tent.

I was surprised as anyone that my resolve not to complicate things for Lonan lasted through the night, but I was helped by an impromptu goodbye party. The Daweses joined us, and as they left after midnight, I took Daniel aside and asked him to promise to keep an eye on my mom for me. I didn't have much confidence he'd be much help if things got hairy (or scaly?), but then, my mom was pretty capable herself.

I also called my dad back, and with Corriell acting as a buffer and keeping us to safe topics, I wrapped up the convo with a warm feeling. And a little more sympathy, since I could see Corriell was worth fighting for. Maybe when I got back, we could have a talk about Dad's methods, though.

Mom was lying on her cot when I got back to our tent, but she sat up wearily when she saw it was me.

"You're leaving in the morning, then?" she asked.

"Yeah, but I think we'll have time for breakfast together first."

She was already shaking her head. "No, I have an early shift in the infirmary."

"Oh," I said. "So this is the last time we'll see each other for a while."

I didn't make it a question, since I knew there wasn't any room for negotiation. Her eyes caught mine and she made an attempt at a smile.

"Avery, about what you said back in the doctor's office...do you really feel like my work is always more important to me than you are?"

Put on the spot, I stammered, "Well...maybe not exactly more important. It's more like I'm your daughter, but your work is—your work is you. Like, your complete identity."

She opened her mouth like she was going to argue with me, but then frowned and looked like she was giving it some serious consideration.

"It's not entirely a bad thing, you know," I said, trying to soften my accusation. Because really, I would have hated it if she was with me all the time. Maybe we'd actually come to the best sort of compromise for each other's personalities, and I'd been too self-absorbed to see it before? And unable to see *her* before.

"And if you didn't have this, what would you do when I left for college?" I asked. "At least you have something to do, something to be, besides my mom. Some of my friends' moms get a little lost once their kids fly the nest."

She raised her gaze from her hands; she'd been twisting them in her lap while I did all the talking.

"But that's just it—going off to college or leaving the nest is a natural progression. But what happens when my daughter goes off to Faerie? And under circumstances like these. There's no guarantee you'll make it back for holiday breaks, let alone come visit me once everything is safe again. If you're ever safe again."

It was my first clue she might be scared she'd lose me to Faerie entirely; she must have been practicing her nursing poker face all this time. I sat beside her to give her a hug. "Of course I'm coming back. You're my normalcy in a shitstorm of crazy."

"Don't say sh—" She her cut herself off with a shaky breath. "Avery Girl, I need to know I haven't messed up our relationship permanently. That you will turn out okay."

"I'm already okay. Better than okay, okay? You do you and I'll do me."

She laughed in spite of herself at my use of her pet-peeve phrase; she'd heard it way too many times from hippie stoners who ended up in the hospital.

I could tell she was pretty tired, though, so I went to bed so she could. Later, I felt her smooth my hair and give me a kiss before she left for her shift. Even later, she managed to get away long enough to see me and Uncle Tam off.

I turned to wave as Mom blew me a kiss and I pulled Nykur in line behind Epona, heading out the gates.

As we veered towards Crow's Rest, we passed abandoned vehicles on the road: some completely intact as if the owners had decided to park mid-lane, and others with some degree of damage. A few with flat tires, a couple more with their axles broken from the weight of all the belongings people tried to bring with them.

One SUV had its roof peeled back like a sardine can, looking so cartoonish I had to ride over and peek inside, but I wished I hadn't when I saw the dark splashes of blood on the upholstery. Flies buzzed around a few blobs of something I didn't care to identify, and a torn, stuffed bunny grinned at me from the backseat.

I rode on, flinching at the "Baby on Board" sign still hanging from the back window.

"Uncle Tam?" I called. "Are you sure we need to go this way? It doesn't feel real safe."

He turned Epona's head and waited for us to catch up. "We needn't stay on the main roads, if you'd rather go cross country, but I'm not sure it will save time. My magic-sense is thrown off, and I can't guarantee we won't wander for a while until we come across an arm of Faerie, where we can travel much faster by magic."

"Oh, that's easy, the nearest magic is over there." I pointed to a ridgetop to the east. "Or wait—it kind of flickered out. Now it's coming from—" I turned to look the way we had come. Nope, it wasn't there anymore either. Not that I was sorry whatever attacked the SUV hadn't come back for dessert...

"I see what you mean," I said. "The magic's jumping around like Bobbin on Red Bull. I guess we stick to the road."

I tried to urge Nykur closer to Epona as we continued, but he shook his head and kept a healthy distance from her rear end.

"Hmm, been on the receiving end of those hooves before, eh, Nykur?" I felt a trembling in the horseflesh under my knees and I patted his shoulder. "I'm sure you deserved it."

He ignored my comment, and I was forced to go back to watching our surroundings. If it weren't for the silent houses we passed, it would have been easy to convince myself we were only out for a pleasure ride. But this time of year, I'd expect to see more people outside clearing the last of the summer gardens, or cutting hay in the fields for their livestock, or hosing off the patio furniture to store it.

Instead, the tall weeds drooped under the weight of their own seedheads. A lone windchime sounded from an empty porch as we passed a house, and I realized that any signs of birds or insects were oddly absent. Whether because they'd fled or been taken, there wasn't much life on this road. The street sign should have said No Man's Land, instead of the punny Haveture Way.

I started humming, and Nykur shied beneath me. "Hey, my singing isn't that bad."

Uncle Tam said, "Since when do you like Steeleye Span, anyway? Has my good taste finally rubbed off on you?"

"Huh? Oh, I wasn't humming Steeleye Span, I was humming the corbin version. The one about how Merlin was born."

"Ah, yes. Now that's a cheery song for a road trip."

"Well, I thought it was kind of sweet, from what I remember. Something about 'the sure touch of my dear is his solemn vow' and turning a cell to bower?"

"Yes, but the ending—tragic songmaking at its best..."

"What do you mean? Lonan didn't sing the ending. He quit, and that's when he got all angsty."

"Well, then, let's leave it as a sweet love song, yes?"

"No," I insisted. "I need to know Merlin's story before we meet him, and this is as good as time as any."

Uncle Tam didn't answer as Epona picked her way around a sinkhole in the middle of the intersection. I carefully avoided looking down into it as Nykur followed. I didn't need to know what had melted the asphalt from beneath...

Once we were clear, Uncle Tam asked, "How far did you get in the story?"

"After they'd lain together, the sun was going to turn him back to feather."

He nodded. "As you may have guessed, that was when Merlin was conceived. Typical of corbins and other such rascals, once his father had seduced the princess, he didn't come around quite as often."

Nykur gave a snort and a wicked-sounding whinny. I smacked him on the neck and said, "Go on, Uncle Tam."

"The princess was alone when she gave birth, and lost a lot of blood. Her servant had to go for help, so of course her father—the king—found out about the child. He was furious she'd disobeyed him once again, and that she'd ruined her prospects as a virgin bride as well. He dragged his daughter and grandson up to the top of the tower, where he meant to throw them both over the edge. In desperation, she called the Name of her corbin lover, and begged him to make good on his promise to take her to Faerie.

"The corbin heard, and convinced his brothers to cross over with him and try to save them. The flock of nine sped to the tower, arriving in time to see the princess and her child cast from the height. The corbin dove to save them—but in this world they were still only crows. Their wings bore the child to the ground, but had no hope to support a grown woman. She lay broken, and her only justice was that her father, driven mad by the corbin's vengeful spell, soon entombed himself in the tower with her body."

Served him right, and ewww. "But Baby Merlin had nothing but puppies and rainbows and a happy childhood ahead of him. The end," I said.

"I'm afraid not." Uncle Tam shook his head. "He stayed with his father for a time in Faerie, but it became clear the child's wild magic was too much for a simple corbin to handle. The boy was taken into the Court of King Oberon, who didn't know how to manage him either. The king took ever more strict and brutal measures to try to keep Merlin's wild magic in line; eventually, Merlin escaped back into the human world."

"Oh, so that's when the kittens and happy childhood kicked in." But Uncle Tam only raised an eyebrow at me. Dammit, let me have this, you old bubble-burster!

"Merlin didn't exactly blend in with the human folk. He looked about ten years old, but spoke of things which should be far beyond him. He'd seen too much in Faerie, wondrous and monstrous alike. Like a child, he used his magic mostly to get his own way, but his impulsiveness had the potential for great destruction."

Was it my imagination, or did Uncle Tam give me a sidelong glance as he said that? I gritted my teeth against a defense for my impulsiveness, since we'd already had that conversation and I didn't want him to get too sidetracked.

He spoke on. "Even those in our world who knew about the Fae could tell this boy was different, and possibly more dangerous than pure Fae. In spite of his magic's protection, the Fae and humans came together to destroy him, and nearly succeeded. He survived by his cunning alone, but it did teach him to be a little more careful about his actions—and about his place in both worlds. He eventually reconciled with humans and Fae, and acted as a go-between until he matured enough to set up the Border and its rules."

I let all the new info percolate in my head for a bit before asking, "Lonan said Merlin kept to himself after that, so how did you meet him?"

He chewed his moustache before answering, "After I'd been at Court for a time, I grew restless. Because I could see through the glamour, the usual entertainments didn't have such a hold on me and I was sick for my home and family. I would go for rides along the Border, searching for a way I could cross without Queen Maeve's knowledge.

"Remember, the queen beguiled me when I was hardly more than a lad—and only a raw country lad at that. I appreciated her lifting me up, and genuinely didn't want to cause her hurt by seeming like I didn't love or appreciate her, but the pull towards home and family was still so strong. It was...difficult to reconcile the farmer's son who I had been, and my new role as the consort of the most powerful Fae."

Even now, I could hear the tension in his voice— something I was all too familiar with. "Do you remember you told me once, about Dad: 'When you're in one land, you always long for the other. Never completely happy in either, no matter your ties to loved ones'? I'm feeling that more and more these days. Even through all I went through at Court recently, I still ache for the parts of Faerie I love." And one Fae who I loved.

He sighed. "That's the way of it. Anyway, on one of those expeditions along the Border, I came across a strange tree—odd even for Faerie. It fairly crackled with power; I didn't dare approach it and wheeled my horse about. Then a voice called out to me, and when I looked over my shoulder, a door had opened into the trunk of the tree.

"Now, I'd been in Faerie long enough to be wary of an enticement, but a man waved to me. And he— he looked so lonely. Orphaned and bereft, like I knew I must have looked. So I chanced it and took a meal with him, and over it we shared stories of the human world. I came back whenever I could get away, and those visits turned into long discussions on whether Fae and human interaction benefitted or hindered both.

"Merlin found a way for me to go home occasionally, and in return, I helped him come up with a plan to restore some balance between Fae and our human kin. You were born in the hopes of creating another source of wild magic to offset the queen's power."

"Well, I hate to break it to you, but your plan may have come back to bite you in the ass." I gestured to the row of kindling where houses used to be, beyond the half-fallen "Thanks for visiting Grantland, Heart of California's Gold Country!" sign. Too bad there wasn't a big enough defibrillator in the world to revive that heart.

"This wasn't the plan," Uncle Tam said emphatically. "You were supposed to take over for Merlin, and continue his work, which meant closing the Border permanently. Saving all the future generations from this torment you and I feel over where we belong, and letting humans set their own course without constant Fae aggression."

And this is where we disagreed—even after sitting through so many of these lectures from Uncle Tam, I still didn't believe Fae and humans were better off cutting ties completely. Rules to help keep things balanced were great, yeah, but what was going to keep humans from surrendering to our own darkness, without the occasional glimpse of wonder that Faerie offered? What destruction could we create, making the Fae look like benevolent leaders, if left to our own devices?

Because in spite of how comfortable I was becoming in my hybrid hide, I still identified with my human side more—but with a healthy dose of cynicism gained from my dealings with the Fae.

And, this conversation reminded me I hadn't asked Uncle Tam about why he'd argued for me to bow to the queen's wishes at Court. I wanted to ask him whether he was his own man, but would he give me a straight answer? *Could* he?

Nykur had told me to be suspicious of everyone. So maybe I should be watching Uncle Tam for signs of thralldom, since the queen had gotten her hands on him again.

Eww, that brought up some mental images I didn't need. I consciously pushed that subject out of mind and gave Nykur a nudge with my heels.

12

We rode for another few hours before we stopped for the night. The coy scent of magic had led us northwest of our course, and we'd set up camp near the ruins of Manzanita, an abandoned Gold Rush town.

Some faded historical markers were all that showed these weren't just random piles of stone and rotted wood, and I wondered if someday that would be all that was left of Crow's Rest. Not like "when the sun burns out" someday, but like "when Crow's Rest is no longer the magical equivalent of Chernobyl" someday.

Not even an outhouse had survived in Manzanita, and the evening started out with me splashing my shoes when I had to pee behind a bush. As if that didn't make me grumpy enough, we discovered we'd left all the hot chocolate packets back at the refugee camp. Uncle Tam didn't want me to draw attention to us by magicking me some cocoa, so I grudgingly sipped a mug of chamomile tea before crawling into my tent and sleeping bag.

I guess the sad story of Merlin's parents combined in my sleep with me missing Lonan, because nightmares overwhelmed me. A confusing jumble of images of Lonan with his hands and feet suspended by bloody puppet strings, and a miniature Uncle Tam being petted, catlike, in the queen's lap, plus more I couldn't—or wouldn't—remember, kept me turning fitfully.

Finally, sometime before dawn a velvet nose pushed its way into the crook of my arm, and I raised my elbow to let the night-dark hare snuggle against my ribs. With Nykur there to warm my heart, I was able to sleep until Uncle Tam roused me with some campfire bacon.

The bacon helped my attitude—come on, when didn't bacon help?—but my lower half rebelled at the prospect of sitting on horseback for another day. So Uncle Tam and Epona scouted ahead while I tried to walk the stiffness out of my muscles.

At first, Nykur was his normal equine self beside me, but then he did this weird thing where he turned his horsehead into a man's head. I did such a doubletake that I tripped over a rock and fell flat on my face.

"Are you okay?" he asked, as I scuttled away from his face, lowered on a muscled black neck. "What's wrong?"

"Nykur, that is seriously creepy. Get rid of that head and go back to all horse! Or all man or something."

"I thought maybe you'd want to talk, and it's awkward to carry these saddlebags and gear in man-form. So, this way we can talk—it's a compromise."

"If by 'compromise' you mean horrifying and bowel-loosening, then yes. *Please* be a horse, or a hare, or a man, or even a car—no more mashups of any of those, please."

He rolled his eyes, but blew a raspberry at me from fleshy horse lips. Horse lips on a horse face, as they should be.

"Thank you," I said in sincere relief. But I must have hurt his feelings, because he soon trotted to catch up to Epona and Uncle Tam, leaving me to walk at my own painful pace.

Truthfully, I didn't mind some time to do my own thinking. I wondered what my mom was doing right now, and whether the Daweses were making sure she slept and ate at regular times. And once I'd finished thinking of all that, my thoughts turned to Lonan—of course.

Why didn't he tell me any of the Host stuff? Did he not trust me, or maybe he was afraid I'd freak out about the queen's other plans—like the one which included killing Uncle Tam? And Nykur had said he'd been sent at first to find a way to get Uncle Tam to go back to her, so being willing to kill him must have meant she was really getting desperate. Or it was like Uncle Tam had said, and Fae don't feel love the same way humans do?

If so, was it true of Lonan too? He seemed to love me, but I had no way of knowing what that actually meant to him. Well, except for him giving me his Name—which I couldn't use right now anyway.

I scuffed in the dirt on the side of the road like a sulky five-year-old, coughing at the dust I'd stirred up. Dammit, Nykur had the water and he was way up—I realized I couldn't actually see either horse, or Uncle Tam, ahead of me. I stopped and shaded my eyes, checking to see if their shapes were lost somewhere in the morning sun. Nothing.

Turning on my heel, I looked behind me for a turnoff I'd missed in my fit of melancholy. But the road was a straight shot, behind and before me, and even though I'd gotten careless about walking in the middle of the road (no traffic), the horses had been mostly sticking to the softer shoulder—which didn't show any hoofprints here.

I paced forward, then second-guessed myself and turned to jog the other way. We should have set up a rendezvous, in case we got separated. Like the Lost Children room at Disneyland.

Failing that, I'd read somewhere to stay in one place if you get lost, so I found a shady spot at the bases of a pine and sat down. The sound of the breeze through the needles helped calm my overactive heartbeat, but I hated the thought of sitting here helplessly, waiting to be rescued. Uncle Tam and Nykur would never let me live it down—they might not tease me about it, but I bet I'd have a lot less freedom.

Maybe I should send up a flare, so to speak...I reached beside me and dipped my hand into the deepest shadows, coming away with a handful of darkness. I molded it into a tiny black horse, more sumi-e than origami, and it trotted in place on my palm.

I breathed "find Kolur Nykur" into its petal-sized ear, and my messenger gave a piping neigh in acknowledgement. Setting it on the ground, I watched my creation gallop off, laying a comet tail of dust behind.

I shaded my eyes against the heat shimmer and watched the inky horse shrink to a smudge in the distance. I decided to move to a bigger patch of shade and walked towards a billboard for Lacuna Caverns—but I hadn't taken more than a few steps before I tripped on something.

As in, full-on faceplant. The scrapes on my hands also complained with a fresh stinging as I sat up, but I couldn't see anything I could have tripped over. I was sitting on smooth pavement—okay, not perfectly smooth, since the county had cut back on the road repair budget—but nothing to make me splat like a toddler. Unless...

I squinted, doing my best to focus my Sight with some of the techniques Uncle Tam had shown me. *Breathe, relax my gaze—any break in the pattern will show up better this way—there!* The heat waves stuttered, right where they met the pavement.

Only, it wasn't pavement: the road dissolved before my eyes into a dusty, red-dirt deer track, hemmed in by scrubby chamise bushes. Now that the glamour had worn off, I could feel the small rocks poking me where I sat, and my dusty tracks led right up to the larger stub of granite I'd tripped over.

When I got to my feet, I could see from a gap in the chaparral I was about halfway up a hillside—but otherwise, I had no idea where I was. How far had I gone off the main road? The passage of time wasn't even a good measure, because if glamour was working here, I could have been walking a Fae road in a Fae timespan.

So—should I climb the rest of the way up the hill, where I can see better, or follow my own tracks back down? Well, considering whatever magic had a hold on me until a few minutes ago was trying to get me uphill, maybe down was my best choice.

But I hadn't gone more than a few steps downhill before the chamise on either side suddenly started thrashing around, like an octopus gone mad. Whippy branches blocked my way, and when I tried to push through anyway, the bushes ripped themselves out by the roots and grabbed me in a tentacled embrace.

And I didn't mean it as a metaphor, or simile, or whatever—the tiny leaves were now more like a sea anemone's tentacles, sticking and stinging wherever they latched on. Some of the branches had eyes on stalks, staring unblinking at me as the limbs immobilized me. I'd frozen in place because it was so damned creepy, but when I felt my body going numb, I started struggling.

But it didn't help. Whether I'd taken too long to react and they had a head start, or these were freakishly strong land kraken, I was being dragged uphill. What's more, blackness was closing in on the edges of my vision. I tried to summon my magic, but my powers moved sluggishly, like they were being tranqued too.

With my last bit of strength, I whispered, "Ennhirr," getting all the breathiness right. Right before I blacked out, I had just enough time to hope Nykur had heard me Call his real Name.

I woke with the feel of fur under my cheek, and breathed a sigh of relief. But...the scent in my nostrils was neither horse nor hare (both of which smell somewhat grassy on Nykur), but more musky. Plus something metallic—like old blood.

My eyes flew open on the heels of that thought. It took a second to focus, and I screamed at weathered bone only inches away from my face. The perspective shifted as the antlered skull turned sideways, the better to gaze at me from a dark socket. No, not completely dark—a burning red ember looked back at me from its depths.

I struggled against my captor, but hardly even rocked him on his horse. A rank exhalation from the Huntsman made me choke as he spoke some guttural words, and I didn't have to understand him to know he was warning me not to fight him. Truthfully, I was too weak to do much—even my short effort had left me exhausted and feeling sick.

"Please...where am I?" I whispered.

He pulled the reins and sidled his horse so I could see we were still on the hillside, but not alone. The other Huntsmen ringed us in a protective circle, and outside it the Hounds were clashing with someone or something I couldn't see. The dogs' enraged snarls, and cries of pain, carried in the twilight.

"What's going on?" I asked. Only the sound of breathing answered me, so I gathered my courage and spoke again. "You talked a second ago, so I know you can do it—do you speak English?"

More breathing.

"If you're not going to talk, will you at least put me down?"

I pushed on the Huntsman's chest, but quickly yanked my hands back. He wasn't *wearing* a deerskin shirt—he *had* deer skin, over a muscled human torso. I shuddered and tried to slither out of his grasp, only to have him tighten his grip enough that I gasped for breath. Once he relaxed and I could breathe once more, I wisely didn't try that shit again.

I got the feeling this one could communicate with me if he wanted to; he just didn't want to.

Mom was right about them doing whatever they wanted to—my measly human-wyvern self didn't have any say in it.

I sighed and settled in to wait him out, but in a break between dog snarls, I thought I heard my name called in a familiar voice.

"Nykur? Are you here?"

"Yes!" His answer sent a thrill through me, until he added, "But I can't get to you; the Hunt has you surrounded. Are you all right?"

"Mostly," I said, watching the Huntsman carefully to see if he objected to me hollering so near to his ear—did they have ears, if they only had skulls? "I think they're maybe protecting me from something?"

My captor grated his agreement. Aha! So he *did* understand me.

I pulled at his hands, which were like human hands but with hardened patches like hooves on his palms. "Are you going to let me go now? My friend is here."

His growl didn't sound promising. "If you won't let me go out to him, will you let Nykur in here with us? At least then I'd be having a conversation with someone who speaks my language."

He was quiet so long I thought he wasn't going to answer, but his rumbling voice made me jump as he called out to his brethren. They parted on one side of the circle, and Nykur stepped through warily. As big as he was, he looked like a child next to these guys.

The furrow in his forehead cleared a little when he saw me, but he didn't try to touch me right away. Instead, he bowed deeply to my Huntsman, staying down until some signal too subtle for me to notice. Finally, Nykur was allowed to grasp my hand.

"What is going on?" I asked. "The last thing I remember, I'd gotten separated from you guys, and then some weird plants attacked me. Is there something still out there that the Hounds are fighting off?"

"Yes—I don't know if it's the same weird plants that attacked you, but the chamise has come alive on this hillside. If you tear it apart, it just creates smaller creatures."

"Like starfish? They kind of reminded me more of sea anemones or urchins."

"Well, they're not like anything I've ever seen, and that's part of the problem."

"Couldn't it be Faerie manifesting here?"

His frown came back. "In a way—but they're shaped by wild magic, Avery. I'm not sensitive enough to tell more than that, but could you have done it? Even subconsciously?"

"I—I don't think so. Even *I'm* not that self-sabotaging. Now do you believe me that it wasn't my wild magic that caused the catastrophe or whatever you want to call it?"

"There's definitely something—or someone—in play here. And it's strong—if those were anything other than the Wild Hunt's Hounds, they would have fallen by now. But they're made of ancient magic, like their masters, and could keep on to the end of days."

"Why is the Hunt here, anyway? Not that I'm not grateful," I added hastily.

"They were helping us search for you, once we got separated. They'd been following us the entire time, of course, but keeping their distance as the queen had asked them to. When we heard your call, they outpaced me and reached you first."

He sounded kind of embarrassed about it. "Hey, they are the Wild Hunt," I pointed out. "You said they don't follow the same rules—maybe they skip through space and time."

He eyed the Huntsman holding me, but my "friend" made no sign he was part of this conversation.

Nykur said, "I don't know. I got here in time to see you wake up enough to start screaming—a sound like I've never heard before, and believe me

I've heard my share of screaming in Faerie. You kept it up until this one grabbed you and took you to the center of their circle."

I tried to recall why I had screamed, but my mind shied away. "I—I remember a burning, deep within my skin, and a feeling of weakness. But I don't remember any screaming, so I must have still been out of it." I cleared my throat tentatively and the rawness I found there convinced me he was right. "I'm still pretty weak, actually—I'm not sure I could even stand right now," I added.

"Well, that could be problematic, since we can't exactly all travel to Merlin's in a big ring of Huntsmen. Do you think you could stay on my back by yourself? Horseback, I mean?"

"Is it still the plan, to go to Merlin's?"

"Yes—it may be even more important to get you there, if you're being attacked. There are others clashing with magical creatures, of course, but yours was on top of a deliberate attempt to isolate you from us. Merlin has always taken steps to separate wherever he's living from both worlds, so it may be the safest place until you're stronger."

Nykur thought this attack on me was personal? That added a whole nother layer of urgency to getting out of here. "Okay—if this dude will let me, I'm willing to see if I can keep my seat."

The Huntsman let out a scoffing breath at my use of "dude," but once Nykur changed form, he gingerly placed me on the waterhorse's broad, dark back. I laid more forward over Nykur's neck and shoulders than I would normally, but otherwise I thought I could manage it.

"Take a few steps?" I suggested.

Nykur strode to the edge of the circle, before turning and making a smooth circuit. *So far, so upright.*

"I think it's okay," I said, and then turned back to the Huntsman. "Hugs all around, and then Nykur and I can be on our way?"

Nykur snorted, but he was obviously the only one who appreciated my sense of humor. Without any ceremony, the Huntsman shifted his attention from me and joined the fight with the hostile hillside. Okay, then.

I sighed and sat up straighter, reveling in the fact I wasn't pinned down under those unearthly gazes any longer. Hoofbeats approached, and I nudged Nykur to meet Uncle Tam and Epona further down the path.

After an awkward on-horseback hug, I asked, "Uncle Tam, do you have any magic salve in your bags? I still have some blisters from those plant creatures and could really use some."

Thankfully, he did, and while I spread it on my arms, he caught me up on the new-normal of magic and the ordinary colliding.

"Since I was searching for you, I didn't stick to the roads so much, and it gave me a chance to see how far the destruction has reached. It's...truly sobering. Those plants attacking you were not the worst of it, I'm afraid. I'm not sure if the damage to the new wastelands can be repaired, and the pace of contamination is accelerating. We need to get you to Merlin's as soon as possible—the good news is there is enough magic in this area now that we can travel in Faerie, and it should lessen the distance dramatically. But it will still be dangerous—are you up for a hard ride on Nykur, Avery?"

Nykur snickered, and I smacked him on the neck. "Grow up, you immature, ancient boghorse." Gathering my dignity, I nodded to Uncle Tam.

"Do you know where we're going?" I asked as Epona led the way.

"We'll start at Merlin's tree," Uncle Tam said. "That's the last place the queen has knowledge of his whereabouts."

"Oh." I forced myself to sound casual. "Are you still in contact with her, then? Or were you at Court?"

He frowned at me over his shoulder. "I haven't spoken directly to her, no. The Huntsman passed that information on to me. Why?"

Dammit, I would have asked the Huntsman about Lonan, if I'd known he had a direct line to the queen.

"I don't get the Huntsmen," I said instead. "Why were they helping me, when a few days ago they would have run me down?"

"They have their own agendas, their own...goals. I've told you they're old, and no one knows exactly how old they are. They've always been around, especially at important points in history. Whether they influence those points or just observe, I couldn't tell you. I don't think even the monarchs of Faerie know what to expect when they show an interest."

Hmm, did that mean they were showing an interest in me, or in this moment in time where something had caused the Border to crash? I hope it's the second one because I wasn't entirely recovered from those plants showing a personal interest in me.

Good thing Uncle Tam was in charge of picking our route, because I couldn't have managed it. Although I obviously was no longer screaming in pain, it didn't mean I wasn't sore. In spite of the salve, my blisters and scratches throbbed a techno-beat of misery. Nykur stepped as carefully as he could to avoid jarring me, but Epona set a cracking pace.

The changing landscape didn't hold my interest, either, and I could have used the distraction. Each breathtakingly gorgeous meadow blurred into the next one, broken up only by malevolent woodlands with grasping trees—the equivalent of taking the Faerie backroads.

I was on the verge of sleep-riding when a whir of wings sounded behind me. Nykur grunted as another weight settled on his back, and I found myself braced by a pair of familiar arms. Lonan was back! Some of my pain eased as tension left me, tension that had been there since he'd flown away.

"You okay?" Lonan's breath warmed my ear as he spoke.

"I am now," I answered, settling into the curve of his body. "I promise I'll kiss you properly once we stop, okay? For now, just keep me from falling."

"Always," he said. "And I'd rather have an improper kiss than a proper one."

"Mmm," was all I could manage as I drifted off to sleep.

I woke up as Lonan handed me down to Uncle Tam's arms. "Where are we?" I asked muzzily. The sky was twilit, but I couldn't tell if it was dusk or dawn. Lonan dismounted Nykur and they both disappeared into the dimness.

"We're at Merlin's tree," Uncle Tam answered as he cautiously set me on my feet. "It's abandoned, and looks like it has been for some time. Lonan and Nykur are doing a more thorough check, but it should be safe to spend the rest of the night here and decide in the morning where to go next."

Lonan reappeared and grabbed my hand, jolting me more awake. "Come on, I've picked us out a room. Unless you need to eat something first?"

"Need sleep more," I confirmed as I followed him. "Is there a real bed?"

"Yep," he said, with a wicked sidelong glance.

"I said sleep." As much as I had missed him, I wouldn't be good for anything without some more time to heal. It felt like I was getting over mono or something, not a magical attack. "Well, maybe chocolate after I wake up, but definitely sleep for now."

We paused on the doorstep of a gnarly oak tree, the windows in its trunk ablaze with a warm light. Lonan led me inside, and we passed through a cozy living room with worn, tufted chairs, and books stacked on every free surface. The gaping hearth was cold, but looked like it had seen centuries of use with only minimal cleaning. *Ugh, I hope Uncle Tam doesn't try to light a fire in there and burn the whole place down.*

Next, we walked down a hall, and I didn't even marvel at how much bigger Merlin's tree was on the inside. Was I losing my sense of wonder, or was it the exhaustion talking? Doorways led off into rooms full of arcane equipment and jumbled furniture, messy as a yellow-billed magpie's nest. So far, Merlin and I had more in common than our wild magic—we both could be guests on an episode of *Hoarders.*

Lonan's destination waited at the top of a tightly spiraled staircase, and but for a leafy canopy, the room was open to the stars spreading above. A double chaise, upholstered in what looked like plush purple fur, drew me like a pimped-out magnet. Okay, here was where our tastes diverged—I didn't think I'd choose to cover my bed in the skin of the two-headed monster from Sesame Street.

But it was comfortable. I sighed as I settled into the chaise, and Lonan climbed in to spoon me. His hand moved sleepily to cup my boob, and I exhaled in a feather-light chuckle. Even the sting of my injuries faded as I relaxed into believing everything was right with the world right now, and I dropped into peaceful dreams.

13

When I woke up, the sun was peeking over the lower branches of the tree. So it must have been dusk when we arrived, and I'd slept all night. Lonan was still sleeping, his arm folded underneath his head and his breath softly sounding.

Of course, my brain was awake and already spinning with anxiety. Maybe getting up would distract me. First, I reached to smooth the feathers flopping over his cheek; his violet eyes cracked open.

"Shh, go back to sleep," I whispered. "I didn't mean to wake you."

He smiled sleepily and pulled me over to him, but I fidgeted under his arm.

He sighed and said, "Unless that's the kind of squirming that leads to something better, go back to sleep."

"Sorry," I said. "I was just expecting...nevermind. You can sleep and I'll go explore downstairs."

But he sat up along with me. "I've been around long enough to know that when people say 'nevermind' like that, they don't really mean it. What is it?"

I hesitated; our last Serious Talk hadn't gone well, and I'd wished he'd never started it. But now it was me who would be putting our relationship under the microscope, and I couldn't help but feel I might regret that too.

No one ever said I was a coward, though.

I bit my lip and said, "It's just that...I know I was really tired last night, but I guess I thought that when you came back, I'd finally know that you were mine. Not 'mine' like a possession, but mine like...the other half of me, with no other commitments."

He raised a brow. "You were so exhausted, we barely spoke. How were you going to get all that from me merely showing up? Though that should count for a lot, by the way."

"I'm not explaining it very well—it's like I'd built it up in my head so much that I thought I would just *know*. Or maybe there'd be some grand gesture..."

"Are you asking me to marry you?"

It was obvious he was teasing me, but I turned red and stammered, "No-ooo, not that kind of grand gesture." No way was I ready for that.

"So then what, like a herd of unicorns bringing you a silken dress, woven from strands of their mane so it glows like moonlight on water? Or a thousand Fae musicians to play an unforgettable tune while I declare my love in poetry?"

He dropped his crooked tease of a smile and said intently, "Because I've done those things for lovers in the past, but I didn't mean them. Or, I meant them at the time but I didn't know they weren't real. What we have—that's real. Real and lasting, if we work to keep it that way. And if we don't let our families and all their maneuverings get in the way. Isn't that enough?"

And he was right, it *was* enough; but I was right too: those words *were* the grand gesture to set my doubts to rest. Or at least, the doubts about us.

A long, languid kiss later, and we were feverishly yanking off each other's clothes.

But then, he left off kissing me and dove under the covers. Laughing as his lips—or was it his feathers?—tickled my ribcage, I asked, "Where are you going?"

"Spelunking," he answered.

"What is—*ooooooooh*." My hands clenched on the blanket, a wave of sensation and magic crashing over me. Fragmenting my ability to think in words.

An alluring scent dragged me out of sleep again later. Chocolatey butter. Buttery chocolate? I opened my eyes to see Lonan circling a chocolate croissant under my nostrils.

I snatched it from him before he could yank it away. "Oh my God, it's actually warm. Where did you get this?"

"Merlin has a pantry to make a hobbit proud. It's magicked to keep everything fresh, and it's full to the rafters."

I swallowed a huge bite before asking, "Why would he go to all that trouble to stock a pantry, and then leave it all behind? What made him run?"

"I don't know. Was he running from something, or to something?"

"Good question." But such deep philosophical considerations vanished when I spied an entire tray of pastries, and a bona fide jar of chocolate hazelnut spread. It had nuts in it, so it was totally healthy and canceled out the other junk food.

When I finally laid back on the pillows, licking jam from a Danish off my fingers, Lonan started to rest his head on my stomach. But at my groan, he raised his eyebrows and looked questioningly at me.

"I love it when we cuddle after sex and junk food, but seriously, I'm too full. Raincheck?"

He laughed and pulled himself up to the pillows, laying my head on his shoulder instead. I reveled in the warm glow of satisfied appetites for a few minutes, but then my mind kicked into gear again.

"Lonan," I said, pulling away and sitting cross-legged. "Now that we have our own stuff settled, I need to know—are you still the Queen's corbin?"

He grimaced and said, "I'm not with the Host any longer. The Queen doesn't have that hold over me, and I can answer any question about it you want."

"But how will I know you're telling me the truth?"

"Have I ever lied to you?"

"Not that I know of, but you can be 'creative' with how much truth you share."

He grinned, unrepentant. "Corbin nature, babe. All that was done in the name of my mission, when I first came to Crow's Rest. I wasn't sure how much to trust you with, however well-meaning you seemed. Ask away, and I promise I'll be completely truthful now."

So I did, and his answers backed up Nykur's version of what members of the Host could and couldn't do. Lonan seemed to be telling the truth with no hesitations, until I got to one crucial question.

"Okay, the queen let you leave the Host—but why? She had some pretty strong leverage over me. And over you."

His face closed down, and he said, "I get to stay with you, Avery. Don't worry about it."

"And you're not spying for her or anything while you're here?"

"Nope, I'm my own corbin. Why so suspicious?" He tackled me backwards onto the pillows, then started nuzzling my neck. One of his favorite distraction ploys. When he moved to my earlobe and tendrils of his magic sped lower, I knew for sure he was up to something.

When Lonan had been selective about his truths before, it was a matter of asking the right questions. Obviously, he was going to continue being selective, as long as I let him get away with it.

I shoved him off the chaise, and he gave a crowish squawk as he hit the hard wooden floor.

"What was that for?" He asked, rubbing his elbow.

"For breaking your promise. Now, what did you have to give the queen in exchange for letting you leave the Host? Are we back to a firstborn child again or something?"

He started to climb back into the bed, but I stopped him with a hand to the chest. He squirmed as the heat from my magic came to the surface of my hand. Oh, yeah, I was getting pissed.

"Avery, it's nothing for you to worry about—"

"Let *me* decide. Lonan, if you're serious about me trusting you, you have to stop with these games and politics, at least with me. I don't have the patience for this shit anymore."

He sighed and said, "Okay. I had to promise Queen Maeve to serve her for three hundred years. Starting after you die."

"Lonan!" I lurched to my feet on the chaise. "What were you thinking? You just handed her a really good reason for me to die. As if she didn't have enough reasons already."

"No, that's the beauty of it—I required a geis in the agreement, so she's not allowed to do anything to shorten your lifespan. Who knows how long your lifespan will be; Merlin has lasted more than a thousand years."

I shook my head. "Of all people, you know there are ways around geises. You don't really have a guarantee of anything, except that you'll be her slave for three hundred years. What does it even mean, you'll be 'in her service'?"

He grinned, but it was forced. "Well, she said something about owing a debt to the Hunt, and if she loaned me out to them, it could cancel out the debt."

I collapsed to the bed. Serving the Hunt would be so much worse than what the queen thought up for him. "What would you be doing for the Hunt?"

"She's punished Fae before by giving them to the Hunt—they use them as prey, for practice. But I got the impression they can also possess Fae. So I could conceivably become part of their pack for a time, and be helpless against whatever they ordered me to do. But knowing how anti-possession you are, you probably think it would be fitting."

A corbin losing himself that way—it was total tragicomedy. "Well, in theory, it would be karmic justice for a corbin, but I don't want it for *my* corbin. Three hundred years with the Hunt, or Queen Maeve, are not worth however long you'll have with me."

"They are to me. For one thing, I don't think you'll ever bore me. You're too contrary."

"If I'm that contrary, how do you know I won't defy your expectations and crochet doilies with the hair from my house full of cats? Or something equally drab, like wearing nothing but Laura Ashley dresses from the vintage section of Goodwill?"

His eyes widened in mock horror. "Not the flower-sack dresses! I've changed my mind—can I sign up with the Hunt now?"

"No, you can't! You're not getting away easily, now that you're back with me." It was my turn to nuzzle his neck and send a shiver through his feathers. "Queen Maeve's plan may have backfired: now I have even more reason to live through this mess, to save you from your bad bargain. So we'd better get it fixed as soon as possible."

"Okay by me," he breathed, as I turned spelunker myself and ventured under the covers.

After a bath (thankfully, Merlin's treehouse also featured a bathtub with hot running water), I ventured downstairs to find Uncle Tam.

"Do we even have to leave here?" I whined. "We could totally just wait out the apocalypse in luxury. Oh, are those pasties I smell?"

Nykur and Lonan tried to get to them before me, but I grabbed two and they had to split one. Since my mouth was too full of pastie to crow in victory, I had to settle for flipping them off.

Uncle Tam rolled his eyes, like he always did when we acted our age. Okay, acted *my* age.

"As soon as we finish packing we need to be on our way again," Uncle Tam said. I hope you managed to get some sleep in between your hot baths and...other things, because we're racing the clock here."

I sighed, and Nykur brushed the pastie crumbs I'd expelled off his shoulder. Shaking his head, he went back to loading stuff into one of the bottomless saddle bags.

"When are we leaving?" I asked, my legs already aching at the thought of the upcoming horseback ride.

"Can you be ready in two hours?" Uncle Tam asked.

"Two hours?" Lonan waggled his eyebrows at me as he repeated the question.

"I—" I started to say, but Uncle Tam interrupted.

"And before you two jump back into bed, may I suggest you spend that time instead by going through Merlin's library, to see if he left anything? Books on wild magic, or a clue to where he may have gone?"

My face too hot to argue, I mumbled agreement and went looking for the library.

Lonan followed me and whispered, "Hey, have we made out in a library yet? Because we should..."

I laughed and held his hand, but once we found the library, I went all businesslike as I scanned the shelves. There were quite a few gaps, so Merlin obviously wasn't as willing to leave all his books behind as he was his food.

I pulled a book down at random, and was soon lost in a collection of fairy tales I'd never seen before, with titles like "The Thief and the Bottle Spirits," "The Bonnie Griffons," "How the Brownie Tricked the Cat," and so on. Were these written for Fae children? It would explain why the Fae always got the best of the hapless humans in these stories, ha.

The sound of falling books pulled me from "The Dryad and the Woodcutter," and I glared at Lonan as he bent to pick them up.

"It's like bookworm Jenga in here," he said. "Who would want to live like this?"

I scoffed. "If you're not going to be helpful in here, go make sure Uncle Tam and Nykur are packing the good food. If we leave it up to them, it will all be whiskey and porritch."

He shuddered. "I'm on it," he said as he left me in the library.

An hour or so later, I still hadn't found anything useful. I'd set aside some enchanting (literally and literarily) books, but nothing like a map with a helpful X labeled "Merlin hiding here," or a printout of Google directions to a secret lair.

When Uncle Tam came to check on me, I dropped another useless scrap of paper and asked, "What happens now? Did we get this far, only to hit a dead end?"

"Look, I've known Merlin for years, and we'd been in touch fairly recently. He'll understand how important it is to get you two together, and he will have left some kind of clue. We just have to find it."

I spread my arms at the chaos around us. "I've *been* looking! But he probably took all the really important books with him—why would he leave them around for whoever this rogue wild magician is to find and use against him?"

"You're right; that wouldn't make much sense."

"Make sense? None of this makes sense, Uncle Tam!" I was pacing now. "There's some psycho out there with wild magic, and a grudge against humans and Fae alike. They don't seem to care if people—and creatures—are losing their homes and maybe dying. The worst part is nearly everybody thinks that psycho is me! I'm probably on the FBI's and the Fae's Most Wanted List. But we're running out of time—if we don't fix this soon, there won't be anybody left to care that I didn't cause any of it."

I took a shaky breath. Whoa, that was a lot to dump at once—I guess it had been simmering for a while. It wasn't the only thing simmering: as my agitation rose, so did my magic.

I'd been really careful not to use it lately—not even to try to heal those sucker marks all over my arms—because my spells had gotten so unpredictable. But now the familiar sizzling/bubbling combo was rushing through me.

I turned my panicked gaze to Uncle Tam, mutely begging him for help. His own eyes widened, and he gestured for me to run. I obeyed, knocking into Nykur and getting a "hey!" as I barreled down the hallway.

Once outside, there was no longer any question of my holding it back. Even this amount of control caused the most intense burning, and the sores on my arms lit up like a swarm of blue fireflies.

Hey, maybe I could make that work for me. I concentrated on each spot where those venomous tentacles had latched on, and set the ache free as living beetles. As each scab became a scarab, it sprouted legs and lifted itself from my skin. I got an attack of the heebie-jeebies and had second thoughts about this method momentarily, but the relief throughout my body as the small army of glowing bugs marched away with my pain made it all worthwhile.

Doing a little happy dance—but carefully, so I didn't crush any beetles—I turned back to Merlin's tree. And that was when I noticed the glowing set of horse tracks, leading from Merlin's front door and heading into the tall grass of the meadow behind it.

My smugness about triggering Merlin's clue with my magic only lasted a few minutes into our journey, until my horse-riding muscles spoke up—shouted, really—and I got down to walk for a while.

Uncle Tam grumbled about losing time, but we discovered if I walked directly in the glowing trail, the surroundings blurred like I was traveling a mile for each step. The view should have been malleable anyway since this was Faerie, but the skipping-around thing usually only worked when you know where you want to end up.

But the speedway Merlin had left for me made everything fly by, literally. Like the legendary seven-league boots, but in the trail itself instead of boots.

Poor Nykur had trouble keeping up, though; Epona treated it like a stroll in the park, but the darker horse had to gallop full out to catch up with every one of my steps. We finally had him change to a hare and I carried him, with Lonan perched on my shoulder in crow form.

The novelty of the step-bluuuuuuurrrrrrrrr-step wore off after a while, and both Lonan and Nykur had a good snooze. Even Epona, with Uncle Tam dozing in the saddle, seemed to be able to move on autopilot, leaving me as the only one who felt like she was actually working.

Granted, it wasn't as hard as walking all that distance in real-time, but still, it was beginning to take a toll. I wanted desperately to stop for a rest, a snack, or even a pee, but my feet kept stepping. More like "The Red Shoes" than "The Seven-League Boots" fairy tale, ugh. There was nothing I could do but grit my teeth and keep going, if I wanted to get to the relative safety of Merlin's location.

The end of the trail came so suddenly I stumbled, with Lonan's claws digging into my shoulder as he tried to right himself. Nykur slipped from my arms as he shifted to his man form and steadied me. My face buried in his chest as I bit back nausea and a few exhausted tears. Oh my god, I never wanted to do that again.

"Are we here?" I croaked.

Lonan gently turned me around, so I could see we were on the shores of a vast lake, rimmed with craggy cliffs. Not far from where the glowing horse tracks ended, another tree spread its canopy over the water and rocks, and set in the cliff face behind it, a dark cleft beckoned.

"You've led us to his stronghold," Lonan said. "No other Fae or human ever knew where it was, only that it was a cavern lined with crystals."

"As long as it has a bathroom—and food—and a bed, I don't care about crystals." My weariness was even heavier now that we'd stopped. "Can we go in now?"

Nykur and Uncle Tam exchanged a look, and Uncle Tam said, "I'll go in first. He can be...moody."

I watched him anxiously as he walked away, with Lonan now also in his humanoid form and bracing the other side of me. As Uncle Tam approached the cave opening, a loud roar flowed out from it.

Lonan tensed beside me, but Nykur had already pulled me into his arms and run a few steps. So that was what the look between Uncle Tam and Nykur was about: "If this goes south, get Avery out of here."

But it didn't look like we'd need a backup plan, as Merlin emerged onto the grass and exchanged back-breaking hugs with Uncle Tam. His laugh, out in the open air, sounded less like a roar and more like a chuckling river. Nykur gingerly set me on my feet again, and I hung back to let Uncle Tam have his time with Merlin.

"So glad you could make it, old friend!" Merlin's speaking voice was nearly as gruff as his laughter.

But after a few minutes of chatting, Merlin called, "And this is Avery? Come here, girl—I never thought to meet another wild magician in my lifetime. I've been waiting a long time for you to come to me."

He enveloped me in a hug, but I wrinkled my nose at his earthy smell—literally, he smelled like soil and old roots—and broke away.

I covered my awkwardness with a grin as I said, "I hope you brought some food with you, because we ate a lot of it at your tree. You'll have to restock if you're going back."

Merlin guffawed, patting his own sizable belly. Although he looked aged, he still carried himself as if he had the powerful build from when he was younger.

"I take it you're hungry," he said. "After your long journey, your first thought is food? You really are a girl after my own heart. No need to worry,

I've plenty of food for all, and Tam Lin can catch me up on what's happening while we eat."

He gestured for us to follow him, and Uncle Tam, Lonan, and Nykur ducked into the dark opening in the rock face. I followed the sound of Merlin's voice through a dim corridor, and emerged into a cavern large as Queen Maeve's hall. As high as the candlelight could reach, crystals and gems twinkled along the walls, and the warm light made the carven stone benches and table look welcoming. The food overflowing the platters made it even more so, and my stomach growled louder than my bladder was complaining.

14

I slipped onto the bench next to Lonan, and filled up a plate, content to let the others talk while I stuffed my face. They were doing a great job of catching Merlin up on the mysterious Border implosion—explosion?—so I felt like my best contribution was to attempt to eat my own weight in some delicious, savory pastries.

And I'd made a pretty good attempt, before Merlin turned his attention to me. "What of you, Avery? Do you also believe your wild magic is the cause of this?"

I swallowed a mouthful of crust, caught off-guard by the accusation hidden in his words. None of the others had said my magic was behind it in their recaps. "I know it's not my magic, but it does seem to be wild magic. Could there be another one of us out there?"

He frowned. "I don't expect so, but I suppose it's possible. Wild magic, by its nature, is often behind the unexpected. What makes you ask?"

I filled him in on the tanginess of the other wild magic I'd detected when Flynnland disappeared, and how the tentacled creatures who had attacked me seemed to have been transformed by wild magic.

"And I know I didn't do either of those things, so that leaves you, or an unknown wild magic source."

My companions suddenly tensed, and I realized it was because I'd just basically labeled our host as a suspect in the worst magical disaster in human and Fae history. Uncle Tam started to sputter an apology, but Merlin waved him off.

"No, no, she's right to question me; I would do the same. At least she's considering the possibility there could be another explanation, which is often more courtesy than I received when brought before the Fae or human courts. And, like all of us, she is only concerned about stopping the perversion of wild magic. Let me assure you, my dear, I share that concern. I most emphatically want to end this. Will you join me in trying?"

"Do you have an idea for a way to stop it?" I countered.

He nodded sagely, his long beard lifting and falling with the motion. I had to stifle a giggle at the sight, and gravely nodded back.

"What did you have in mind?" I prompted again.

"If we join our powers together, I can guide you to a modicum of control. I can also draw on your energies to investigate how the Border's collapse has progressed. It could be key to seeing an end to this."

I had to admit, the chance to hand this off to someone who was more prepared for adulting was tempting. I mean, I hadn't exactly cured cancer with my powers so far—the only thing I had done completely-on-purpose recently was to score some free pizza.

But these days, "it sounds too good to be true" automatically raised my skepticism-antenna. "How would we join our powers together?" I asked. "And is it reversible?"

"It would require a ritual, similar to the one which bound my own powers to the Border millennia ago. I cannot say with all certainty that it will work, but with focus on both our parts, it should be possible. As it has never been performed in this way, I also cannot promise it will be reversible. If it ensures you cause no further harm like you did to your mother, isn't it worth the risk?"

Good point. It was a risk—even though Uncle Tam seemed to trust Merlin, I'd only just met him. The stories Lonan had shared told of another side to the wild magician, and how he could be vindictive. Having had a taste of what it was like to be on the receiving end of some of the queen's "justice," though, could I really blame him if he had lashed out in the past? I'd done the same, more recently.

I looked to my companions, and Uncle Tam smiled in encouragement. But Nykur and Lonan were keeping their faces carefully neutral, which meant this decision carried a lot of weight and they were trying not to influence me.

"Do I have to decide right this second?" I asked. "Could I, you know, sleep on it?"

"Of course. I'll show you to your rooms."

Merlin rose and led us down another corridor. "There are plenty of rooms here, suited to all your needs. Kolur, perhaps you would like to spend some time in the underground lake?"

Nykur's other name—but not his Name name— sounded odd on someone else's lips. For all I knew, they'd known each other for centuries. In any case, Nykur got a bounce in his step at that suggestion, and headed down the branching Merlin indicated.

Uncle Tam stopped at a room where a peat fire burned, the acrid scent bringing a smile to his tired face. Must be some kind of sense memory for him, but that smoke smelled like it would burn my nose hairs off.

Merlin continued on with Lonan and me in tow, and said, "Avery, if you wish, this entire cavern system responds to wild magic. You can shape a chamber to your desires."

He opened a door into a room featuring blank stone walls, crudely hewn from the solid bedrock. As I watched, it melted and reformed in response to my thoughts. With a few transitions, I was looking at the room I'd created for Flynnland, inside the Honeymoon Mansion, complete with its ginormous hot-pink bed and a jetted bathtub.

Some of the tension left my body at seeing something familiar, and at allowing myself to hope it was only the first of many lost things to be reclaimed. I took Lonan's hand and stepped inside, thanking Merlin for his hospitality.

But as I went to close the door, Merlin stopped it with his palm. "Avery, keep in mind that every moment you delay this decision is a moment that the Fae and human worlds lie under threat. Do not take too long to ponder."

Whoa, way to buzzkill the bath I was looking forward to. But I nodded, shutting the door and retreating from the world's demands for now.

I must have fallen asleep in the bath, because I woke to Lonan clumsily trying to dry me off. How did I even get over to the bed?

When he saw I was waking up, he handed me the towel. "Good, you do it. You were so out of it that I was starting to feel like a mortician or a creepster."

"Those aren't mutually exclusive, you know," I said as I took the towel and dried the ends of my hair. "How'd you get me out of the tub?"

"Magic."

"And you didn't think to, I don't know, use magic to dry me off instead of indulging your creepster mortician?" I demonstrated by channeling some magic to my skin, where the heat of it dried me instantly.

"Well, you're better at stuff like that. And now you're awake to do it—problem solved."

I shook my head at corbin logic and crawled under the covers. "Okay, I'm fed, I'm clean, and now I want to sleep for a couple of centuries. Come spoon me."

He did, and started to say, "Hey, Avery, tomorrow—" but that was all I heard before dreams overtook me.

It took the smell of bacon to rouse me in the morning. I munched on a piece while I tried to wake up completely.

"Lonan, I have to ask, did you—"

"Spoon you internally?"

I laughed, in spite of it being the most awkward, cheesy euphemism for sex I'd ever heard. "Yeah. I couldn't remember if it was a dream or a really nice surprise in real life."

"It was real, and it was great. Want me to demonstrate?"

"Later. I'm too hungry now, so is there more breakfast where this bacon came from?"

"Yes, but Tam asked us to come and eat in the Hall with everybody else; I smuggled that out for you. Apparently, rats and bugs have been getting into the caves now that everything's gone haywire, including Merlin's boundary spells, and our host doesn't want to encourage them to linger."

With a sigh, I stood up and stretched. "That may be a true reason, but Uncle Tam also probably really wants to talk to me about Merlin's idea. He never lets up—he's so stubborn."

"It's a family trait, from what I understand," Lonan said dryly.

I threw one of my dirty socks at him, as I rummaged in my bag for something clean to wear. After another bath that I managed to stay awake through, Lonan and I found the dining hall again.

"Avery," Uncle Tam said, "why don't you take a seat beside Merlin?"

Ah, so Tam *was* up to his subtle tricks again. He must think I'd be more likely to go along with Merlin if we bonded before we bind. Hoping to get a read on Merlin and whether I could trust him, I did as Uncle Tam suggested and sat next to our host.

Merlin didn't say anything right away, so I awkwardly opened with, "So, your tree—it's pretty cool. I could totally live there for a thousand years."

Everyone at the table went very still, careful not to look at Merlin. Who, when I glanced over, was gritting his teeth and gripping the edge of the table. Uh oh, what shit did I step in this time?

"Avery, that's not a subject Merlin likes to talk about—" Uncle Tam started to say.

Merlin waved off his warning and said, "No, Avery needs to learn my history, and through it her own. I will truly answer any question she asks."

I wiped my mouth with my napkin as I took in the tension remaining at the table. I needed the right question to get him talking if I was going to see beyond the legendary mask. "Um, okay, so your tree wasn't a happy home?"

"It was always intended to be," Merlin said. "I built it for my love and I to share, perhaps to even raise a family. She helped me with the design and details, and my magic transformed the oak into a comfortable, snug home. Little did I suspect, I was actually building my own cage. My lover, Nimue, was my undoing as she betrayed me; the Fae and humans came together to bind me to that tree."

I frowned. "Nimue? I've read about her in the Merlin legends, and that she betrayed you, but I don't know why."

"She claimed imprisoning me within the tree was the only way to save me from the others, who wanted to destroy me outright. When she could not dissuade them, she offered to help trick me, so that I might at least live out my life with her, as we had wanted."

There hadn't been any sign of a woman's touch in the tree when we were there. "But...with a fully human lifespan, how long did you actually get to spend with her?"

He closed his eyes momentarily before answering, "She did not live long past my binding. So I had my cage to myself, with no companion to lessen the loneliness and long nights."

"Except Uncle Tam, right?" I blinked as I realized what I had implied. "Um, I mean, not that he necessarily helped you with those nights. Not that there's anything wrong with that—I meant, you managed to find some friends, right?"

"Yes, some like Tam Lin came along and helped me."

"Helped break the spell keeping you there, you mean? How was it able to hold you and your wild magic for so long, anyway?"

"I was too weakened by the spell itself. It not only bound me to the tree, it bound my life force to the Border. As long as the Border stood, my magic fueled the laws which ruled it, and would have done so forever."

"Until the Border failed." I said. "That let you escape?"

"Yes, with the collapse of the Border and its laws, I was free to tread my own path once again."

Hmm, on all the crime shows on TV, that would be motive for killing the Border. But he'd already said, more than once, that he wanted to end whatever was happening with the Border. I didn't get the feeling he was lying, either about that or about the betrayal landing him in a tree for a thousand years.

Lonan turned the conversation to something lighter, and we all gratefully let the meal pass in small talk. By the time I'd finished breakfast, I hadn't made up my mind about taking Merlin up on his offer. I felt a lot of empathy for him and the hatred and fear he'd faced in his life, but I still had unanswered questions.

Since I think better on my feet, I asked our host if he'd mind if Lonan and I took a walk and explored the caverns.

"Help yourself," Merlin said in his gruff way. "Don't venture outside, though—my spells can't protect you out there."

I stopped halfway to the corridor. "What do you mean? Have there been more wild magic attacks since we've gotten here?"

Merlin and Uncle Tam exchanged a look, but it was Merlin who answered, "There have. As I said last night, I would have a better chance of investigating the attacks with your magic combined with mine."

I nodded to show I understood, and then practically dragged Lonan from the dining hall and down a random turning.

"Jeez, no pressure, Merlin," I whispered to Lonan, even though we must have been out of earshot.

"You did ask," he pointed out.

"Yeah, I did. That one's on me." I sighed. "Is he what you expected?"

"Merlin? I suppose so. I mean, he looks old, but I can feel the power coming off of him. He reminds me of an old bull elephant."

I laughed. "He does have a bit of a gut, but how would you know what an old bull elephant is like?"

"Hey, I've traveled more than you have. Ox-pecker birds are enough like crows for corbins to take them over." He squeezed my hand to let me know he was about to get serious. "But what I meant is, there's a sense of restrained power with the old bulls—like they still have the ability to go on a rampage, but their age and experience has made them more wise about using it."

"Yeah, that sounds like what I was thinking, too. Without the elephant comparison, of course, since I've never been that close to one. But just because he has the experience and restraint to use his pow-ers wisely, should I be adding mine to them? And how do we know having all that power won't change him?"

"We can't *know*—you'll have to use your best judgment."

I snorted—since when did I have a "best judg-ment" setting? And I knew first-hand how having more magic than you can handle coursing through

you can be overwhelming, and even Merlin was only two-thirds human. Maybe being mixed with
corbin wasn't quite so unstable as having wyvern in
the mix? He'd seemed sane, if you allowed for him
being betrayed by his lover and stuck in a tree for a
millennium.

Lonan must have seen my thinking-face, because
he left me to my thoughts as we wandered. But
without me concentrating on my magic, most of the
rooms we poked our heads into were the same kind
of blank-walled chambers my bedroom had started
out like. The few which had another format, like a
library and a junk room, seemed to resist me even
stepping through the door.

Not like they were locked or anything—more
like they were already saturated with magic and
couldn't take on any more. Hmm, did that mean
worrying about combining my powers with Merlin's was a moot point? That they were somehow
incompatible?

Merlin's rooms at the tree hadn't felt like this—
they obviously had been transformed in wildly
magical ways, but none of it was active by the time
we got there. Except the pantry, where the food
preservation spell still worked. Maybe it was a
normal Fae spell, and not wild magic at all?

Ugh, I didn't know enough about any of this to know if my guesses were way off-base. Which might be an argument for letting Merlin take over the world-saving for a while. Or at least asking him some more questions.

"All this walking and thinking is making me hungry again," I said. "Wanna head back to the dining hall?"

"Or...we could find something to do that doesn't require walking or thinking."

He pinched me hard on the left buttock, in case I didn't get what he meant. We had time for both—bedroom first, then the dining hall. But any afterglow from the former was quickly dampened when we saw Merlin waiting for us at the table, not even pretending he was there to eat.

"Lonan, would you mind if Avery and I speak in private?"

Lonan raised an eyebrow at me and I nodded. He grabbed a bottle of whiskey off a sideboard and saluted me with it as he exited to the corridor Nykur had followed to the underground lake.

"Don't let me stop you from getting something to eat," Merlin said wryly, after I sat and folded my hands in my lap politely.

I pulled a covered dish towards me, and lifted the lid to find a fresh batch of lasagna bubbling away. It smelled familiar...

"Is this from Vulcan's? The Italian restaurant in Crow's Rest? That shouldn't be possible. Unless...did you fix everything already?"

He shook his head, with what seemed like genuine regret. "I'm afraid not. Tam Lin brought me some of this lasagna once, and I enjoyed it so much I laid an entire supply into my magicked pantry. It stays as fresh as the day they made it, until I take it out and pop it in the oven. Clever, no?"

"Yeah," I said, as I moved some noodles and sauce around on my plate. Somehow, it didn't taste as good as I'd expected, since who-knew-what was still going on in the outside world. I still wasn't convinced either Merlin or I was the solution.

As if he could read my mind—or maybe just my mood—Merlin said smoothly, "We're not so different, you and I. Our wild magic sets us apart from human and Fae—and always will. Wouldn't you rather trust me, so that together we can reach our full potential?"

I dropped my fork, and leaned towards him. "Why did you have Uncle Tam create another wild magic child, anyway? To spread the misery around a little?"

He gave a bitter smile and growled, "You know nothing of misery, child. You think a few months of uncontrolled magic entitles you to judge me? I have lived with wild magic—and its consequences—for a dozen human lifetimes. I have made more mistakes, and wonders, than you will ever conceive of."

We obviously share that "zero-to-fierce in six seconds" trait, ha!

I nodded, refusing to be intimidated by him. Or at least, not to let it show. "I'm asking you again—why did you have Tam Lin create another source of wild magic, knowing all the problems with it?"

"Wild magic is as much as a blessing—"

"—as it is a curse, yada yada. I've read all the superhero stories, so I get that—and yeah, up until a few weeks ago the good parts outnumbered the bad. But why did you think the worlds needed another one like you?"

He frowned at me for a moment, but then gave me a grudging, faint smile. "Honesty, yes? Because I could see something needed to be done about the Border, with a more permanent solution for both worlds. Bound as I was with the Border's magic itself, I couldn't do it on my own. I knew I would need more wild magic if I wanted to find a new way. I feared I would never see my aims realized, until I sensed your wild magic beginning to manifest. At once, my faith was renewed. You can make that possible."

"You could feel my magic, from the beginning? Then, can't you tell if there's someone else out there who caused this collapse?"

He stroked his beard—OMG, so wizards actually do that—before he answered. "The one who is responsible will only be able to hide their involvement until our powers are combined—then, it will all come to light. The sooner we perform the ritual, the sooner we may have our answer."

I sighed. "And...we're back to that again. Listen, what happens if we don't combine our powers? Won't the Border try to seek out some natural balance again on its own?"

"Do you genuinely not understand, girl? The Border is no more—it has been destroyed. Do not let your fears make you blind to the truth."

"About those fears I have," I said, "they're perfectly legit. We could destroy the balance and the Fae could take over Earth, or permanent access to magic by big governments could supersize human wars. And probably a thousand worse scenarios I can't even think of right now."

Merlin stood up, the better to loom over me. "Both those things have happened in my lifetime, to some degree. However, the worlds are more resilient than you give them credit for. Even if the worst happens, as you see it, be assured that from endings come new beginnings."

I opened my snarky mouth to ask if he'd read that in a fortune cookie, but Merlin's intensity was enough to shut me up as he continued.

"You were born to usher in a new era for Faerie and Earth. From all that Tam Lin has told me of your sense of loyalty—of justice—I know you would not willingly allow countless people and creatures to suffer because you hesitated. But that is what's happening—another town has been overcome by Faerie, including a school where refugee families were sheltering. None of them have been heard from since, and if we sit by and do nothing, it will indeed get worse before it gets better. You are asking me for guarantees which I will not offer, nor *can* they be offered when real stakes are involved. So I am asking you once again, Avery Flynn—will you trust me, and help me to end this?"

Dammit, he really knew which buttons to push. He was right I wouldn't be able to bear the thought that more people and creatures were dying or disappearing, all because I feared the unknowns more than what was actually happening. When it was put like that, it sounded really stupid and shortsighted— not how I like to think of myself.

Maybe I knew deep down I'd have no other choice, because once I made the decision it didn't seem so bad after all. "Fine, I'll do it. Only, I want everybody else here—Lonan, Uncle Tam, and Nykur—for the ritual."

Merlin rubbed his hands together, and said, "That is easily arranged. I cannot thank you enough, Avery."

Apparently he'd had plans for this in place for quite a while, because things moved quickly. I finished the lasagna while he left to collect the others, and then we all tramped down a dark corridor to the appropriate chamber.

Even Lonan and Nykur seemed impressed by the setup, which featured smooth rock walls opening to the twilit clouds above. A stream of water ran in a channel in the floor, and fire burned on an altar. A roll call of elements: earth, air, water, and fire. Merlin already knew the spell, since it had been used to bind him to the Border, and his tree, originally.

He took my hands and asked soberly, "Are you ready?" At my nod, he continued, "For this spell to work, I must speak your Name, Avery—the Name which was worked into the spell at your conception. Do you trust all those here with that power?"

"I do," I said, then laughed nervously because it felt as solemn as a wedding in here. *If any of you has reasons why these two should not be joined, speak now or forever hold your peace.* "Can you—will you give me an idea of what to expect? Will this hurt?"

"It shouldn't hurt—but I can make no promises. Directly after my binding, I felt a profound sense of relief, and you may feel the same. Shall we find out?"

There was a challenge in his gaze now, and I felt my own stubbornness rise in response. "Let me know what I need to do."

"You need only be willing—and surrender your trust to me. I will manage the rest."

He began chanting in an unfamiliar language, which somehow felt ancient and dusty in the damp air. I couldn't follow a word of it, but did my best to stay focused. When he spoke my Name, *Tan*, it resonated throughout my bones. It was followed by a rush of peace and relief, as he said it would be.

My entire body relaxed into a trance, and even the tanginess crossing my senses wasn't enough to throw me out of it—*wait, why is this familiar? Is that—*

15

The next thing I knew, I was snogging with Lonan, his tongue nimble on my lips and face. It was only when his dancing tongue turned into a slimy tentacle, pushing into my nostrils and smelling of meat, that I realized I was dreaming. While I struggled to awaken, a panting breath moistened my ear—*hang on, that's real.*

I raised an arm, my hand flopping weakly to my head, and felt fur beneath my fingers. A stout body wriggled into my armpit, and a tail thumped out a tempo of joy. Through bleary eyes, I recognized the faint brindle pattern in the fur.

What was going on? My saliva did its best to wash away the taste, something like mushrooms grown in an old jock strap, lingering in my mouth.

A sharp nip on my nose brought me back to the present.

"Bobbin?" My voice was a harsh rasp, my tongue leaden in my mouth.

"Close," a voice whispered. "It's Daniel, in Bobbin's body. Keep your voice down."

"I don't think I could manage more than this croaking sound if my life depended on it," I replied, struggling to sit up.

"Your life may depend on it, so listen up," Daniel said. "We're going to get out of here, but you've been asleep for a long time and it will take a while for your whole body to wake up. We don't have that kind of time, so you're going to have to be like Westley after The Machine, and move anyway."

"Westley-after-The—oh, yeah. So am I mostly dead?" I wheezed a ghost of a laugh, but Daniel only jabbed me with his sharp, doggish nose so I'd keep moving.

I managed to sit upright, and then had to stop and rest. "Where are we, anyway?"

"We're in Merlin's caverns, in your room. We have to get out of here."

"Jeez, you've turned into a nag. Wouldn't it be easier to have Nykur carry me? Or Lonan could come prop me up."

Daniel jumped off the bed and ran to the door, anxiously peering into the corridor. He returned and tugged on my pantleg.

"They're not here," he said, "so we're on our own. Come on!"

His urgency finally penetrated the fog enough to get me on my feet. I swayed like a drunken sailor trying to find his land legs, but I was able to sail into the corridor.

"No talking from here on out," he said anxiously. "Just follow me."

I did as he said, and it took all my concentration to focus on the jogging dog rump, and to keep it in sight. We passed some turnings which looked vaguely familiar, but Daniel kept us in the shadows and the back ways. Finally, a light shone up ahead, with the soft luminescence of clouds and sunshine and the outdoors.

We needed to cross a larger chamber to reach the exit, and Daniel held me back, his nose twitching. When he judged it to be safe, he started across the space, with me practically stepping on his tail.

I could almost feel the breeze on my face, when a voice halted me in my tracks.

"Leaving without saying farewell, Avery? I am crushed."

Daniel actually scream-yelped, and I nearly fell as I tried to rush for the outside. I came to a stumbling halt as I saw Merlin leaning against the opening in the rock wall. Blocking the way.

At the sight of him, some primal instinct rose up in me and I reached for my magic to defend myself. Only...nothing happened, unless you counted me feeling even more tired. Unable to stop myself, I slid to the cavern floor.

"What did you do to me?" I rasped. "Whatever's going on, it's not what we agreed."

"Isn't it? You no longer have to worry about your powers getting out of your control, with them firmly in my hands. You were happy enough before your friend woke you up, weren't you? You can still go back to sleep, and find peace again."

When I stared at him blankly, he turned to Daniel, who was trembling beside me. "There was no need for all this subterfuge, my boy—not at this stage. Avery is free to go, if she likes."

"But—you wouldn't let Lonan leave. Or Tam, or Nykur," Daniel said. "They had to escape."

Merlin waved a hand dismissively and took a few steps into the cavern. "That was earlier, but things have progressed enough it truly doesn't matter now. My keeping Avery here was a kindness, nothing more. But if she prefers to spend her final days out in the world, then so be it. Perhaps it will give her more comfort than her own dreams could offer."

Either he wasn't making sense, or my brain was still too foggy to make sense of his glib words. Or were they threats?

"My final days?" I asked. "What does that mean?"

"Exactly as it sounds—but it's not personal. In a matter of days, every living, thinking creature will be no more. Thank you again for making it possible, and enjoy the time you have with those dear to you."

He started to walk back into the main cave system, but I grabbed his arm as he went past.

"Hey! You don't get to tell me I've possibly helped you start Armageddon, and then wish me well like a demented flight attendant. *What* is going on?"

His anger blazed—literally burning my hand on his arm—and he spat, "I owe you nothing! Leave here."

Without my telling them to, my feet moved me towards the outside. I fought it, I tried to argue, but I had no say in what my body was doing. Just like when I'd been so afraid whether I could trust Lonan or Uncle Tam if someone else was playing puppet-master, now I knew exactly how that felt. Helpless and utterly maddening, that's how.

Just as I felt the sun on my face, Merlin called, "On second thought..." and my feet froze in place. Now I wanted to move, to join Daniel where he ran in panicked circles in the dead grass, but I couldn't do it.

"You said you were letting me go." I panted against the force holding me.

"And so I shall. Once I have given you a message for Tam Lin, that is."

He threw a string of syllables at me, full of hard g sounds—in Welsh, maybe?—and then made me repeat them. I knew he was satisfied when I fell onto the ground outside, released from his control.

Daniel came and pulled on my sleeve, trying to get me to move, even if it meant crawling.

"Wait," I gasped, and turned back to Merlin's cave. "There's no way I trust you now. I won't give this message to Uncle Tam if it will hurt him."

Merlin shrugged. "As if you have a choice, child. It likely will hurt him, but not how you mean. Greater than any hurt, it will be his opportunity to die a free man. Do not deny him this."

And the rockface sealed shut, leaving me to kneel in the dirt with a frantic dogboy urging me to run. A zombie's pace—the old-school, slow kind of zombie—was all I could manage as we made our getaway. The landscape was truly post-apocalyptic, with dead trees and plants crumbling into dust as far as I could see.

Once we'd topped the next hill, though, we found a dark horse waiting for us. I touched my cheek to his and breathed, "Nykur, thank you for coming. But I'm not sure I can stay on your back—how far do we need to go?"

Muscled arms came around me, steadying me on my feet. "It's far enough that horseback is the best way to travel, since there's not enough reliable magic to trust my car form. Could you manage in a litter?"

At my blank look, he added, "Here, I'll show you."

Nykur took his horse form again, but a large box rode high on his back. Woven from bamboo or something, a cushioned frame protected Nykur's spine and skin. I walked around it and found a small door, which opened onto a cozy space the right size for me to curl up in. Totally genius design, but no way would this model have worked on a regular horse. Maybe an elephant?

I shook off my wandering thoughts and said, "We'll have to try, because I don't think I can walk."

I boosted Daniel in, and then used a group of boulders to scramble in after him. Sinking into the layer of pillows in relief, I barely felt Nykur's careful trot as it sent me to sleep.

I slept undisturbed until familiar voices called my name. Lonan and Uncle Tam's faces crowded the opening of the litter, anxiously urging me to wake up. Gentle hands helped me out of the horse litter, and I got hugs all around. Even Daniel was back in his own body, with Bobbin barking joyfully around our feet.

But I was afraid this reunion scene was too perfect; what if this was a dream, too? Maybe I was still sleeping in my cavernous bedchamber—or maybe in the outer chamber, where Merlin had been waiting. I started crying, sobbing so hard it turned into hiccups.

Lonan and Daniel seemed so stressed that they weren't much use, so Uncle Tam ordered them to make me welcome, and soon I was parked in front of a roaring fire. A cup of soup in my hands reassured me this was real, and I calmed down enough to see we were sheltered in the corner of a shattered stone building. A few lanterns lit the immediate area, but otherwise the starry night was unbroken by lights into the distance.

The soup warmed me through, and I was able to ask, "Are we in Crow's Rest?"

"No," replied Uncle Tam. "We're in the—a place everyone is calling Spellmeet. It's the zone around Crow's Rest, where magic and natural laws both operate."

Nykur snorted. "Or don't operate. They're both pretty unstable here."

I frowned, still confused. "So we're near Crow's Rest? Like, in Skinners or someplace?"

Daniel answered me. "This place is too far gone to say which town it was. No landmarks left, and it's not worth digging in the rubble for some street sign or something. We're at least—what, six miles east of the ruins of Crow's Rest?"

The others nodded, and the scope of the destruction started to sink in. "How long was I 'asleep' at Merlin's, for all this go to hell?"

"About a fortnight," Uncle Tam answered gravely. "It's been getting steadily worse—and spreading. But it all went to hell, as you say, as soon as Merlin took control of your powers."

"So...you know for sure the two things are connected?"

I didn't hear anything after Uncle Tam's "yes." It was too much to handle, so without a word I walked into the scrub, finding a log to sit on not too far from the camp. Uncle Tam told the others to let me go and I felt a flash of gratitude that they listened and let me sort out my thoughts.

And my thoughts were all pretty negative. Like, even though they were saying Merlin was to blame, it was actually me who had caused this. If I had genuinely tried to learn to master my magic earlier, if I had let the queen kill me in her dungeon, none of this would have happened. Everything I'd done, or hadn't done, was based on childish impulses, on what I wanted or needed. It took me handing over the entire world to its death for me to see how much I needed to grow up. If only knowing that now made up for everything which came before.

I still wasn't clear what exactly Merlin had done in the weeks since I gave him access to my powers, and in the years—centuries—before. What did he mean that every living thing would be "no more," and that I'd helped make it possible? From what I thought I knew about his history, he'd gone to great lengths to stop the endless warring between the Fae and humans. So how did he go from that, to being the instrument of destruction for all thinking beings?

I ran my fingers through my hair, accidentally pulling some out in my anguish. Lonan came to sit beside me, but I noticed he leaned heavily on my shoulder and it jarred me out of my own head.

"Lonan, have you had any sleep lately?" I asked. "Have any of you?"

He answered, "I haven't gotten much sleep lately while we were trying to get you out, but I'll be fine."

"No, really, you should sleep. I've had two weeks' worth, remember? You'll be taking a watch later, I'm sure, so you need your rest. Uncle Tam and I can talk."

Hand in hand, we returned to the camp and he crept into a bedroll without arguing further. Nykur snored from another pile of blankets, and Daniel's form was black against the stars where he stood watch seated on top of a boulder.

Uncle Tam huddled near the fire. He seemed unsurprised to see me, and set a cup of chamomile-peppermint tea to brewing without asking.

"So," I said wearily. "Catch me up. How did you get away from Merlin?"

He topped off his own mug of tea before answering. "It was obvious something had gone wrong as soon as Merlin finished the ritual."

"Obvious how?"

"You collapsed, but you weren't dead—your eyes were moving like you were in REM sleep. When we all tried to rush to your side, Nykur, Lonan, and I found ourselves separately wandering the cavern's tunnels instead. But all the tunnels eventually led us to the same dead end, and we were able to put our heads together then and make a plan.

"I used my link to the queen as an escape—since I was her consort once again, she had cast a spell to trigger if I tried to escape my promises. Any attempt to remove or destroy the pendant she gave me would return me to her side, no matter where I ran to."

"So much for not smothering you this time around," I muttered.

Uncle Tam gave a grimace and continued. "Lonan shifted into a blackbird form, and Nykur into a hare, like when you were following the trail here. I tucked them inside my jacket, and smashed my pendant to activate the spell. The queen's magic swept us all right through Merlin's barriers."

"Where did you go?" I asked. "And the queen's magic worked, even though everything else went haywire?"

"Yes, her magic seems to be intact. But the queen refused to openly attack Merlin, and by the time we'd gotten a rescue party sorted...Merlin had shut his barriers tight. We hunkered down to watch the caverns, but there didn't seem to be any way in or out.

"That is, until Lonan spied a rat coming out with some of Merlin's stash of food; we realized natural creatures could come and go at will. Lonan's and Nykur's forms don't count as natural, so they were blocked—but Daniel had been in Bobbin's body often enough the two of them are able to fit together nearly seamlessly. It took some convincing for Daniel to risk himself, but he was willing once we saw how destructive the wild magic had become in Merlin's hands."

I hunched my shoulders under the weight of my responsibility—not only had I failed to find a solution for the rampant wild magic, I'd given Merlin the ability to double his powers. "Uncle Tam, what do you think turned Merlin so—I don't know, mad, in both meanings of the word?"

"I honestly don't know—I thought I knew him as a kind man, a warrior for mankind. Something changed him."

Damn—if we knew what had changed him, maybe we could change him back. I sipped my tea in silence for a few moments, and then asked, "Uncle Tam, if Merlin gave me a message for you, would you want to hear it?"

He sat up straighter as he considered. "A message? It could be a trick."

"That's what I thought—but he claimed it would be your only chance to die a free man."

A shadow crossed his features, and it wasn't a trick of the firelight—I'd struck a chord somehow. "Aren't you a free man?" I asked.

"I—I want to say yes." He sounded like he didn't quite believe it, though, and like he hadn't noticed it until I'd pointed it out. And doubting it obviously troubled him. "I think...perhaps you'd better give me the message."

Before I could ask him if he was sure, I felt another phrase bubbling up. It was the message, coming out whether I wanted it to or not. My eyes grew wide and I pulled the neck of my shirt up to try to stuff it in my mouth, to try to stop the words coming out. But Merlin was right when he said I didn't have a choice.

In spite of myself, I leaned forward and repeated the phrase Merlin had taught me. When the last syllable died away, Uncle Tam's jaw dropped, and his eyes filled with horror. He leapt to his feet, pacing and muttering in Gaelic, and before I could reach his side, he threw his head back and howled in anguish.

"Shit! Uncle Tam, what's happening?" My voice was my own again.

He strode over to me and clutched my shoulders. "Don't you see? It was me, all this time! I did this! I made you, who shouldn't have been made, and so many other wrongs."

"What are you talking about—"

But Uncle Tam pushed me aside, and ran out into the darkness, wailing like a lost child. I started to go after Uncle Tam, but Nykur appeared at my side and stopped me with a hand on my arm.

"Let him go," he said. "I'm afraid he'd try to harm you—or himself—in his state, if you push things. I'll try to see if I can talk him down."

I nodded reluctantly, and took my seat by the fire.

16

After spending a few sleepless hours huddled by the fire, hoping every sound meant they were on their way back, I finally climbed Daniel's rock and told him I'd take over the watch. Dawn broke with no sign of either Uncle Tam or Nykur.

Lonan and Daniel joined me for some breakfast, but none of us ate much, since we were too on edge.

"What if they don't come back?" I asked. "Were you guys headed somewhere specific so they could meet up with us?"

"Our plan was pretty much to get you *away*," Lonan said. "And we weren't even sure we could. If Tam had any plans beyond your rescue, he didn't share them with us."

"Then, what? We sit here and let Merlin continue with his spells? That's not really my style. Isn't there somebody we should warn—or join up with?"

"Like who?"

"I don't know...somebody more powerful than Merlin?"

"The only one more powerful—or equal to—Merlin is the queen. Is that who you had in mind?" Daniel asked. "Last time you saw her, you were burning up her Court. If you think she gives out heavy punishments to her own people, what do you think she'll do to you when she realizes you're vulnerable? Do you really think she'll go easy on you now, just because you don't have any magic?"

At his words, I jumped like he'd poked me with a hot marshmallow-roasting fork. Beside me, Lonan turned a quizzical look my way, but I avoided his gaze.

"I saw you, Avery," Daniel said. "You were up on the rock trying to light a pile of pine needles on fire for like an hour. You can't do magic anymore, can you?"

The silence stretched, until I finally whispered, "No."

"Nothing? No magic at all?" Lonan asked.

I shook my head. "I've tried. I can't even find my wings—or my inner wyvern—whatever you want to call it. And I don't think my link with Nykur is there any more. I've Called him like a dozen times, and he's never ignored me for this long. I can't even heal myself." I rolled back my sleeve and showed them a series of shallow cuts on the inside of my arm.

"What is that?" Lonan peered closer at my skin. "Now you're cutting yourself?"

I tried to jerk my arm back. "Well, not *cutting myself* cutting myself—I only did it because it's the best spell I know by heart. The healing one Uncle Tam first taught me. But it's not working either."

Lonan sighed, and said. "Okay, well, we have some time while we wait for Nykur and Tam to show up. How about I try some spells designed to detect magic and magical abilities? Then we can at least tell if it's gone, or dormant, or exhausted, or what."

"So if my magic is there, but I'm—I don't know, enchantingly constipated—you'd be able to tell? But what if you messing with my magic somehow lets Merlin get his hooks into you too?"

Lonan chewed his lip as he thought about it. "I don't think that would happen..."

"But you don't know for sure?" I prodded, after exchanging a worried look with Daniel.

"No—but do you have a better idea?"

I sat in silence, and so did Daniel, before I finally sighed and said, "I've charged into a spell without all the information one too many times; I'd rather wait until Tam and Nykur come back. Let's give them some more time."

But in spite of me sounding somewhat rational on the outside, that wasn't how I felt on the inside. I wasn't just a member of the Blame Avery Club; I was its president. And two voices in my head were currently duking it out.

I was trying to do the right thing. I admit it was a relief to think somebody could take over saving the world for a while.

The right thing, or the easy thing? You had to ignore some red flags to agree to bind your powers to his.

Well, yeah, but there weren't any other real choices. Plus, I had no way of knowing what his real plans were—Merlin had centuries to put the gears in motion, and I was supposed to figure him out in a matter of days? He had Uncle Tam fooled, and maybe even the queen, so that's not exactly fair to expect me to do better.

The people who lived on this street before it was destroyed might have their own opinions on what's fair; let's ask them. Oh wait, they're dead, along with a lot of others.

ANGELICA R. JACKSON

I deflated—there was no sassy comeback for that comment. Merlin himself had said his plans wouldn't have worked without my powers added to his. Which made the end of the world my fault—again, no matter what I did. Tears sprang to my eyes, out of equal parts frustration and regret.

I crawled into a sleeping bag and managed a fitful few hours of napping before I woke up tossing and turning, grumbling about having to sleep on the ground. Lonan mumbled that my whining better not keep him awake and then rolled over.

Nearby, Daniel slept through it all—wait, if he was sleeping, who was keeping watch? There on the lookout rock, slouched a familiar figure. I gasped and climbed up to give Uncle Tam a hug, and he let me hold him for a few seconds before disentangling himself.

"I was so worried you weren't coming back," I said. "Where's Nykur? Tell me what happened—"

"I'm not here to stay, and Nykur is taking some time away," he said in a weary voice, like all his years had caught up to him at once. "I came back to tell you—I owe you an explanation, but I need you to let me get through it without interruption. I don't think I have it in me to confess my sins twice over. Will you listen?"

I nodded wordlessly at his plea; the lump in my throat would have kept me from talking anyway.

He nodded gratefully. "First off, you can stop blaming yourself for delivering Merlin's message—I know you *are* blaming yourself, Avery. It was indeed a blessing; Merlin was not lying when he said it was my chance to be a free man again. You see, I haven't been my own man since the queen stole me from my human life, and moreso since I met Merlin. After I met him at his tree, I have been under his thrall ever since, all unknowing."

He had to stop speaking for a moment as his breath caught, and it took all my willpower not to ask him questions. Or offer him comfort.

"The creation of a wild magic child, and the secret fostering of your magic—these were his ideas, but my actions. His theft of your powers was inevitable as soon as I gave you the pendant linking you to him, and that allowed him to manipulate your magic from a distance."

My gasp made him pause, and he gave a weak smile. "Allow me to anticipate your question. Yes, the pendants we had were forged by Merlin, so he could control and watch us from afar. At first, the pendant's job was to keep your powers hidden and concentrated. For the eventual joining with his own. When Drake destroyed it, it broke the connection, allowing you to thwart Merlin's plans of letting the Border unravel. But Merlin discovered the connection between your magics was still there, and through it he could fan the flames of your own magical flareups, to force you into seeking his help."

At the news that Merlin had been exaggerating my magical tantrums, I had to get up and pace a few laps on the top of the rock while I sorted out my feelings. A wave of relief at knowing not all the things that went wrong with my magic were my fault was overwhelmed by anger at how Merlin had used me so...so mercilessly. And Uncle Tam too, for hundreds of years.

That pang brought me back to Uncle Tam's side and I touched his chest, over his heart. Where his own Celtic knot used to lay.

He nodded. "The connection through my pendant was more powerful. He could act through me at times, and used my relationship with the queen to manipulate her and the Court as he saw fit. I had no awareness of these gaps of lost time while he occupied my body, but the memories have since come back with the breaking of the geis. I betrayed those dear to me—my family, even my queen when she was still dear to me. All that time, I was convinced I was protecting you and humanity, that he and I were going to create a lasting peace. But his peace comes at the cost of the end of everything."

I couldn't stop myself from breathing, "How?"

"The binding of Merlin worked too well. His life force is so entwined with every living creature in both worlds that he cannot die—as in, he literally cannot perish while the worlds live. He is not immortal, so each passing year has brought fresh agonies for him, both physically and mentally. Whether Nimue and those who bound him knew it could happen, I cannot say.

"He has tried every way to end his existence, and it seems it is not possible without taking all of us with him. Burning the last of his ties in some great, final conflagration fueled by the life force of every conscious being. Such a thing would have been unthinkable to the young Merlin, who fought so hard for human lives, but is acceptable to the mad, twisted thing he has become after many lifetimes of being used as a magical reservoir."

"That's—" I started to say, until I remembered my promise to let him talk and stifled the words into a grunt.

Uncle Tam barked a laugh. "Go ahead. I've covered most of what I have to say, and I'm surprised you lasted this long."

In my head, questions warred to be voiced—but did the answers ultimately matter, if we would all be space dust soon? Ashes on this Earth? There were so many details of Uncle Tam's story I wanted to question, wanted him to expand on, until I realized they weren't so important after all.

There was only one real question: "How are we going to stop him?"

"I do have a plan, but there is no 'we' in this scenario. Especially not without your magic in play—yes, I know you have no connection left to your own magic. Merlin couldn't risk it. I don't know if there is any real, human sympathy left in him, but I'm going to try to appeal to him. If I can get him to bind to me instead of all living things, then he can use my mortality for his own ends. I am very possibly the only person he may trust enough to die with, and I have to see if he will. And let my death sink him down with it."

I made a small noise, but he held up his hand. "Before you protest, know that I've had more than my own lifetime as well, and it's past time for me to move on. The fact that I've spent so much time in Faerie, absorbed some of its ambient magic, gives my death more weight on the magical scale—hopefully enough to accomplish Merlin's aim. If my death can have meaning, so much the better. I have not always lived my life with meaning, let alone with selflessness."

"From the sound of it," I said, "you haven't gotten to live much of your life at all. Don't you want the chance to?"

He turned his gaze to mine and I could see all the way into him: weariness lay at the bottom of all his brave talk of finding meaning in his death. Just like Lonan had commented last summer, about Uncle Tam wanting to end his life as a human man should, he was determined to make this happen.

Instead of answering my question, he got to his feet and said, "I must be on my way, Avery. If I stay, I will only get more maudlin, so I'll say my goodbyes now. I have no idea what the afterlife will bring for one such as I, but know that I wish a life without hardships for you from here on out. And may the worlds finally find peace."

He leaned in to kiss my forehead, and I said, "Wait, Uncle Tam, I'm not ready for goodbye—" before a wave of his hand froze me where I stood.

His whispered, "Goodbye, Avery Girl. I am sorry—for everything," before he disappeared into the scrub. Tears blurred my vision, and I couldn't move to wipe them away.

And it occurred to me that he had sounded so different, when he'd talked to me just now—was I hearing Uncle Tam's true voice for the first time in my life, and for the last time in his?

Once I thawed out, shaking in reaction, I paced atop my lookout rock. I was too overwhelmed to talk to another person right away, so I didn't go down and fill Lonan and Daniel in. I didn't try to follow Uncle Tam either, because he'd probably just freeze me again.

I did try to think of any way I could help with or without magic. And...I couldn't think of anything. I mean, what was I going to do—fall back on my only other skill and smartass Merlin to death?

It wasn't even that I'd become dependent on magic in just a few months—it was the scale of Merlin's scheme, so huge I couldn't imagine one person standing against it, whether it was Uncle Tam or me. I was going to need some major help.

As if in answer to my thought, the sunlight flashed on bleached bone. A Huntsman—*the* Huntsman—was standing in the distance and even with the scrubby trees and chamise between us I could feel his gaze catch mine. He seemed to be waiting for something, or maybe trying to communicate.

I could always ask him what was up, but he hadn't exactly been Mr. Chatterbox before. I was about to wave at him with a select finger and go back to camp when a thought occurred to me. Well, more of a memory, about Daniel saying there was only one magic that could compete with Merlin's.

With a sigh, I climbed down from my post—on the side facing away from camp. I picked through the rocks and pine needles until I found a trail. My friend, Silent Knob, waited for me, with the rest of the Wild Hunt arrayed behind, mounted and ready to ride out.

"You knew, didn't you?" I kicked at the dust, sending an angry cloud his way. "You knew there was only one hope against Merlin all along, didn't you? You could have told me."

I don't know how a skull could grin any more, but this one did.

"Fine. Let's go."

He mounted his horse and held out a hand to me. "Um, couldn't I ride a Hound or something? Or maybe you have a spare bicycle?"

He held out his hand longer. With a shrug of surrender, I let him pull me into the saddle in front of him. I shivered as a gust of tomb breath spilled onto the back of my neck, and we leaped into motion.

The scenery blurred into a muddy collection of streaks, kind of like I remembered from my first visit to Faerie. But this was more extreme and nausea-inducing—like going from impulse engines to warp drive with no transition. If I puked right now, would it end up in some other place and time? Like, if the Galactic President was in the middle of his inaugural speech, would he get hit with a vomit-pie-in-the-face, smack out of nowhere?

Before I could even let out a chuckle at the idea, we lurched to a stop, so suddenly I fell out of the saddle. The Huntsman's hamhand caught me and lowered me the rest of the way to the ground.

I wobbled over to a pair of guards and said, "I'm here to talk to Queen Maeve. Tell her I want to negotiate my surrender."

And then I hurled on their shiny boots.

Queen Maeve put me under guard before I could see her, but I was just grateful she didn't kill me on sight. After all, my fiery tantrum was the reason she was hiding out in a cave in the first place.

It was a beautiful cave, warmed by a roaring fire in the hearth and furnished with rich, um, furnishings, but still a steep fall from her Court and its charms. Judging by the coat of arms over the carven entrance, it must have been the home of the Oread family that Lonan mentioned she'd holed up with, after the flames ate even her throne. When they'd thought I'd been trying some kind of takeover.

So yeah, I was lucky not to be struck down when I showed up unannounced—and I knew it. I even offered up the Downward Dog of Humiliation bow she expected, without any expectations of my own.

When she released me from my bow, I said humbly, "Please hear me out, and you'll see I'm not a threat to you. I don't even have anything left to bargain with."

The queen inclined her head, so I took a seat on a cushion and told her everything we'd seen on the way to Merlin's place, and what happened after we got there. "To sum up, some things are totally my fault, and other things not. We both know, without my wild magic, you could kill me without breaking a sweat. Can we hold off on any punishments for now, and concentrate on what we're going to do next?"

I held my breath as she tapped a pointed finger-nail against equally-pointed teeth—a new look for her. That couldn't be good—the better to eat me with?

"You are fortunate much of your story has been confirmed by Tam Lin," Queen Maeve said, "else I might have destroyed you on sight."

My shoulders rounded as the tension left them. She not only wasn't going to kill me immediately, but she also believed me. "So Uncle Tam was here? Or, is he still here?"

"He is not here. He must have come to me before visiting you."

The queen looked up at my heavy sigh, giving me a canny smile as she said, "The lifting of the geis upon him does make one wonder if Tam Lin has ever been himself in our presence, does it not?"

"You mean like how I had to sometimes wonder how much Lonan was into me, and how much of it was your orders? How is that any—"

I took a deep breath; this was exactly the kind of shit that had gotten me into trouble before. And without Merlin continuing to egg me on through my magic, the anger issues were all on me. Time to prove I was trying to grow up.

"Enough is enough. I'm not going to keep this cycle of blame going," I said. "I'm truly sorry if you'll always doubt if Uncle Tam ever really loved you; for what it's worth, he's told me he did. I'm sorry both of our worlds may be ashes before we can stop Merlin...I could go on about all the things I regret, but it wouldn't get us any closer to a solution. So what are we going to *do*?"

Fingernails tapped on the teeth again. "I fear there is only one power which can derail Merlin's plans at this point, but it would require me to have an extraordinary amount of trust in you. It would also require you to trust me, and what is more, to be bound together for all of our lives. However short or lengthy they may turn out to be."

My stomach gave a funny lurch. "Whoa, wait a minute. You're starting to sound a lot like Merlin, and we both know how well that joining of powers turned out."

She shook her radiant head. "But the consequences point us to the solution, girl. I believe Tam Lin is also thinking along these lines."

"You mean, like how he mentioned he wanted to bind himself to Merlin? I don't think we should let him. We need to stop him—"

She tut-tutted, which was such a startlingly human sound that it cut off my words more effectively than any argument.

"I do not want to lose him either," she said. "But I am thinking ahead and I do not see many other solutions. You may wish to try thinking, rather than merely reacting, yourself."

Ouch, that stung. But it was true I'd only had that realization recently, about how acting impulsively was no longer working for me. And maybe never had; the consequences were just smaller then. I hung my head, humbled, before I nodded to acknowledge the wisdom in her words.

"I'm sorry, you're right," I said. "So, what are you thinking—are you going to fight Merlin?"

She smiled, all sharp teeth again, and said, "No, my child, *you* are."

I gaped at her, with my brain short-circuiting as several different arguments tried to wrestle to the front of my tongue. "But—how would that even—no magic...is this how you've decided to kill me?"

She let me get through my stumbling question and said, "Has Lonan not told you that I am the longest-lived monarch Faerie has seen in millennia? We do not generally live long as rulers before our rivals kill us off, since bloodless coups are unheard of."

Was that why she had such a fierce reputation? Because she'd killed off all her rivals before they could kill her? I hoped she still didn't see me as her rival, though since I'd never wanted to rule anyone or any place, that had been a one-sided rivalry.

As if she had read my thoughts—or maybe just my face—she continued, "Yes, I have had to be ruthless in my punishments, but what my predecessors failed to realize is that there must be a balance of absolute rule and the illusion of democracy. I say *illusion* of democracy, because the occasions where I have shared power or delegated tasks were mainly an opportunity for me to shift blame if it became necessary."

That fit with how she'd treated Lonan (a possible rival?) in the past: sending him to stop his brother, but not publicly acknowledging his mission. Making him think it was vital that he stop Drake, when she already knew that his attempt was just the first of many to come. Taking the credit for the discovery of another wild magician, but letting me take the brunt of the Fae grumblings about restoring the Border and its laws.

It was a necessary reminder that I'd be better off working with her than against her, and my expression must have once again shown my realization. She stared me down until my gaze dropped away; if I'd still had a wyvern tail, I would have tucked it like a dog.

"Now, if we may return to my proposal, did you not hear how we will be bound for the rest of our lives? If this does work, can you offer me any sureties you will not abuse that relationship?"

I frowned, thinking this through. What did she mean about us being tied together from now on? Would I be a slave forever to the queen and her own plans? I'd gone to a lot of trouble to avoid that very scenario, but here we were full circle at it again.

But it sounded like the risk went both ways, if she was worried about me abusing her. She didn't strike me as a person who casually allowed herself to be vulnerable—in fact, all the totalitarian things she'd done could be a mark of how unsafe she felt.

Unsafe in her self, not only as a ruler or leader of her people. Especially when everyone around her had their own agenda, their own questionable motives, for every interaction they had with her.

Over the last few months, I'd had a glimpse of what that would be like—but what if it kept happening over hundreds of years? Thousands? No wonder trust was such a precious commodity for her.

I sighed. I didn't really want to feel sympathetic to her; it was easier to hang onto all the things she'd done to piss me off, or to hurt me. Easier to travel those familiar, indignant pathways in my brain.

But maybe Merlin had felt that way, too, and if he'd been able to trust again after Nimue, we wouldn't have gotten to this point. Maybe helping others, trying to save them, meant learning to let yourself be saved too. For me, it could be the hardest lesson of all, since it meant setting aside all my defenses and trusting the queen completely. The same queen who was waiting on an answer.

Okay, time to drop my own walls. "I can't promise I'll be the perfect partner from day one. In fact,

I'll probably screw up a lot. But I can guarantee I will try my best, and wholeheartedly. Is that enough?"

She tilted her head to one side, as if gauging my sincerity. "I think it will do."

But she still hadn't been all that specific about what I would be agreeing to, other than it would leave us bonded for life. And it might possibly be the only way to defeat Merlin. "Okay, tell me more about this binding."

"I think perhaps, in this case, it would be better to show you. Your understanding will be greater then." She gestured for me to come closer.

"We're just...jumping right in? We're doing it now, with no preparation?"

She nodded, still waiting with her hands out-stretched. "There are parts which are impossible to convey in words. We must trust each other, or we will all die."

Survival made for a damn good argument. I exhaled my last reservations, and took her hands in mine. She was absolutely right—nothing she could have said would have prepared me for what it was like to take on her magic.

17

When I popped into view back at camp, I was met with ungraceful scrambling, for weapons in Lonan's case and for escape in Daniel's. Only Bobbin seemed to take my return in stride, with his enthusiastic snuffling of my shoes.

The boys demanded answers about where I'd been, but I had trouble focusing on just their voices. I was willing to explain, but first...

I went over to an oak tree, sagging half-charred in the ruined house's yard. Wrapping my arms as far as I could around the trunk, I pressed close to its corrugated bark. Warmth passed through me and into the tree, where it cycled back to my own body—like sharing a sleeping bag with a warm-blooded alien. Not an ultraprecise description, but I didn't know any other way to put it.

The life in this damaged tree was struggling to survive and thrive. Sap coursed like blood through its arteries and veins, ordered by the oak's slow-moving consciousness. I followed the quickening energy into the roots, splitting my awareness as I followed each ropey limb to its tiny filaments.

From there, I jumped into an earthworm, quiescent in the cool loam beneath the surface. *Not much stimulation there, Mr./Mrs. Worm...* Instead, I rose up through the branches and into the sun-warmed leaves, where I hitched a ride with a robin, winging over the devastated street. I, robin, cried an alarm at a slinking cat—*ooo, I bet a cat is interesting on the inside...*

With a shudder, I pulled back from the glimpse of feline wishes for blood and guts and feathers, and hopped into the mind of a lizard basking on a curb—

"Tan!"

My Name snapped my attention back to my body. It took some effort to separate myself from the tree, and to turn and face Lonan.

"Yes?" I murmured in answer to his Call.

Anger—and fear—spread from him like a radio-active aura. "What is with you? You disappear without a word, making me crazy with worry, then show up and act like a tree is a long-lost relative and ignore us. And is your magic back—is that how you healed the tree?"

I looked back at the oak, and it was now standing whole and hearty, stretching its unburnt limbs to the sky. In a way, it was a long-lost relative—as was every living creature—but my musing was cut short by Lonan's exasperated sound.

Instinctively, I stepped over to take his hands and offer him some comfort, but as my energy flowed into him, he flinched and jerked away.

"I know this magic," he blurted. "It's the queen's magic—how do you have it?"

"She gave it to me, of course. We agreed it's the only way I stand a chance at beating Merlin."

Lonan and Daniel exchanged a look, and it was fascinating to see a visible spark of understanding pass between them. Like, an actual spark. With the aid of Maeve's magic, I could see so many more levels of energy and life.

"She gave it to you?" Daniel asked. "No negotiations, no tricks?"

"I didn't say there weren't any negotiations," I answered, "but there wasn't much choice. Hello, have you noticed the world is ending?"

Lonan's lips thinned in irritation. "Yeah, we have—but why isn't the queen taking on Merlin herself? That's got to be a red flag for you right there. So what did you promise her in exchange, assuming you survive?"

It wasn't time yet to get into how irrevocably linked the queen and I were now. If we didn't survive this, it wouldn't matter, and if we did then the queen and I had plenty of time to work out what exactly it meant day to day.

"I'm...the queen's agent, I guess. She stayed behind to keep up appearances, since we didn't want anyone to know she gave me her magic."

"She never gives anything for free—"

"And she still hasn't—she's playing a long game. If I beat Merlin, she can take credit for the bold move of binding me to her magic. If I fail, no one will be around to know and it's moot. If I'm able to save everyone but not restore things, Queen Maeve can blame me and use it as an excuse to take me under her wing—or her thumb. She even has the option of using the restoration of damaged areas as leverage for her Favour."

"And she told you all this?" Daniel and Lonan exchanged skeptical looks.

"No, I saw it after we joined," I said. "Anyway, it doesn't matter right now. What matters is we stop Merlin, and all these questions are wasting time."

I grabbed a hand from each boy and tried to transmit some of my resolve, and also to physically remind them I had the queen's powers on my side now. Their palms shivered under mine, but some of the tension left them.

"So what's the plan?" Daniel asked. "How are you a match for Merlin now?"

"It's about connections. It's always been about connections—that's how the queen maintains her power, and how Merlin was bound to every life in the first place. We think Uncle Tam figured that out and is going to try to drag his former mentor into a true death, along with himself."

"Somehow, I don't think it's going to be that easy," Lonan said.

"I'm not going to let Uncle Tam sacrifice himself out of guilt. I'm going to use the queen's magic to turn Merlin's spells back onto him, and let him die on his own—no one else needs to go with him, if I can help it."

Daniel attempted to get me back on track again by asking, "So what's next?"

"Merlin has blocked himself away pretty effectively in his cavern, but I'm sure Uncle Tam has made a start on getting inside by now, and I can get us to Uncle Tam. But I can feel we're approaching the point of no return, where Merlin will have too much life-energy on his side to stop him, so we need to move."

"All of us?" Daniel asked. "What good will Bobbin and I do? I think I could be more help back at the refugee camp."

I turned to Daniel, ready to say he had a point, when I noticed dark threads stretching away from him. I was getting better at perceiving the connections between living things as actual, visible networks—so it was obvious these two threads were turning from healthy colors to thinning black lines.

Hurriedly tracing them to their source, I gasped and said, "Oh no. I'm so sorry, Daniel."

He was more puzzled than alarmed at my sympathy. "Sorry for what?"

"Your parents...I don't know if I can save them, but I can send you there." I picked up Bobbin and whispered in his ear, pouring out a little magic along with my breath. Thrusting the dog into Daniel's arms, I added, "Brace yourself. And make sure Bobbin licks your mom and dad as soon as you get there."

"Wait, what are you talking about? Are my parents—" His voice cut out as he disappeared.

Lonan raised an eyebrow in inquiry, and I hugged him hard. "Oh my God, it's so sad—Daniel's parents are dying. It's so stupid—they ate some home-canned food another refugee brought, and it wasn't cooked properly. They were trying to help stretch the food for the camp, and now there are people dying from botulism."

Lonan rubbed my back as I cried, and then he asked tentatively, "You didn't... Did you send Daniel to his parents' deathbed with no explanation?"

"No!" I sniffled and drew away. "I sent him to Agent Boulder's tent, since I thought he'd be the least likely to shoot Daniel if he appeared unexpectedly, and he can tell him what's going on."

"That's...messed up. I liked the Daweses—this is really going to be devastating to Daniel."

"I know." I took a shaky breath and added, "But there are going to be a lot more people dying if we don't get started to Merlin's."

We snuffed out the campfire, but left everything else where it was; we might need to regroup here. After leaving a "Gone to save the world!" note in case Nykur came back, Lonan and I headed on our way.

As we walked, I tested out my new powers by brushing against the invisible energies weaving through and around every living being. Some connections were straightforward, like the living mat of entangled roots from the trees, grass, and weeds, and the tiny things who lived among them. Even the flying birds had tendrils reaching from the sky to mingle with the earth-bound creatures.

The threads thrummed like a toddler on Easter candy, as energy flowed and ebbed. All those sparks of life inexorably tied—a strength Merlin was exploiting like a weakness.

I couldn't stop myself from trying to heal the damaged areas we passed, though I wondered at first if it would siphon out some of the magic in my tank. But each healed place acted as a hub of energy, helping its neighbors without any further draw on me. If there was enough time, life would surge back into these poor, blasted spots on its own. *If there was enough time.*

Reaching out for my connection to Lonan was as warm as reaching for his hand, and as comforting. I sighed, and heard him do the same simultaneously, as our moods synced. Was I controlling his mood, or were we really that connected? I was seeing things on both a micro and macro level, so it was hard to say.

Curious, I zeroed in on the thread connecting us, until I was so focused that I could see the individual bits of energy traveling along it. Bits of energy—that couldn't be right. Molecules? Electrons? I should have paid more attention to those *Magic School Bus* episodes. In any case, the pattern looked more like a one-way street than equal traffic.

With the most delicate touch of my mind, I adjusted the flow. The particles stalled for a moment, and then flooded me from Lonan's direction. I was filled with a sense of love, worry, fearhorninessamusementsadness—*whoa*. I pulled back on the throttle in my mind, and let things equalize a little better. Now it was like our energy was co-mingling, taking a moment to sway in time and sing a verse of "Kumbaya" before moving on its way.

I laughed aloud, and looked up to see Lonan watching me with a bemused half-smile. "You're getting better so fast—a natural."

"You could feel what I was doing?" I asked.

"Yeah, but maybe only because we already had a connection. Or maybe because it's Maeve's magic, and I'm pretty familiar with it. I've had it turned on me more times than I could count."

"I didn't mean to—"

"No, I could tell you weren't trying to intrude. But now that you know better, you'll do better, right?"

I rolled my eyes. "Sure, Oprah."

"Maya Angelou."

"Whatever." But my nonchalant tone was contradicted by the pulse of delight traveling down our connection because he knew it was Maya Angelou.

He winked at me, and I smiled before going back to my exploration of the connections. How far could I stretch my awareness, anyway? I followed threads leading to the west, until I could taste the saltwater lapping on the Pacific shore, and east until the dust of the desert parched the salt off my tongue. Every thing, every being, connected—except—

Except for a dead zone, somewhat nearby. The network of life told me it was hitting a wall, a circle of void, though new tendrils were even now forming to go around it. Everything shouted that it shouldn't be there, shouldn't be possible.

I hacked into the visual feed of a passing bird, and sent it soaring to the dead spot. I dreaded what it would find—another black hole thing, like the one that sucked up Flynnland? The true beginning of the end of the world? My body tensed as the rest of me flew, waiting to see into the dead zone.

My breath released in relief as the figure of a huddled old man came into view. Sitting on a log with his head in his hands, he looked harmless enough. Broken down and weary, yeah, but not like a life-force vampire or anything, as far as I could tell.

My bird made a querulous noise, and the old man looked up. His face—even with the added lines of pain and age etched into his skin, I knew his face.

On instinct, I grabbed Lonan's hand and tugged on the thread connecting me to the bird with my other hand, pulling us to that spot. The old man cowered under his folded arms as we appeared.

I knelt by him and said, "It's all right now. We're here, Uncle Tam."

"Avery?" His voice cracked, and so did part of my heart. This was not the strong, vital man who had helped raise me. As many times as I'd been angry with him for some borderline evil thing he'd done (or Merlin had done through him), Uncle Tam didn't deserve this.

I held my arms out to hug him, but my hands ran up against a barrier, sort of like the force field the St. John's wort creates. It didn't hurt for me to touch it, and it didn't seem to hurt Uncle Tam if I brushed up against it, but it felt solid and immovable.

"What happened?" I asked softly.

He rubbed his watering eyes before he haltingly answered. "My attempt to bind Merlin—I tried to make it so he wasn't connected to the rest of the worlds any longer. Tried to save everyone. But he was too strong for me. I'd barely started the spell when he discovered it, and he laughed that I would dare to take him on. When I kept saying the spell, kept at it in spite of his power, he stopped laughing and turned his anger on me."

I reached out to Uncle Tam, seeking a spell on him that I could reverse or transform. It was still like he wasn't even there—the dead log on either side of where he was sitting held more life and energy than he did.

"But what did he actually do to you? He made you old and..." I trailed off before I could say "pathetic," but he must have heard it in my voice because he gave a bitter smile.

"He set me apart from the worlds. Said my punishment is to watch as he draws the life from everything and everyone around me, and then to wander the wastelands for the rest of my days."

He shuddered. "I never realized before what it is to be truly alone—I've been lonely, but this is different. I can't feel the sun on my skin, or hear a bird's song as music—it all has nothing to do with me any longer."

And he dissolved into the most heartrending sobs. I tried to comfort him, but it was no use. Merlin had reduced Uncle Tam to the husk of a man, and on top of what he'd already done to him, this felt even more wrong than the lives that wild magician had already stolen in his bid for death.

I stood up to pace, gnawing my lip as I tried to figure out a way to beat Merlin. The queen's magic was itching at me, like something here was the key. If I could only see it...

For now, I had the beginnings of the plan I'd made with Queen Maeve, but I needed to make sure of what Uncle Tam had already tried.

He answered all my questions in a monotone. "He didn't know what you were trying until you started the actual spell?" *"I don't think so."* "And you used a variation of the original binding spell?" *"Yes."* "And he aged you to punish you?" *"No, I think the disconnection from the Queen's magic aged me."*

Every answer was another piece to the puzzle, but I still couldn't see the solution—until I nearly tripped over a strong thread of energy. It had an actual physical presence which I could touch, though Lonan said he couldn't see or feel anything. Despite Uncle Tam's claims that he was no longer connected to anyone, it led right up to his bubble of dead space.

The other end seemed to be anchored at the epicenter of Merlin's wild magic, to the east. How was this here, when Merlin had supposedly cast Uncle Tam out of the worlds? I carefully examined the tether, trying not to send too much vibration down it to alert Merlin. It had a familiarity to it...a taste. Or a smell?

Wait—this was what I had sensed when Flynnland disappeared. So, was the similarity something to do with my magic, or Merlin's? I sat back on my heels, thinking.

"Lonan," I called. He looked up from his experiment of throwing things at the force field to see if they'd get through, and I continued, "Didn't you tell me the queen had tried to get a spy into Flynnland, and they found something weird about it?"

He nodded. "Yeah, he said he couldn't find a way in there because there was no there."

"Even for a Fae, that doesn't make sense."

"Aunt Maeve wasn't happy with his answer either. I think she put him in the hedge for it."

"Typical. And that's all you know?"

"Well, when I was in the Host, I did see some reports on her desk once. It said further investigation showed that Flynnland was actually a pocket of space—a void—outside of the worlds. Like a bubble habitat at the bottom of the sea or something. That's why not just anybody could get in: you were the conduit."

I rocked to my feet. "And you're just telling me this now?"

"Um, a few things happened since then and pushed it out of my mind. Plus, you weren't exactly reacting well with weird news about your magic and I was trying to protect you."

"Oh. Thanks?" I managed to keep my tone at about 35% sarcasm/65% sincerity.

"What are you thinking?" He asked. "That Tam Lin is in a bubble like Flynnland?"

"Maybe...I mean, if Merlin was telling the truth that he wanted Uncle Tam to survive everybody else, he would have to do something to set him apart. The tether might be here because he has to maintain it in some way, like a power cable."

"But then why didn't Flynnland survive the first big blowup on the Border? Once you were back in your world, it disappeared, right?"

I deflated a little. "Um, I don't know...I wasn't specifically trying to do anything that complicated when I made it. I really had no idea what I was doing, and used my wild magic to create what I wanted. Maybe it wasn't stable enough, since I hadn't written it into the coding?"

Lonan made a skeptical noise, but I barely heard him because I was crouching by the tether, examining it closer. I could run my hand along it with no resistance, until I hit the barrier—but wait, there was something like an edge, where the tether disappeared into the force field.

I hooked my fingernails under it and carefully pried. It gave slightly, expanded, like a half-frozen Fruit Roll-Up. With some work, I was able to fit my forearm into the bubble, snug against the ropiness of the tether.

"Are you sure that's wise?" Lonan asked, breaking my concentration.

"No. I mean, I don't know," I replied. "What's the worst that could happen—I blow up the world?"

"Fair point."

"Uncle Tam," I called, "can you touch my hand?"

He leaned forward, listless, and reached for my fingers. We both jumped when he made contact, and I laughed at the jolt. But Uncle Tam closed his eyes and gripped my hand hard as I acted as a conduit, connecting him once again to another living thing. I felt his aloneness leaving him, and his hold relaxed.

As soon as I tried to withdraw my hand, his eyes flew open in panic and he grabbed me again.

"Uncle Tam, I'm sorry, but I need to try something. Can you trust me?"

After a long hesitation, he nodded and let my fingers retreat back outside the bubble. I felt around for the opening, and it didn't seem like it had collapsed or gotten any smaller without my energy holding it open.

"Find me something little, Lonan, like a—nevermind, I have something." I gently plucked a darkling beetle from its roving path, and closed it into my fist. Breath held as I stretched into the bubble again, Uncle Tam received my gift into his trembling palm.

He petted it with the gentlest of fingertips, and smiled. "Thank you."

Lonan cleared his throat. "Um, Avery, it's great that Tam Lin isn't alone now, but don't you think we should get back to stopping Merlin? Before, you know, everything burns up?"

But while he was talking, my brain and the queen's magic were working a mile a minute. No, like a parsec a second. Whatever it was, a plan unfolded in my mind's eye, and the magic gathered to fulfill it.

My awareness stretched to the farthest corners of both our worlds, while simultaneously reaching into the net of energy pulsing into my feet, through my body, into the sky...

"Avery?" Lonan's voice echoed through the reaches of space. "You look—you look weird. What's going on?"

"I can see it...It's too late to stop Merlin. He's been putting this plan in place for too long, and it's passed the point of no return. I can't stop it..."

I looked at Lonan, seeing him through a color cast of spinning nebulae. "But I can save most of you."

"What do you mean, 'you?' You need saving too, Avery."

But I was already reaching to expand the sleeve of an opening around the tether, letting the magic within me do its work. The opening of the bubble yawned wide, swallowing the energy I sent into it; Uncle Tam fell to his knees as the flood hit him.

"What's happening?" he gasped.

"It's the only weakness I could find in Merlin's spells: he set this space aside, so it would withstand his death and the implosion of the worlds. I'm going to take advantage of it by tucking the worlds and their lives, their energies, into this bunker.

"Some will still have to die with him—his spell will have to run its course—but I can save nearly everything. Every*one*."

Lonan and Uncle Tam both started talking at once, but I ignored them and focused on my job. As long as I didn't overthink it and get in the magic's way, a steady stream of energy flowed through the bottleneck in front of me, and into Uncle Tam's ev-er-expanding space.

It was like sending the worlds through some Willy Wonka contraption. As I watched, entire sections of the surrounding landscape distorted as they squeezed through the opening; once on the other side with Uncle Tam, they expanded back to normal and took their proper place in the lineup. Both Fae and Earth spaces alike. The process startled a few birds, but didn't seem to bother anything else.

The flow picked up speed, so I slowed my own perceptions, the better to track the progress. From this side of the barrier, the safe space drew the world through a straw, like chasing the dregs of a milkshake in a glass. I laughed aloud, growing giddy at the flow of magic through me, and by the bright spots of energy from each living thing as they passed over.

I eventually noticed the slowed-down figure of Lonan, looking like a mime in a windstorm, trying to get my attention. But as I let time speed up again, he stepped into the riptide of magic, which swept him into the rush of passing matter. He dwindled to the size of a blackbird—how appropriate!—and popped out the other side.

Uncle Tam grabbed his hand before Lonan was carried who knew where, and they collapsed on the rotting log to catch their breaths. But then he said something to Uncle Tam, and they both got to their feet and waved at me.

I could see their lips moving in a shout, but couldn't hear anything over the streaming magic.

"What?" I called.

They redoubled their efforts, but I still couldn't hear them. I shrugged, not having much attention to spare from the magic anyway. Finally, Lonan and Uncle Tam resorted to charades and I was forced to guess.

"You're...you're doing The Twist? You want a garlic twist? Wait—are you gesture-singing 'turn around, Bright Eyes?' Seriously—oh, you want me to turn around."

So I did, and discovered Merlin's stronghold was much closer than it had been, since a lot of the terrain in between us was now on the other side of the barrier. *That's not good—let's save that bit for last.*

18

I visualized the cave and its hillside as a boulder in a stream, and the rest of the worlds eddied and flowed around it. Cool—I didn't know I could do that. Or the queen's magic could do it, whichever it was.

But my smugness was disrupted by Lonan once again waving to get me to look their way. It was harder to drag my attention to him this time around; splitting my awareness between directing the magic and seeing what Lonan wanted was giving me a headache.

After a shorter bout of charades, he showed me some of the sections weren't fitting together properly once they'd funneled into the bunker. I guess taking them out of order to avoid Merlin's cave was disrupting their pattern or something;

some patches of Faerie were even jumbled in with stuff from the human world. Like, a corner of one of the Fae darkwoods was now smack in the middle of a city—was that Sacramento?

I strained my brain and the magic to its limits, but couldn't quite stop the effect, so I had to go back to taking chunks of the worlds in order. I'd have to take my chances that Ol' Beardie Weirdie wouldn't catch on—

As if on cue, Merlin emerged from his lair with a roar of fury. I sped up the flow of magic and matter—no time to be careful now.

"No! Do not interfere, Avery!" Merlin hollered as he approached.

I would have made some snarky comeback, but I honestly couldn't spare anything. Speeding up the flow was drawing more heavily on the magic and my own flagging energy, meaning I would have to do my best to ignore him and continue with my work.

Too bad Merlin didn't get the memo to leave me alone, because he started throwing wild magic at me—literal balls of contained magic—which exploded on impact. The ground near me spurted dark pools, or boiled with knots of thrashing black snakes: manifestations of Merlin's anger made solid by wild magic.

I sidestepped a particularly nasty batch which proved to contain magma or acid, but the next one he lobbed caught me on the shoulder. I screamed as red-hot tendrils ripped into my flesh, and a black rosebush burst from my skin. Roots of pain spread through me, pulsating along with my heartbeat. A rosebud swelled, stained in the center with my heartsblood, and I fell to my knees.

With a sneer, Merlin left me to his magic's mercy and turned to the slowing tide of the worlds.

As he strode toward the opening, Lonan and Uncle Tam attempted to plug it from the other side. They scrambled to stuff it with leaves, mud, whatever they could grab quickly. But although the exodus of landscapes had slowed, it hadn't stopped entirely and each of their meager barriers fell away.

Meanwhile, it was getting harder for me to breathe as the roots of the rose used my veins and arteries as pathways. It felt like only a matter of moments before my lungs and heart would be caught in a tangle of dire vegetation like one of the queen's hedge creatures.

With what strength I had left, I reached out and created a whirlpool at the entrance to the bunker—a spinning pit of energy so well-balanced nothing would be getting in or out.

Rebuffed, Merlin stalked back to where I knelt. He snarled, "You still don't understand. You still want to save what is not worth saving."

I shook my head, and fought off the dizziness. "You're right, I'll never understand why you don't think it's worth saving. There are good people— innocent creatures—who are dying for your ego."

"And what of the bad ones, the ones who are not innocent? Like the queen, or any number of tyrants making their citizens' lives unendurable? And don't forget the petty evils of everyday life."

"The petty evils of everyday life?" I laughed weakly. "Like when somebody won't hold the elevator for you? That's not enough to earn them a death sentence."

He scowled. "That's not what I meant—you are..." He sputtered to a halt, then gathered himself. "And what are you doing with the queen's magic, anyway?"

"She couldn't let both the worlds die with you any more than I could. Tricksy bitch that she is, she's still a thousand times better than you."

"Better? *She* is the reason for all of this; she is the one who made me this way."

"So take it up with her, and leave the rest of us out of it." But the fire was leaving my voice, and my defiant suggestion sounded more like a sobbing plea.

Seeing that I was fading before his eyes, he abandoned his Villainous Motivation Rant and turned back to the whirlpool. Through the haze of my pain, I watched as he tried a number of spells on my barricade: to freeze it, to push it aside, to burn it. So far, the queen's magic proved stronger than his, what with its more direct connection to the beings of her kingdom.

But I noticed something curious: each time he spellcast, the wild magic rooted within my body pulled towards him. Not so much physically, but like it felt...an affinity. What's more, it wasn't an entirely unfamiliar sensation to have that wild magic acting within me. No, more like acting *inside* me instead of within me—yeah, like that made sense.

But it was enough like having my wild magic back that I wondered if I could use it to my advantage. I reached out mentally to the wild magic taking over my tissues, and it seemed to respond in kind—until a surge of the queen's magic sparked against it, and the wild magic recoiled. I tried again and again, but got the same result every time, until the wild magic grew wary and was slow to respond. I think it only responded at all because some of that magic was mine, and wanted to come back to me.

And I wanted it back. But if these magics were somehow incompatible, where did that leave me? Maybe...if I wanted a chance of tapping into the wild magic, I would have to renounce the queen's magic? To set it free from me so it could continue to act.

But would that be a betrayal of my agreement to the queen? Would it return to the queen on its own? She had given me the magic to defeat Merlin, but part of our bond also demanded I care for the magic in my charge.

She had made it clear to me that the magic of the ruler of Faerie needed an anchor, a living being to hold together the bonds of the ruler's own magic and that of the kingdom and its citizens, or it would dissipate. That was why she couldn't share just some of it with me; she had to hand over the entire bundle, with her own magic included.

It was only now I'd experienced the vastness of the connections that I understood the extent of the gift she'd entrusted me with. And how she'd left herself completely vulnerable in the process, relying on me to win this battle and to restore her magic intact. But I couldn't if I died with the magic still anchored to me.

Plus, Merlin's progress on attacking my barricade—he'd managed to create a few spikes that held the whirlpool in place for a few seconds before they shattered—showed his wild magic could eventually overcome the queen's magic. Leaving us right smack in the middle of the fiery Armaggedon scenario once again. Not much of a choice after all, especially since I was already losing to this parasitic rose.

I drew on the queen's magic for the strength to reach out along all my connections, searching for a suitable host for this gift. My strongest ties were to Lonan and Uncle Tam, so my awareness found its own way over the barricade, through the opening and into the bunker, and to them.

The magic itself would have to decide, and I thought Lonan would be the obvious choice. After all, he was the queen's blood, and he was young and strong, with a familiarity of how her magic worked. After a swirl of indecision, it gravitated instead to Uncle Tam.

Maybe it recognized its queen still had feelings for him, or maybe it had already spent so much time keeping him young that he felt familiar to it. Or maybe his lifelong determination—hijacked by Merlin's plans—to do right by humans and Fae convinced it he was the best champion.

In any case, I could feel the moment the magic decided to choose him over me, its dying host. As the queen's magic flowed away, it left me bereft and so alone.

Gone was the interconnected web of life which had filled and surrounded me, and the wild magic rushed in to fill the void. I gasped at the renewed onslaught, and then I couldn't breathe at all as it seized my lungs and heart.

As things grew dark, I reached for the lifeline of my wild magic intertwined with Merlin's, as his cursed rose sapped the last of my strength. I had nearly given up hope, when I felt the gentlest nudge, like from a hesitant kitten's nose.

With the mental equivalent of baby talk, I convinced my magic to stay, and join with me once again. I sighed as every thorny root inside my body instead became a reservoir of power, as my wild magic found its home within me.

Merlin was too absorbed to notice the defection of my wild magic, so it gave me time to really settle into my own power again. How could I have ever wished this gone, back when it first made itself known? I drew myself up and flexed all my magical muscles.

Before I could go all heroic though, a shining figure stepped out of the bunker. Merlin and I actually had to shade our eyes, the light was so bright from his armor. It was Uncle Tam, gone all Galadriel and "they all shall love me and despair." And he was not happy with his former geis-master, that much was obvious.

Merlin fell to his knees under an onslaught of magic, but still he bared his teeth and struggled. The fight between them hit a stalemate as neither was able to overpower the other, but also didn't have any energy to spare to thwart the other's spells once and for all.

Uncle Tam would need my help.

My wild magic lashed out at Merlin's weakened form, but with a wave of his hand Uncle Tam unexpectedly swept me aside. My wings unfurled and kept me from hitting the ground with the full impact, but even so I ate some grass and dirt.

This time I approached with more caution, and with the threat of my magic tucked away. "Uncle Tam! I'm trying to help!"

He turned his gaze to me, and it was like the sun going behind a cloud as he dimmed down the wattage. Now he looked merely like an illuminated angel, instead of a god.

Wow, did I look like that when I had the queen's magic? I wish I'd gotten selfies.

Uncle Tam's voice snapped me back to the current crisis. "Avery...you should be with Lonan."

"No. You need my help—if the queen's magic was strong enough on its own, Merlin would never have been able to get this far with his plans. We're going to have to use wild magic against him, too."

As if to prove my point, Merlin took advantage of Uncle Tam's distraction and surged to his feet. I hit him with my wild magic, curling tendrils of thorny rose vines around the old wizard. Not quite what I meant to do—could the rose which had taken root in me be shaping my magic now? It could have been worse: he could have gotten me with the snakes, and I'd be stuck with those.

While Merlin struggled with the roses entangling him, Uncle Tam let me approach him this time. Merlin snapped at me like an abused chihuahua as I passed, but he couldn't move from his place.

"Okay, so what's the plan here?" I asked Uncle Tam.

"We stop him," he said through gritted teeth. I knew from experience how difficult it was to manage the queen's magic plus a conversation, so I filled in some blanks for him.

"Well, that's not so much a plan as a wish—I felt it before, you know. The worlds are already doomed to a fiery death, like a lit fuse. We can't stop it this point, and all we can hope for is to lessen the damage. So how do we do that?"

Uncle Tam didn't answer, but his attention turned inward so I assumed he was communing with the queen's magic. While I waited, I snuck a glance at the bunker—the pace of the worlds' flow had picked up again under Uncle Tam's hand, so Lonan couldn't have exited if he'd tried. It would be like a salmon fry trying to swim upstream in a fire hose's spray. Instead, we waved at each other through the barrier and I blew him a kiss.

Finally, Uncle Tam spoke. "Come take my hand, Avery."

I stepped closer and did as he said. When his hand grasped mine, I nearly fell to my knees. The queen's magic rushed into me, sussing out every corner of my body. Then, like when I had experimented while holding Lonan's hand, Uncle Tam pulled back and let the magic hit more of a balance.

Now my wild magic and the queen's magic intertwined like otters at play. Not sparking against each other, or fighting for dominance, but forming a harmonious whole stronger than any separate magic. Everything now streamed into the bunker smoothly and efficiently, while Merlin's magical network simultaneously disintegrated.

Merlin's struggles quieted as our combined magic overwhelmed him. With the aid of the queen's magic, I saw all the threads of life he'd gathered to him falling away. Each one meant a soul spared from sharing his funeral pyre.

I wanted to pump my fist in victory, but didn't want to throw Uncle Tam off; he was doing most of the driving, so I helped by cleaning up a few things around the edges of the real-estate exchange. Things like an outbuilding that didn't make it through the same time as the rest of its farm, and making sure families of raccoons stayed together (I'd seen a nature show about the bonds in raccoon families, so I knew how important it was).

Patrolling the edges was how I noticed it: another smaller rope leading from the worlds into the bunker. The main coil of energy was how Uncle Tam was getting the worlds into their new home; in fact, there was more mass in the bunker than out here, I could tell. But then there was also this other cable snaking from Merlin into the bunker, and somehow this one seemed newer. Fleshier.

I carefully got Uncle Tam's attention and pointed it out. His brow furrowed as he let the queen's magic play along it. We were still connected by our hands, so I knew as soon as he did, without him saying anything.

Even though we were incredibly strong together, as long as the portal into the bunker was open, Merlin could still insinuate himself into the "saved" portions of the worlds. We hadn't permanently saved anyone at all, unless we were willing to cut ties between this original dimension and the new one. This new thread was a line of metaphorical gunpowder.

Closing the portal would leave whoever was on this side to perish with Merlin, and how did you make a choice like that? The characters in *The Hunger Games* had decades to get used to the idea of "tributes," and even then they rejected the notion that a random choice determined who died.

This selection would have to be even more stark and arbitrary—and wouldn't only affect me and Uncle Tam if we stayed. We'd also have to make the decision for all the creatures who hadn't gone through the portal yet. Should we even be considering it, knowing that on one side of the line you lived, and on the other you died because a maniac needed kindling? Some of the zones out here were dead zones, like the fuse had already burned through them. It was a no-brainer not to feed those through.

But, I could feel how close we were to running out of time. There wasn't any time to negotiate with fate. Or even yell at it.

I met Uncle Tam's eyes and acknowledged what he already knew: we were going to have to close the portal. Like, now. And then probably die.

I took Uncle Tam's other hand in mine, so we had two points for our magic to join. My hair whipped around like inside a tornado, blinding me. Parts of both worlds swirled past as we tried to send as much as we could through the portal before we closed it. From what I could tell through my connection to Uncle Tam and the queen's magic, it was working, but there would still be places and beings stranded on this side.

Oh no—that whale is too far away, it will never make it—and Yosemite! What kind of Earth will it be without a Yosemite? But even in the time it had taken me to anguish over it, a thousand other places and creatures had made it to safety. Fae and Earthen creatures who maybe didn't even know it had happened.

My mind couldn't keep up with the magic and I felt buffeted and battered—but somewhat at peace, since I knew I was making a difference.

I had so resigned myself to making this sacrifice that when a complete absence of noise and movement hit me, I thought *This is it—this is death.* But hands on my shoulders made my eyes fly open, and I found myself staring into Lonan's.

"What? What is—No!"

I was inside the bunker, safe with Lonan, but Uncle Tam was still out there, literally wrestling with Merlin. Without my wild magic in the mix, Merlin was strong enough to fight again. I tried to run back through the portal, but Lonan hung onto me.

Struggling against his hold, I screamed, "Uncle Tam! Leave him there—come in here and we'll close the portal from this side!"

He didn't answer me, but there was enough of a connection between us I could tell that wasn't what he intended to do. He was going to end his life with selflessness and meaning, like he'd said.

But our magics were still intertwined, so I used it to reach through and try to pull him in. He dragged closer to the portal and I bared my teeth as I gave another tug. Uncle Tam was fighting me, though, and Merlin was fighting him—with no clear winners.

Uncle Tam turned his head to me, and I had a moment of hope before I felt him closing the portal. Like a puckering pair of lips—or some other more unsavory orifice—the opening drew tighter in front of me. I gritted my teeth and drew on as much magic as I could, trying to pull Uncle Tam through before it closed entirely.

Instead of only fighting him though, Merlin was now actively keeping Uncle Tam in place. My last sight of them was their matching expressions of crazed determination as they grappled while the portal shut tight. With a shimmer like a spreading dome, this offshoot dimension separated permanently from its parent.

I had a moment to stand there with my mouth hanging open, hands reaching for nothing, before I started screaming as my nerves burst into flames.

I thought something had gone wrong, and we were all going to burn with Merlin after all. But as the sensation dragged on, I realized it was the backlash from the suddenly severed, conjoined magic hitting me. The queen's magic had never felt more like a sentient thing as it sought its anchor, questing helplessly where the portal had snapped shut.

I tried to wind my wild magic around the remnant, to show it it wasn't alone. But it wasn't enough, and the queen's magic fled along the only other connections it had known—back into the network of Maeve's subjects, who were scattered in Faerie and Earth.

With a final pulse of energy like a sobbing moan, it was gone from me. I collapsed into Lonan's arms, breathing raggedly but grateful that at least my nerves weren't shrieking any longer.

But it wasn't over yet. My own wild magic had become so entwined with the queen's magic that it too was ripped from me. Again, there was a touch of sentience as I felt its regret—but then it went scampering off like a wild animal released from a cage. Its trail was marked by distant shouts and cries. And not happy ones.

Lonan caught me as I collapsed, and he rocked me in his arms as I gasped for air, too far gone to even sob. He offered me some water from the canteen on his belt, and it helped enough that I could begin to calm down.

"I'll probably be blamed for everything the wild magic does now, too," I said wearily. "Do you think we should find the queen to tell her what happened, or does Uncle Tam's—does Uncle Tam being gone mean she'll kill me on sight now? Especially since I won't be bringing back her magic like I promised."

Lonan paused before he answered, "Let's not worry about it right now. Maybe we should, I don't know, lay low until we see how things shake out."

"But we have responsibilities, and I think the queen needs to know in person that Uncle Tam is...is gone." All the urgency went out of me with those words. "He's really gone, isn't he?"

And Lonan held me while I cried.

A few days later, we stumbled into the camp we'd left behind, and my heart ached anew to see Uncle Tam's tidy bedroll. He never used a blanket; he always insisted on this piece of patched, plaid wool. I had asked him once if it was his family tartan, from back before he was taken by the queen, but he'd never answered. Now I'd never get the chance to tease him into answering me.

We'd been avoiding contact with most other people—and creatures—over the last few days, to give us a chance to process our grief. But one of Lonan's cousins had just left the campsite, after delivering the news that the Daweses lived through their botulism poisoning with the help of the queen's magic I'd sent via Bobbin. But since they'd been saved by magic, they were stuck in Faerie now—returning to Earth would just start up the organ failure again. Still, good news, along with word that my own parents had survived too.

Near the rekindled campfire, Lonan and I crawled into our sleeping bags, which we'd zipped together into one big bag. We were dozing off when the sound of hoofbeats made us go on alert.

"Nykur!" I called, trying to disentangle my legs from the covers as a huge black horse came into view.

A spray of mud from his hooves caught us as he braked. Then it was a man standing there, glaring at us.

"You really are a pair of idiots, aren't you?"

"What?" I stopped a few feet away from him, and lowered the arms I'd raised to hug him with. "Are you pretending to be mad, to cover up how much you've missed us?"

"No, I really *am* mad," he answered. "It would be just like you to survive whatever the Hell happened, and then get killed by an angry mob because they found you sleeping by the fire."

"What angry mob—" But Nykur cut off Lonan's words with a wave of his hand.

"Get your stuff and let's get out of here. I'll explain on the way."

But I didn't move right away. "Is this a trick? The last I heard, you weren't bonded to me anymore, and had taken your chance to get away from me. So what changed?"

He rolled his eyes—an oddly equine gesture—and started shoving stuff into my pack. "Because I started to hear all these rumblings—rumors—about what Avery Flynn had done and how she should pay. I know things with you are never that straightforward, so I decided to try to find you before the bounty hunters do."

Now I did hug him. "Aww, Nykur, you do like me. I missed you too."

He harrumphed. "If they kill you, I'll never get to hear the full story. You know how Nykurs love to know secrets."

"It's true," Lonan put in. "They're notorious gossips—worse than corbins."

Nykur snorted, and they bickered softly as I finished rolling up our sleeping bags. We scuffed out the fire and slunk off into the darkness, hoping our flames hadn't already led anyone near.

"So tell me more about these mobs," I said, once we'd walked in silence for a time. "Why are they after me?"

"Everybody is talking about how everything that's gone wrong is your fault. The blowup of the Border, the consuming patches of dead zones, the queen—"

Lonan stopped and laid a hand on Nykur's arm. "The queen? What's happened to my aunt?"

Nykur, uncharacteristically gentle, patted Lonan's hand. "I should have said the former queen. She's not well—she's lost her magic, and her mind along with it. Her Court is saying it's the result of a bad bargain she made with Avery Flynn."

"That wasn't Avery's fault," Lonan said sharply.

But I knew the truth, didn't I? She trusted me with her magic and her people, and I let her down. I still owed her my service, and more—even if there was no magical connection left between us.

"What else?" I asked hoarsely.

"Then there's Spellmeet: geographically, it's near where Crow's Rest used to be." At the small sound I made, Nykur paused before continuing. "It's a weird place, like parts of Earth and Faerie have been patched together in a quilt. Magic is unreliable in Spellmeet, and so is technology—they both work, but erratically."

"Also not Avery's fault," Lonan said, with a hard glance at me.

But I didn't bother to acknowledge his defense of me. "So much lost, and yes, it *is* my fault—if I hadn't given Merlin control of my magic, if the queen hadn't given me her magic—"

Lonan gripped my shoulders, forcing me to meet his gaze. "I knew you'd do this—try to take it all on yourself. Some of the best magical minds in Faerie failed to see what Merlin was up to. How could you—someone so inexperienced in magic—hope to see it?

"And the queen—no one tricked her into anything. She knew the risks, and also knew it was our best chance. If you hadn't brought her magic for

Tam Lin to use with yours, we wouldn't even be having this conversation. We'd all be dead with Merlin—everyone would. If a Spellmeet is the price we paid for avoiding annihilation, then I for one will take that bargain. So will everyone else, once they know the truth."

I shut my eyes against tears. "Even if your version is the real, true version, how will anyone believe me?" And what I meant was, *how will anyone forgive me?* I wasn't sure if I'd ever forgive myself.

"We'll tell whoever will listen," Nykur said softly. "And those who won't, they'll eventually forget—"

"'They'll forget'?" I asked bitterly. "The humans maybe, but what about the Fae? The ones with eternal memories? And grudges to match."

Nykur answered. "They have other things to worry about. There's no queen, and already all the powerful families are jockeying for some kind of upper hand."

We all stood in place for a long while, until I broke the silence. "Well...if I'm on the run, we'd better get moving. Unless you're not coming with me?"

In answer, Nykur and Lonan took their places on each side of me, and our steps kept time as the night swallowed us.

EPILOGUE

When Gracie Shore unlocked the front door of Shady Grove Nursing Home, the pair sitting out on the steps caught her by surprise. Sure, she'd read through their applications (no references to speak of) and invited them in for an interview, but these days you couldn't count on much. Too many of the young people would rather run wild in Spellmeet than clean up after some old and sick people.

Gracie cracked the door enough to say, "Good morning. And you are...?"

"I'm Calluna," the girl replied. "And he's Starling."

"Hmmph. Are those names made up? If you're on the run from something, don't be bringing trouble to our doorstep. We have enough to do here."

The boy made an innocent face (but his eyes stayed cocky) as he answered gravely, "No, ma'am, we are not looking for trouble. We're a couple of harmless refugees from Amish country—"

Calluna cut off what was obviously going to be a long story with a hand on his arm. "Ms. Shore, we just want a new start, and we're willing to work. You've seen our applications and it seemed like you were willing to give us a chance—has that changed?"

"Hmmph," Gracie said again. "Well, you're here and I'm shorthanded, so come on in."

They all stopped at the front desk so she could get them temporary badges—no sense in printing up the good kind until she knew if they would be staying. And, as she suspected, both of them hesitated before writing the names they'd told her, as if their hands wanted to give them away by forming different letters.

Once Gracie started showing them around, they listened well enough. The questions they asked showed they had a pair of brains too. In fact, if she didn't know better by their lack of references, she would have guessed they'd done this kind of work before.

The boy, Starling, seemed comfortable in the kitchen and they left him to help dice melon for fruit cups.

After an appraising glance at the girl's clothes—nondescript but sturdy—Gracie said, "Callie, you come with me and see what it's like on the front lines."

Gracie had meant it as a joke, but when she saw how the girl blanched at the term "front lines" she knew this one had a history with the chaos. If the girl had lost her family or her home in the devastation, it could explain why she wasn't one of the kids who were dazzled by the attractive nuisance of Spellmeet.

The way Callie didn't show any disgust at the worst of the residents—the ones who had disappeared when the Border first fell and reemerged weeks later with bodies and minds twisted—reinforced Gracie's theory that the girl had seen tragedy. The gentleness in her voice and hands made Gracie relax a little—and hope a little.

Callie seemed eager to prove herself, but when she stopped outside a closed door Gracie tried to move her along. A woman's hoarse voice, spewing what sounded like curse words in an unknown language, carried into the hallway.

"Oh no, Honey, that resident is not a first-day kind of project," Gracie said. "Poor thing was found wandering with no one to claim her. It takes four of the staff to bathe her, feed her, change her bedding—that one's vicious."

"Then why do you let her stay here?"

Gracie shook her head before the question was even finished. "And leave her on the streets, helpless? She'd end up dinner for some monster—give it indigestion, though—and it would be on my conscience. No, she stays here until she gets her wits back or until she passes on. Even the outcasts deserve that dignity."

Callie nodded and Gracie turned to continue down the hallway, but the creak of door hinges and an increase in volume of the cursing made her wheel around. The girl was already stepping into the room and Gracie rushed to catch her.

Too late. The woman in the high, wing-backed chair launched everything in reach at Callie, who ducked each object and continued to approach. Gracie pulled the radio from her belt, ready to call for help.

But then Callie did a strange thing—she crouched so low her belly was near on the carpet, her face resting in a milk stain from yesterday's refused breakfast. Gracie thought for sure the submissive posture would only make it easier for the shrieking resident to kick the girl, but instead the woman sat up straight in her chair.

An almost regal expression came over her, even with the spittle drying on her chin, and she intoned, "You may rise."

"You speak English?" Gracie blurted. "The whole time you've been here, all we've gotten from you is what sounds like a curse on us and all our descendants and you could've told us what you wanted—"

"Only this one will care for me now," the woman interrupted. "Make it so."

Gracie sputtered, but Callie spoke up. "I don't mind, really, Ms. Shore. I want to do what I can to help."

As if she assumed it was a done deal, Callie wiped the woman's face and then started picking up the thrown objects.

"Hmmph. All right then. You get paid every two weeks, and if you and that Starling need a place to stay we can work something out for rent on the apartment over the garage. But you're on probation for the first month, so this isn't a final call."

Callie nodded her understanding and continued tidying the room while the now-quiet resident watched.

Gracie headed to the kitchen to let old Randall know it looked like they could free up the scheduling for that room. "You won't believe it, but the new girl charmed Maeve right off the bat—"

The *clang* of a dropped prep bowl interrupted her before Starling muttered an apology and picked it up.

"Anyway," Gracie continued, "if she's that good with all the far-gone residents, she's a keeper."

And that was how it worked out, with both Callie and Starling staying on and becoming essential personnel. Even that hyper little dog, the one they were watching for a friend while he traveled, was a welcome spot of brightness.

Which is why Gracie ignored how sometimes Starling would disappear for a few days (Callie always covered his job), and how Callie's black hair grew tired brown roots every month before she touched them up with fresh dye.

By the time Callie slipped up in a conversation and called the boy Lonan, they were such a part of the Shady Grove family that no one remarked on how "Lonan" was the same name printed on wanted posters all around town.

Or how this Lonan character was known to be traveling with a universally hated criminal—a girl just about Callie's age and height.

A girl named Avery Flynn.

ACKNOWLEDGMENTS

Although Avery's adventures always continued in my head after the first book, her story would not have made it to the page without the support of my family and friends.

And once again, a team of editors and critique partners helped make my words fit to read. They included: Elizabeth Buege, Rich Storrs, Susan Burdorf, and Kathleen S. Allen.

Thanks are also due to Brenda Scott Wlazlo for bringing my characters to life in the audiobook versions of the Faerie Crossed series.

ABOUT THE AUTHOR

Angelica R. Jackson is a writer, artist, and avid naturalist, who shares a home in California's Gold Country with her husband, and far too many books (if that's even possible). A pair of rescued dogs and a reformed-feral tabby named Pippin keep her from spending too much time on the computer.

An active volunteer in SCBWI's CA North/Central region, she served most recently as the Illustrator Coordinator. Her photos are collected in *Capturing The Castle: Images of Preston Castle (2006-2016)*, also from Crow & Pitcher Press.

FEB 2 6 2019

CPSIA information can be obtained
at www.ICGtesting.com
Printed in the USA
FSHW02n1513081018
52825FS

9 780998 721446